*Occasional*

# THE DIAMOND THIEF

# J. A. MCLACHLAN

EDGE SCIENCE FICTION AND FANTASY PUBLISHING
AN IMPRINT OF HADES PUBLICATIONS, INC.

CALGARY

The Occasional Diamond Thief
Copyright © 2015 by Jane Ann McLachlan

This is a work of fiction. Names, characters, places, and incidents are
the products of the author's imagination or are used fictitiously and are
not to be construed as real. Any resemblance to actual events, locales,
organizations, or persons, living or dead, is entirely coincidental.

Edge Science Fiction and Fantasy Publishing
An Imprint of Hades Publications Inc.
P.O. Box 1714, Calgary, Alberta, T2P 2L7, Canada

Interior design by Cath at Expert Subjects
Cover design by Marija at Expert Subject

ISBN: 978-1-77053-075-1

EDGE Science Fiction and Fantasy Publishing and Hades Publications, Inc.
acknowledges the ongoing support of the Alberta Foundation for the Arts and
the Canada Council for the Arts for our publishing programme.

  Canada Council  Conseil des arts
for the Arts    du Canada

Library and Archives Canada Cataloguing in Publication

McLachlan, Jane Ann, author
    The occasional diamond thief / Jane Ann McLachlan.
ISBN: 978-1-77053-075-1

    I. Title.

PS8625.L3245O23 2015      C813'.6      C2014-907639-8

FIRST EDITION
(A-20141130)
Printed in Canada
www.edgewebsite.com

*For my daughter, Caroline,*
*Who always pays attention to what matters.*

*With love and laughter*

*"People pay attention to things they love. That's what*
*makes them beautiful."*
*Kia, p. 25*

# Table of Contents

# Chapter One

"She speaks Malemese?"

I stop walking mid-step in the hallway. Dr. Eldrich's voice carries through the closed door of my parents' room, even though he's speaking quietly. They have to be talking about me—I'm the only one who can speak Malemese, besides my father.

"She has an ear for languages, like Itohan." My mother, Owegbé's voice is low but clear. They must be standing just on the other side of the door, where they can speak privately without disturbing my father. If I hadn't been walking past right at that moment, I'd never have heard them. I creep closer to the door to hear them better.

"He taught her?" Surprise makes Dr. Eldrich's voice rise.

"She taught herself four years ago from language discs at the library. I suppose she thought it would please him. Itohan was ill for months after hearing Malemese spoken again, by his own daughter."

"I remember." Dr. Eldrich's voice is low again, mimicking Owegbé's hushed response. "You didn't tell me what had set him off."

There's a moment's silence. I feel a rush of heat to my face, anticipating what Owegbé will tell him. But all she says is, "There was no need. I made sure it wouldn't happen again."

Right. Of course she wouldn't tell him the whole story. But I remember that day, and how she "made sure."

My father was sitting alone in his den, scrolling through the bills and invoices on his business comp, not really doing

1

anything; Etin handled most of the financial details of their independent trading business. When I walked in, his eyes were half-closed in the vague, listless look he always had. I glanced around to see if there was anything new. The room was a jumble of things to look at: shelves with artwork and knick-knacks from his travels; vivid alien landscapes on the walls; holos of strange-looking people he had met as well as of family, crowding his desk. He began to smile when he saw me—and then I made the stupid announcement I'd practiced, in Malemese, "Father, I have learned to speak like y…you…"

I stuttered to a stop as he leaped up, his chair crashing to the floor behind him. A garbled cry, half-shout, half-whimper, came from deep in his throat. Owegbé, Etin, Oghogho, all came running to the door of the study where I stood terrified before my father.

Why hadn't I noticed he only spoke Malemese when he was ill with one of his fevers? but I was only eleven then, a kid.

Father's arms never left his sides. I stood there, frozen with fear, watching his fists clenching and opening as the force of his emotion battled the strength of his willpower. Owegbé realized what I'd done by my father's shouted accusations; she ran in and slapped me so hard I fell to the floor.

She would have hit me again except that Etin rushed in, yanked me to my feet and pushed me out of the room. I ran down the hall and outside, and just kept running. I don't even know where I went, I was crying so hard. When I finally crept back home at dinnertime, father was ill in bed. I never called Owegbé "Mother" again.

I shake off the memory and glance down the hallway. Owegbé could wave open the door at any moment and find me here, listening. The room I share with my sister Oghogho is just steps behind me, across from our brother Etin's room. I should move back so if Owegbé opens the door it would look like I'm just leaving my room. I start to step back, but then Dr. Eldrich speaks again: "His lungs are failing."

Instead, I move closer to the door.

"They no longer send sufficient oxygen to his brain. We could give him a new lung, but his heart is also weak…"

"He doesn't want to live."

"I'm sorry." Dr. Eldrich's voice trails off for a moment. I lean right in against the door.

"I'll have an oxygen tank couriered over. Perhaps if we can build up his strength a little…"

"No. Let him find peace at last," I hear Owegbé say.

I almost fall into the door. She can't mean what I think she means, she can't just give up on him—

The door swishes open. Owegbé stares at me. After a startled moment, her face turns dark and tight, her eyes so furious I start to tremble and can't speak, though I want to yell at her, tell her she can't, she can't just—

"It may prove useful now, if Akhié can still understand Malemese," Dr. Eldrich says, still looking at my father. He hasn't even noticed us. "But don't let her speak it. I don't know what the effect might be if he heard it spoken around him." He turns and sees me standing outside the open door, frozen in my mother's glare. He doesn't say anything. He just comes over beside her. I'm totally caught eavesdropping, but I'm too relieved to be embarrassed, because she can't kill me with him standing there.

She takes a deep breath, like it's all she can do not to hit me despite him being there. "Your father will speak only Malemese, now," she says. I can't even look at her anymore, because her voice is so calm, is such a lie. "You must translate, tell me what he needs. Can you still do it?"

Why won't he speak Edoan? I want to ask, Why Malemese? What happened to him there? But I know she won't tell me—maybe she doesn't know herself—and I'd only anger her more. I nod without looking up.

"You heard the doctor? You won't speak Malemese?"

I nod again. I want to scream: I get it! But even more, I just want to get away from my mother.

⁊

My parents' room, which is now my father's sickroom, is beige like the rest of the house, but instead of the usual clay tile flooring it has a thick, soft rug, terra cotta, the color of dirt. It looks okay with the simple, bare beige walls and the white oak dressers. Owegbé has 'impeccable taste'. But I wish I could take my father into his cluttered, colorful den. Maybe his gaze would focus again if he had something to look at. I get up from the chair beside his bed and turn to leave.

"Vienada preem." Come closer.

He's speaking Malemese. I've been called in often over the past weeks to translate. For the last few days he hasn't spoken Edoan at all. I'm the only one who can understand him now. I'd be happy about that, about sharing something only with him, if he knew he was talking to me.

"Vienada…" Come.

What would have been impatience when he was well comes out now as only weariness. I go closer, stopping two feet from the side of the bed. I can't look at his face, so I stare at his arm lying on top of the bedcovers, long and limp alongside his covered body. It's dark against the white sheets, and so thin I can see the veins standing out under his skin.

4

Slowly his forearm rises. The fingers move slightly, beckoning me even closer before his arm drops back onto the pale sheets. I creep forward until I'm nearly touching the bed.

"Look at me," he whispers in Malemese.

I don't want to raise my head. I'll look into his eyes and he won't recognize me. I should be used to it by now. But each time I hope it will be different. Maybe this time, I think as I lift my head, because he seems to be speaking directly to me. But then he calls me Owegbé or Etin and gives me nonsense instructions that I can barely understand to translate. Mostly, he just calls for water, or fumbles about in agitation until someone guesses his need and helps him.

"I haven't given you much reason to love me, Akhié."

I stare at him. I can feel myself grinning like an idiot but I don't care. He knows me! He recognizes me, even if he is still speaking Malemese. He's getting better!

I mustn't upset him by answering in Malemese.

"No reason at all to love me," he repeats sadly. He turns his head, glancing restlessly over the sheets that cover him to stare unseeing at the air in front of him.

"I do!" I cry in Edoan.

It's no good; he hasn't spoken or responded to Edoan for over a week.

"I love you, Father!" It's like he can't even hear me in Edoan, like I'm not even answering him. What if he dies thinking I don't love him because I didn't answer? It might be too late already, the way his mind wanders. He's staring into the empty air, no longer focused on me at all.

"I do love you," I whisper, this time in Malemese.

He starts as though I've hit him, and pulls himself onto his elbow, leaning toward me eagerly. "Ahhh!" he cries, staring just above me.

The look on his face… a second ago I wanted to hug him, and now I can't help backing away.

"Sariah! At last!"

I look over my shoulder. There's no one there.

"All these years I've pitied you and hated you, because of it. At last you've come to claim it back!"

I peer around the room, afraid to move. Who is he talking to?

"Take it! Take it!" His hand moves in a jerking gesture toward the dresser. The agitated movement nearly makes him fall back against his pillows. He holds tight to the side of the bed.

What if someone hears his raised voice? Only its weakness has prevented it from carrying beyond the room, but someone could walk by any moment and hear the shrill urgency of it. "Shhh!' I whisper, "shhh!"

"There, in the top drawer!" Again the desperate gesture. Whoever he thinks I am, my only means of quieting him is to do as he insists. I hurry over and open the dresser drawer.

"Back. Left."

I hear him gasping for breath and half turn to tell him to lie down, to rest. His eyes are bright with fever. He gives a sharp nod toward the open drawer. I give up and reach into it.

What am I looking for? I pat at the folded clothes. Should I pretend to find something? Would that calm him? I hear a soft rattle in his breath that frightens me. I have to get him to calm down.

"The corner… behind… wood." Every whispered word is punctuated by that horrible rattle. He's so certain, there has to be something here; he'll only be satisfied when I bring it to him.

I'm about to give up when I feel a narrow crack between the backing and the bottom of the drawer, in the far left corner. A piece of leather seems to be stuck in it. I pull on it, but it resists. I hear a gasping breath from the bed. Getting a firmer grip, I pull with all my strength. Slowly, the thing comes free. A leather pouch, no bigger than my two thumbs curled together, lies in my hand. I hold it up to show him.

He nods, a small jerk of his chin as he sinks back against the pillows. "… inside, just as… it from you." I can barely make out his whispered words over the rattle of his breathing.

"What is it?" I hurry over to him, risking Malemese again.

"You know! It's yours…your heart…"

I almost drop the pouch. Does he really believe it holds someone's heart? It seems to grow heavier in my hand, and colder…

He whispers something. I bend over the bed, my ear only inches from his mouth, trying to sort the breaths that are speech from the background of labored breathing.

"…no one knows about it …take it away …I'm done with you at last… Sariah!" His words end in a sudden, harsh rattle. With a soft sigh his head slides sideways, mouth half-open.

"Father!" I grab his hand, shaking it. "Father!"

My scream brings everyone rushing to the room. Owegbé pushes me aside. "Itohan," she moans, her voice so low she might be whispering a secret to him as she bends over the bed to embrace him. Her face is so twisted with grief I hardly recognize her.

I can't breathe. In all my fourteen years I've never seen Owegbé like this, never imagined her capable of tenderness, or grief. It's awful to see her so changed, and terrible to know that she has so much love, but none to spare for me. My sister pushes me further aside, crowding up close to Owegbé. Neither one of them has spoken to me since I started caring for father. The way they push me aside now makes me want to scream again.

"Come away," Etin whispers, pulling me out into the hall.

He puts his hands on either side of my head, his thumbs wiping away the tears I didn't know till then were on my cheeks, ignoring his own tears. "You spoke Malemese to him, didn't you?"

I start to pull away but he holds onto me. I open my mouth to deny it—

"He was already dying, Akhié. He's been dying for years. It isn't your fault." Etin pulls me into a hug. After a moment, I hug him back, and begin to cry harder. He holds me and lets me cry for a few minutes. Before I'm anywhere near ready to stop, he releases me. I feel like I'm going to fall, but his hand is still on my shoulder, supporting me. "You should go off somewhere. Don't return until evening. Let them mourn without seeing you." He gives me another quick hug then pushes me gently toward the door. "Don't look so guilty when you come back."

I watch Etin go back into father's room. The whole family's there, all but me. I look down at my hand, curled around the leather pouch. Stuffing it into my hip pocket I run down the hall, pull the front door open with an angry jerk, and leave. It shuts noiselessly behind me.

All I can think is, they don't want me, as I hop onto the transit strip and drop into a seat. The people around me block my view of the city rushing by as it picks up speed. Usually I stand at the edge, my arm wrapped around one of the poles, where I can feel the speed and see the low, almost seamless line of pink and copper brick buildings racing by on either side. I like the way the sun shines brightly on the hollow red clay tiles of their roofs, shaped to deflect its heat, and turns their windows into rubies as I flash by.

Today I don't notice anything, even when the crowd of people dwindles and the buildings are clearly visible. I look up only when the ruby reflections have long ceased and most of the remaining walkers have swung off to enter the low, windowless hotels for space travelers. A little farther and there are no buildings at all, only rough fields of red dirt and scraggly weeds, and a few clumps of tall, spindly trees, their long fronds drooping in the hot sun. I'm at the edge of the huge fields that surround the landing areas of the spaceport.

I get up and move to the edge of the transit strip, balancing myself hand-over-hand against the poles. The tug of the wind increases. I ignore the cord that will signal the strip to slow down—I haven't used it in years, nobody between the ages of twelve and thirty does. Instead, I lean with one hand against the cool curve of a pole and stretch out my other hand, slipping it into the looped strap hanging just above my head. The strap is attached to a rotating metal disc at the top of the edge pole. Pushing off lightly, I swing myself over the edge of the transit strip, dangle a half instant watching it move just below my feet, then let go. I drop with my knees slightly bent onto the ground. The entire manoeuvre takes only a few seconds. It's so automatic I barely noticed what I'm doing, until someone jostles me from behind.

"Sorry," the man mutters, grabbing my shoulder to keep from falling. I step aside, wondering why the idiot didn't take a second to adjust to the change of speed before dropping, or pull the cord and wait for the strip to slow, like most people his age do.

"You going to spaceport?" He says in Central Ang with the heavy drawl of Coral, one of the Inner worlds. I stare ahead, pretending not to understand.

"…backward people with archaic travel-ways…" I hear him mutter in Coralese as he turns and heads for the spaceport.

The mid-day sun is hot. I scuff my feet on the dry, red dirt, feeling the heat in the soil through my sandals. I squint up at the sky, brilliant with sun from horizon to horizon, as constant as people are inconstant. I hate my family for sending me away, for wanting to grieve without me. Maybe that's not fair—Etin was only trying to protect me from revealing my secret—but it amounts to the same thing. I wish I never had to go home.

Then it hits me: my father's dead. I'll never talk to him again, or see his smile, or even wave my hand in front of his unfocused eyes when he's thinking about something or remembering something or whatever he does when he goes away like that. I'll never again be mad at him for it, when I'm trying to get his attention; or feel the way I feel when I have his attention, when he looks at me like there's nothing else in the world as important to him right then as I am. No one will ever look at me like that again.

I stumble and almost fall, but I catch myself and blink hard. I can't think of my father, not yet. I need to get somewhere no one will see me. My legs are trembling so much they barely hold me up. I force them to keep moving, up over a small rise and down the other side to where I can't be seen from the walkways or the transit strip, if someone rides by.

I sink to the ground. I want to cry, it hurts so much, but I guess I did too good a job of holding back my tears because now they won't come. I reach down and grab a handful of the warm, dry soil of Seraffa and hold it against my cheek. A single tear runs into it, leaving a narrow trail of red mud across my face.

I hear the piercing whine of a space shuttle approaching the distant landing field. The ground shakes beneath me as it settles on the landing site, the weeds around me swaying crazily. I stare at them numbly, waiting for the ground to stop trembling.

How can anyone stand to live in a spaceship? Cooped up without the feel of the sun and the breeze on their skin, without the warmth of soil beneath their feet or the sight and the sweet, pungent smell of familiar growing things around them? Better even to be a weed, unwanted and despised.

I reach for one of the tall stalks beside me, brushing my fingers up the sturdy, maroon stem and across the lighter, copper-colored

# Chapter One

leaves, plump with stored water, smooth and waxy to touch. They're tough, weeds. They take what they need on this desert planet. What do they care if no one wants them?

I lie down, stretching my arms and legs wide to crush as many weeds as I can, breathing in the fresh-sap smell that rises from the thick leaves and the similar, sharper scent of broken stems. I lie there, motionless and dry-eyed, with the sun on my face, the hot breeze in my hair, the firm earth with its cushion of vegetation underneath me.

And inside an emptiness that all Seraffa's warmth can't fill. It disappears into a small vacuum inside me, leaving nothing but an ache. All I can feel is that ache: not the sun, not the wind, not the soil with its weedy softness, just the emptiness and the deep ache of it.

Two more ships come in. One departs. The sun droops lower until the spaceport casts its shadow across me, making me shiver. I shift sideways and feel something hard pinching my hip. Half-rising, I dig down into my pocket. When I touch the soft leather of the pouch, I take several deep breaths before I can steel myself to pull it out.

In the daylight it no longer looks so ominous. It's just a commonplace little sack with a small, hard object inside it.

I have to use my teeth to untie the leather cords that hold it shut. The thin cords are dry and tough in my mouth, and when I finally work them loose they still hold the shape of the knot. Reaching inside with my thumb and forefinger, I feel a jagged stone the size of a marble. I pull it out and drop it onto my palm. The sun hits it, and I gasp in disbelief. It is stunningly, frighteningly beautiful.

The stone is clear and brilliant, like the diamond in Owegbé's wedding band, except that this one is ten times the size of hers. It has a brilliant circle of darkness at the core, as though I am staring straight into the sun. Light shimmers across this dark center like lightning in the night sky, and shoots out through the surrounding diamond in a rainbow of colors. I stare at it, mesmerized.

And quickly close my fingers tight around it. I look down at my closed fist for a while, before I pick up the pouch and slip the stone back inside. How did my father come by such a thing? And why didn't he tell anyone about it?

He was hallucinating, his sentences disjointed, when he talked to me. "It's yours" was clear enough, but who did he think he was talking to? I shiver, remembering his intense stare, just above my head, as though he was looking at someone behind me. Just thinking about it makes me turn and look over my shoulder.

"Sariah," he said. A word or a name? Either way, I've never heard it before. And he called it… what? A heart? Someone's heart? None of it makes sense, because he wasn't making sense. He was dying. I close my eyes. That's a word that doesn't make any sense. How can I live with that word?

The pouch slips out of my hand. I open my eyes and look down at it. What should I do with the diamond? If I show it to anyone, they'll ask where I got it. Then Owegbé will find out I spoke to Father, that I broke my promise and spoke Malemese, and she'll blame me for his death.

She's right. I did kill him. I spoke Malemese, knowing I shouldn't, and it was too much for him to bear, just as the doctor warned me. He warned me and I did it anyway—

I lean sideways just before the spray of vomit spews from my mouth, and then I heave and heave, unable to stop. When nothing more will come out I spit onto the ground, trying to clear the taste from my mouth with saliva. I grab a handful of weeds and wipe my mouth, then grab a fresh handful and chew on the stems until their bitter flavor drowns out the other.

# Chapter One

The pouch is lying on the ground, like a written confession. I scoop it up. No one knows about it or the diamond, I think with relief. And then I think: no one knows my father had it, or that he gave it to me. They'll think I stole it.

Would they put me in jail?

My hand tightens around the pouch. Not if they don't know.

# Chapter Two

I step off the transit strip in front of the block of residences where I live. The interlocked clay bricks feel hard under my sandals after the springy feel of the weeds, but they're warmer than the cold metal of the transport strips.

As independent traders, our family is respectable enough to live in this section close to the inner core of the city, and Owegbé insisted on it, even though my father's single trade ship earns barely enough to maintain a ground-level, corner apartment at the back. That's fine with me. I like being grounded. I wouldn't choose one of the upper level apartments with their sunroof skyscapes even if it was free, so I'm glad we're too poor to afford one. I wish we had a door, though, or even a window, opening directly onto the narrow courtyard in the center of the block of apartments. It's not much—a couple benches, redgrass underfoot with shrubs and a few flowers at the corners. Costs a planet to water, which is why it's so expensive to live here, but in the middle of the clay and steel city, it's a place I can go to breathe.

Thinking about it makes me realize how breathless I feel now. What if they won't let me in? What if Owegbé guesses what I did, why I ran? I'll have to pretend I needed to be alone. That's what Etin would have told her. I'm walking so slow you'd think I was crossing a dune, my feet sinking in sand at every step, but I can't seem to make myself go faster. I reach the corner of our complex, and turn down the narrow alley between our building and the complex next to ours. As I approach our apartment, I hear a hum of conversation, too subdued to make out individual words.

I turn onto the street behind our building, which our apartment faces onto, and slow up even more. Through our front window I see a crowd of people moving about inside. The sight makes me stop dead. I can't face all those people. It'll be hard enough to hide my guilt from my family. I have to get out of here. I look around nervously, and then think of the Traders' Library, my other refuge when I need to be alone. I'm on the verge of running back to the transit strip when someone moves across the window and looks out, straight at me.

I want to flee more than ever, because she's wearing the blue and white habit of a member of the Order of Universal Benevolence. But when she looks at me, I freeze. It's impossible to keep anything from a Select of the O.U.B. They train from childhood, heightening their six senses to a nearly inhuman level. The smallest twitch of a muscle in my cheek or shift of my eye will tell her I'm lying as clearly as a full confession. It never worried me before, but I never had anything to hide, before.

What is she doing here, anyway? Father would never have let her into our house. But Owegbé believes in the O.U.B. I remember her taking me to worship services as a child. I shouldn't resent my mother taking what comfort she can from her faith, but I do. It just seems like she couldn't wait till Father died to change things.

The Select stares back at me, making sure I know she's seen me, then crosses behind the window back the way she came, toward the hall and the front door. She's coming to see me!

Running away now is out of the question. She's probably already seen that I want to and she'll be wondering why. It's one thing to disappear all day to mourn alone, another to appear to be avoiding the O.U.B. Might as well just tell them outright I have something to hide.

My left hand moves reflexively to the pocket of my pants. I jerk it away, and clasp my hands together behind my back. I'll never get away with this. I ought to show her the diamond as soon as she comes outside, and tell her where it came from. If I delay at all… But I've already been away all afternoon. Won't it look suspicious that I didn't turn it over earlier?

Besides, if I tell her told how I really came by it, I'd have to confess to speaking Malemese to my father. The pouch was so well hidden I'd never have found it unless he told me where to look. And he did. He gave *me* the diamond. He didn't give it to Owegbé, or the O.U.B. There must be something special, something secret, about it. Some reason he wanted me to have it.

Right then and there I know I won't give it up. Even though as long as I keep it, I'm as much a thief as—

As my father. A thief. How else could he have come by something so precious? Why else would he hide it so carefully, for so long, would he only talk about it in a language no one else understood?

Alright, a thief. But no one will ever call him that. No one will ever know, even if I have to be a thief, too, to keep the secret.

There must be some way to hide something from a Select. I remember a saying: "to fool the Select, you must fool yourself." That's impossible—how could you deliberately fool yourself? Maybe hypnotism could do it, but there isn't time for that.

I'm still trying to think of something when the front door slides open and the Select steps out. Think of something else, I tell myself desperately, which just makes me even more aware of the gem in my pocket, so I picture my father in his bed, as I saw him this morning.

Only this morning? Only so short a time ago?

*I haven't given you much reason to love me.*

I've tried not to think of his words all day, and now grief hits me like a physical blow. I shudder and my legs go weak; I'm falling when the Select runs forward and grabs my arms.

"I can't face them," I whisper, "I'll cry." And then, of course, I start to. I blink the tears back, horrified that I really will cry in front of everyone. Owegbé would be furious over such a public display of emotion. But not as angry as if she learned the truth. I hate myself for it, but I stop resisting the tears.

"Come." The Select leads me back into the alley, where we have a small measure of privacy. This is even worse! I don't want to be alone with a Select of the O.U.B. I pull away, wiping my face with my sleeve. Only now that I've started crying, I can't stop.

The Select waits quietly. When at last I pull myself together, she asks, "Would you like to pray?"

"Not really." The words slip out between a hiccup and a sob, before I have time to think. I look up, horrified. Refusing to pray with a Select is like spitting in a Worship House. Owegbé will kill me when she hears.

But the Select doesn't look angry, she looks relieved. "I don't have very much experience with praying out loud," she says. "For others, I mean. Not that I don't pray for others, I do. All the time. Just not with them listening…"

What is she talking about? Is she blushing? I edge toward the front door.

She appears to pull herself together. "I'm very sorry, my dear."

"Thank you," I mumble. My tears were convincing because they were real, but I don't dare push my luck. I have to get away from her before I betray my secret.

"Oh, don't thank me. It's not a nice thing, being sorry. Far better not to have anything to be sorry about. At least they tell me so. Often." The Select sighs.

What is she talking about now? I look at her more closely. She's pretty young for a Select, maybe in her early twenty's? And not much taller than I am, 5'3 or 5'4, with skin as pale as mine is dark, and wide blue eyes that look—uncertain. Uncertain? I look again.

"Are you a Select of the O.U.B.?" As soon as I say it, I wish I could take it back. But everything about her is so unusual for the Order that I can't help wondering if I've mistaken the habit.

Instead of being insulted, she looks embarrassed. "Not a very accomplished one," she says. "I'm kind of still in training."

"Oh." Then I remember what the O.U.B. are trained at, and begin moving toward the front door again. She follows me, looking a little dejected.

I pause before lifting my palm to the infra-red dot beside our front door. "I'm sure you'll get better at it," I say awkwardly.

"Do you think so?" She smiles hopefully as the door sweeps open. I step into the narrow hallway, with the Select right behind me. "I try very hard, but I always seem to say the wrong thing. They tell me it would be better if I just didn't talk—" she breaks off abruptly.

"No, it's okay. I like the way you talk. It's better than asking questions—" I break off. I don't even want her to think about asking me questions.

"But people respect the other Select, especially when they ask questions. I just can't think of the right questions to ask."

Good. I look around the front room. It's packed with people. I recognize some friends of my sister and brother, and neighbors, a few relatives. Across the hall, the dining room is also crowded.

"I suppose it's just as good to be liked as to be respected," the Select is saying beside me.

I almost say, take what you can get, but stop myself this time. The Select's candor is infectious.

Perhaps she's trying to get me to talk, to see what might come out? She might be more cunning than she seems. I nod without answering, and glance toward the dining room again. Someone shifts sideways and I catch a glimpse of the table, laden with food. The sight makes me hungry. I haven't eaten since breakfast. Then I see another Select, an older man, speaking to Owegbé. Two Select in our home? My father would *hate* that. Today, at least, should be about him, not Owegbé, even if she does follow the Order.

The older Select straightens and turns his head, and sees me looking at him. I quickly turn back to the Select beside me, so I won't look like I'm avoiding the O.U.B.

"I'm Select Agatha."

"You have names?" For the second time I'm surprised out of my natural caution.

"Of course we do. I've never understood why we don't use them in public. It's a silly thing to keep secret, don't you think?"

Behind Agatha, I see the man make a sign of comfort over Owegbé. Then he turns and heads directly toward us. There are too many people and conversations between him and us for even a Select of the O.U.B. to have picked up our actual words, although you can never be sure; it's more likely his intuition is bringing him our way. Or something he saw in my face. He looks calm and reserved, the usual Select expression that actually expresses nothing. But there's something in his eyes as he looks at Agatha that reminds me of the way Owegbé looks at me.

*...keep secret, don't you think?* Agatha's words register on me belatedly. Are they meant to trap me into saying something I shouldn't, or are they another weird confession that could get her into trouble? I look at her pale face with its slightly anxious expression. She looks the way I feel, trying to please Owegbé. I decide to trust her. A little.

The older Select is close enough now to hear what we're saying.

"Did you know ...Itohan?" I can't say 'father,' can't even let myself think the word, not with my face still tight with dried tears. Even saying his name causes a pain so sharp I miss a breath. But this is something we might be saying to each other, and certainly safer for both of us than the topic of secrets.

Agatha's expression transforms at once into the serene face of the Select.

"I did know him," she says, "years ago, when I was an Acolyte, younger than you are now. Before he turned away from the Order. He was a good, kind man."

I feel my face crumbling.

"Not now," Agatha says. "Not here. Go and wash your face, and change. I'll tell your mother you're back."

"Thank you," I stammer. I hurry down the hall before the older Select reaches us.

Select Agatha will never know how close we both came to being caught.

# Chapter Three

"I'm looking for Messer Sodum of 'Sodum's Jewelry'." I force my voice steady despite the pounding of my heart. What if the station concourse peddler lied to me about this jeweller? What if he demands proof of ownership before he'll pawn the ring? I smile to hide my fear. I'll think of something, if it comes to that.

"Yu've found him. What's yer business?" The old man turns to face me on his stool, frowning. He's bald, with huge ears and slightly protruding eyes which stare piercingly through a pair of archaic spectacles. Spectacles! I struggle not to show surprise. Surely he's had laser surgery. Even the poor are entitled to necessary health care, and although his store is small and far away from the main shopping station, Messer Sodum is obviously not poor.

His outfit is unusual for Seraffa, but it's so carefully cut and fitted it has to be the latest fashion on some planet or other. The top, a long tunic with bloused sleeves, is ornately embroidered with swirls of turquoise and midnight blue. The threads stand out against the softer blue of the material itself, which looks so cool and light and rich it might actually be real Earth silk. The high-back collar fans away from his neck in a way that will give protection from the sun and yet allow easy movement and cool air around his neck and the back of his head. I wish I had a collar like that on my jumpsuit. The rest of his outfit is hidden by the counter, but an arch of sapphires and turquoise jewels glitter around the edges of both his overgrown ears.

"Yer business?"

I blink, embarrassed at being caught staring. Quickly I unseal one of the side pockets on my pants and pull out a small ball of folded tissue, which I drop onto the counter. He looks at me a moment, before unwrapping the tissue to reveal an ornate ring with a pattern of small, brilliant diamonds encircling an emerald. I can't help giving a small, tight smile at the sight of it. The minute I saw the ring it screamed 'escape!'

"And who's's this?" Messer Sodum lifts the ring negligently from the nest of crumpled tissue. His right hand, which holds it up to the light, is unadorned, but on his left hand are two large rings, glittering with diamonds and sapphires. He's watching me, waiting for my answer.

"It's… my mother's." I glance around, moving my head as little as possible. There are no other customers, but an assistant stands a few feet away, rearranging a display of precious necklaces while the clear plexiglass hums above his hands in self-cleaning mode. I lean in toward the old man and say, in a carrying whisper which will surely reach the clerk, "she can't come herself. She needs the money without my father knowing."

Sodum's left eyebrow slowly rises into a scornful arch. "I'll have t'evaluate this." He picks up the ring. "See we're not interrupted," he tells the clerk, who smirks at me until his master gives him a look.

I follow Sodum to a small back room. As soon as the door is closed he turns on me. "What d'yu think yer up to here? Who sent yu?"

I stumble against a table and stammer out the name of the concourse peddler, thinking, the peddler lied! I've been set up! I back up to the door, ready to grab it open and dash out.

His expression changes from suspicion to anger. "Bringin' me somethin' in daytime? He told yu that? No, no I didn't think so! Yu didn't think t' ask how it's done, did yu? I should turn yu in, yu little fool! Yu let me know when yer coming and yu come at night. There's a door in the back there." He juts his chin sideways toward the darkened end of the room. "Opens onto th'alley behind the shop. Use that."

I gape at him. What makes him think I'll ever come again?

He glares back at me. After a moment, I nod. He might give me a better price if he thinks I'll come back.

"Yu have an eye fer value," he says sullenly, and I guess that's the only reason he hasn't kicked me out on the street. He settles on a stool and lays the ring under his jeweller's eyecomp. I watch him move it slowly, recording each stone. "People yer age don't often reco'nize quality when they see it. They go fer big and flashy. Fake stuff." He snorts in derision and checks the numbers flashing across the rectangular screen at the base of his eyecomp before looking down into the eyepiece again. "Mmmm. Nice, very nice. Could be beginner's luck." He glares at me. "Who taught yu?"

"No one." I'm feeling a little sick, hearing that it's so valuable, but I tell myself to douse it. Why take it at all, if it wasn't valuable? "I inherited the skill," I say defiantly.

"Don't be cute. Tell me how yu came by this. The truth, or I'll send yu away with it."

I narrow my eyes and stare back at him. But when he picks up the ring and holds it out to me, my resolve breaks.

"In a washroom. A woman took it off to wash her hands. Then she turned to fix her face, and forgot it." My face feels hot. I could have called her, told her she'd forgotten it; instead I watched her leave.

"She saw yu?"

I shake my head. "I was in a cubicle. She'd moved to the make-up mirror before I came out. She was focused on it, listening to its instructions." My mouth twists in disgust. Why would anyone let a communal mirror tell them how to make up their face? Couldn't the woman even pretend to have some originality?

"No cameras in a washroom." Sodum nods, looking satisfied. "Come 'ere." He places the ring back under the eyecomp. When I move closer he ignores me, as though he didn't order me over. He rotates the ring gently with his electronic tweezers until each of the stones has been exposed once again to the light of the 'scope. After a final look, he stands up and motions me onto the stool. I hoist myself up and peer down into the eyepiece. A huge diamond gleams fiercely up at me.

"Looka its planes—the angles it's cut at. See how they draw the light t'the centre and toss it out again? Now look at it with yer eye alone." He slides the ring out from the groove of the eyecomp and holds it up so I can see the diamond I've been looking at through the comp. The fire in it leaps from plane to plane as he turns it slowly.

I nod, bored. Fine, it's pretty. Is it worth as much as I need it to be?

"Now looka this." He pulls out a drawer underneath the table and lifts up a necklace. It's got a single diamond, half again the size of the one in the ring; but where that one sparkles with life, this one is dull, its center oblique. He moves it around in the light. Its edges shine flatly, taking light in without throwing it back.

"I understand." I don't really care. It's not like I'm ever going to do this again. And compared to my father's diamond, neither one is worth breaking a sweat over.

Sodum smiles. Most people's smiles widen their face, plumping out their cheeks to create a younger appearance. Sodum's smile emphasizes the cadaverous thinness of his face with its long, narrow chin and avaricious eyes, slightly protruding as though there isn't enough room for them in his face. I try not to grimace. He appears not to notice my reaction.

"Shame to break down a piece like this. Looka that beautiful work."

"All right." I'm done with this. What do I care if he thinks the thing is lovely? The woman didn't, or she wouldn't have left it lying there. People pay attention to things they love. That's what makes them beautiful.

Messer Sodum frowns through his ridiculous spectacles, then he shrugs. "Long as yu can recognize quality, yu don't have t'appreciate it. This ring's worth a thousand creds." He points to the final numbers on the base of the eyecomp. I've heard that the meter can be 'fixed' and if it's possible, this is the guy who'd do it, so I just look at him, as though I know more about this than I do.

"I've got t'melt down the gold and cast the jewels into fresh pieces. My clerk saw yu, and he saw the ring. If there'd been a customer in the store— Yu put me at risk. I should send yu away. But since I like yu, I'll split it 40-60 with yu. Next time, come at night and I'll give yu 50-50."

"50-50 this time. 30-70 if you want me to come again."

Is the gleam in his eye amusement or anger? I don't care; I'm the one who took the risk getting the ring. And I need the money. Five hundred creds will barely be enough. Of course I'll never do this again, but it's clear he wants the future business, so if I seem to be negotiating for it, he may let the more reasonable 50-50 go.

"50-50 now, 40-60 next time if yu bring me the same quality, and nothin that's known outsida its owner. No one will offer yu better." He holds the ring out to me.

"All right," I say, hesitating just long enough to let him think he's won.

Sodum opens the drawer under the table again and gets out an envelope. I watch him write something on it, slip the ring inside and seal it, then shut it inside the drawer.

"Come back in two weeks. At night, that door. I'll teach yu t'open safes."

Back in the front of the store, he slides his card through the credcomp and keys in his password and account before he steps aside. My hand shakes slightly as I complete my end of the transaction. Is this really happening? I watch my account go from C75 to C575.It's all I can do not to shout out loud.

"Tell yer mother she can reclaim her ring within ten days."

I look at him blankly.

"Standard practice." His eyes narrow and flick sideways, where his clerk's waiting on a customer nearby.

"Of course," I say. "My mother will expect that."

On the way home I stop to purchase two space-bags. This is really happening.

Etin walks by my room as I'm packing my belongings into them. He stands at the bedroom door watching me.

Don't speak to me, I think. I'm going and nothing you can say will stop me, so don't say anything at all. He doesn't, but he keeps standing there. I find myself packing more slowly. Why should I be glad to see him? He'll offer to take me out for a caf and gel, or to an action holovid—he knows I love them. Then he'll ship out again tomorrow, next week at the latest.

I'm not being fair, even if it is true. Etin has to go on every run the *Homestar* makes. He lost money hiring a professional trader for some of the runs during our father's illness and has to make it up now with continuous runs. Oghogho gets to go with him as an apprentice trader between study terms. Eventually they'll be able to take turn about, as Etin and Father used to, and Etin won't be gone so much. Well, that's no help to me now, living with a mother who never speaks to me, rarely even looks at me, and a sister who's little better.

I walk to the closet and take down three jumpsuits—the last of my things.

"I hear you translated at an Immigration Investigation. How did it go?"

"Fine. They paid well." I answer too quickly. He knows me enough to hear my nervousness. I take a silent breath and say, "I'm leaving." Let him blame my tension on that. "I've registered with the College of Translators."

"You're only fifteen." He hasn't moved from the door, but his voice has changed, is softer.

"I turned sixteen last week."

"I'm sorry, Akhié. I'm away too much."

I shrug. What good are regrets? It's not as though anything will change. I've found my own way out, anyway.

"You're still too young," Etin continues. "No one there will be your age."

He thinks I might be lonely. I almost laugh out loud. As though I could be more lonely anywhere else than I am right here. But that isn't Etin's fault.

"It's what I want to do," I say instead. "It's what I'm good at." I begin folding the first jumpsuit into my bag, not looking at him. "They've given me early admission. Why not? I'm already doing the work."

Etin smiles. "One job and you're a translator? But I'm glad it went well. It was good of Dr. Eldrich to recommend you."

"They needed me." Etin always assigns good motives to people, deserved or otherwise. "No one else can speak Malemese." Why would they want to? If Seraffa wasn't a port world of traders and merchants for all the outer inhabited worlds, I would never have found lesson flashdrives on such an insignificant and little-used language. I know that now. When I was ten I thought it must be an important language, because my father spoke it.

I couldn't understand why my brother wasn't studying it as an apprentice trader.

Etin is silent, watching me fold the second jumpsuit carefully into the space-bag. "She can't help it, you know," he says.

I feel my stomach clench. "She could if she wanted to," I answer after a moment. I can barely get the words out. My hands fumble, folding the last jumpsuit. Etin comes in and takes it from me. Shaking it out, he begins to fold it again. I sit on the edge of the bed with my head bent. I thought the hard part would be getting the money.

"When you were born she called you 'babydoll'. I used to watch her bathe you. You were so small, and bright. One day you looked at her and said, as clear as anything, 'mommydoll'. Mother laughed with happiness. I heard her telling Father about it in a netcast.

"She thought it would make him smile. But after that trip to Malem he never smiled. And he used to smile all the time, and laugh—you got your sense of humor from him—and lost it with him. We all did, especially Mother."

"Why did he even go to Malem?"

"I was eight when he left. I remember them quarrelling about it. Mother said it was too far; the trip would take too long to be worth it. But the O.U.B. wanted transport there and they were willing to pay well. And Father thought by taking them he might get a foot in the door to trade with Malem."

"No one trades with Malem."

"That's what Mother said, but Father was always an optimist. He even went to the trouble of learning Malemese."

"An optimist?"

"You didn't know him then. He changed after Malem. When he came back... I don't know. He was feverish, not always rational. When his fever broke—well, you know how he was.

Dr. Eldrich tried everything, none of the meds would work on him. He embarrassed me. I was nine years old and ashamed of my father."

"What happened to him there?" I don't want to hear Etin's confession. I idolized my father. When the other kids laughed at him I cut them off cold. Just as well. I don't need any friends prying into my secrets.

Etin shrugs. "He never spoke about it, not even to Mother. I guess we'll never know."

"At least he didn't name you something awful." Etin means "strength" in Edoan. A good name, unlike mine, which means "sorrow." Who names their kid that?

"Akhié isn't your official name. Mother wouldn't name you sorrow. But that's all he called you when he got home, and he was so fragile, always on the brink of fever and despair, she was afraid to openly name you something else. Soon everyone was calling you Akhié."

"What's my real name, then?"

He frowned. "Mother called you pet names—little bird, babydoll—your first few years. Then she called you Akhié, like Father did. I don't think you have an official name; just your birth registration number. I guess you could pick one and register it, if you wanted." He grins at me.

What does he want from me? *'Oh goody, I don't even have a real name'*?

"I'll think about it." I get up and seal the two space-bags shut. The lining around them begins to hum and gently swell as oxygen is sucked out through the tiny nozzle and replaced with helium. In a few minutes they are so light, despite their contents, they gently bob beside me as I hold their strings.

"You don't have to go, Akhié. You can live at home and attend the College of Translators. Oghogho commutes to her college."

"Hers is closer. Anyway, I can't stay here. You don't know what it's like." How could he? Even when he's home he only sees how things are for him.

So I tell him: "Owegbé hates the sight of me. She'll always remember that at the end I could understand Father when she couldn't."

"Try to see it her way, Akhié. Malem took her husband from her. Malem devoured him. Even on his deathbed Malem claimed him. She hates Malem; hates the people, the language, the planet, hates the thought of it being in the same universe as us. How do you think she felt when her daughter began speaking Malemese too?"

"That's why she hates me?"

"She doesn't hate you. She's afraid for you. And maybe afraid of loving you too much."

"No fear of that."

"Try to understand."

"No! It's more than that. She blames me for his death even though she doesn't know… what you and I know. And when she looks at me like that…" I swallow, and choke out, "…I think she's right."

I know she's right. I killed him. Etin knows. And now I'm a thief, as well, which he can't ever know.

"I'm afraid of what I'll become if I stay here—if it isn't already too late."

"Come on the ship with me. You're too young to start college. You'll learn a lot, and you'll be with family."

I smile a little. "I'm a land-lover, Etin. I couldn't live in space for months and months, without the wind and the soil and the sunshine." The thought makes me shudder.

"How will you pay to room at the college?"

"I told you. The job paid well." This is the question I'd feared. C75 would never have got me into college, let alone a room on campus. "I got a... grant. And I'll work. Next year, I'll get a scholarship. I have Father's gift for languages, remember?" And other gifts of his, as well, I think, resisting the urge to touch my pocket where the small leather pouch lies hidden.

How well did either of us know our father? Perhaps I'm the one who followed his real trade, not Etin.

The space-bags bob gently behind me as I walk down the hall to the door. I don't look back, even for Etin, as it closes behind me.

# Chapter Four

It takes me two months—the last week barely eating—before I go back to Sodum's shop. Tuition and residence cost more than I thought, and the part-time job I expected to find—well, who's going to hire a college freshman when they can hire a senior? The money I made from the diamond ring is spent.

I could move back home and commute two hours to the College of Translators. Owegbé wouldn't turn me away, but she wouldn't welcome me, either. I don't need that. So here I am in the middle of the night, somewhere near the back of Sodum's store. It's cloudy, the only light comes from the narrow, solar-powered panel that runs along the jutting edge of the roofs in front of the stores. Here at the back of them, it's almost pitch dark. I've been up and down this unlit street twice, looking for the entrance to the alley. If I could just walk past the storefront and orient myself it would be easier, but the front street is too well-lit with sidewalk panels as well as the rooftop panel, and I don't want to be seen near the store.

Why shouldn't I steal? I ask myself as I walk slowly in the dark. My father did. Apparently not very successfully or we'd have been better off—unless it was all used up during his years of illness. All but the magnificent diamond with its black, secret center. He wouldn't sell it and neither will I, not ever. I only wish I knew its secret. According to the info-net, GoTo, there may be diamonds mined on Malem—extraordinary ones, if it's true—but no one's ever brought one away from Malem to verify the rumor. It could just as easily have come from a dozen other places where my father traded, but none of them describe a stone like his.

Wait, there: I stop at a break between two buildings and look down a narrow dirt walkway littered with garbage. On either side the dirty walls of buildings rise up, barely discernable from the black night as they recede into the alley. I shiver, peering into the pitch-black alley.

This is only temporary. Next year I'll win the second year scholarship. But that won't feed me now. My empty belly is more insistent than my fear, so I step into the dark. Four paces in and the darkness becomes tangible, a midnight space I have to force myself to walk into.

I grope with my hands along the wall that I think is the outside of Sodum's store. If I've got the right block, the right alley. How far along is his store? It's been months since I sold that ring to him, I can't remember the block front clearly, let alone the back. If I hadn't passed him by chance at the station, where I was trying to shoplift something to eat, I wouldn't have remembered his offer to teach me at all. On impulse I dropped my bag in front of him and, bending to pick it up, set the date for tonight's meeting.

I feel the indent in the wall that means a door, and knock quietly. No answer. I knock a little louder. Why doesn't he open it? He should be waiting for me. What if this is the wrong alley? What will I say if someone other than Sodum opens this door?

A sudden, sharp hiss makes me jump. Further down the alley, a door has opened silently.

"Come here! Quickly!" Sodum whispers in a fury. He's dressed in black; all I can see is his white, skeletal hand on the door and his pinched face stretched over a bald skull. His archaic spectacles catch the thin light coming through the door and shine out at me with what appears to be black, empty sockets behind them. I back away.

The hand not on the door appears, making small, rapid gestures at me as he scans the alley. "Get in! D'yu want t'be seen?"

The hiss of his voice is creepy, but I didn't come all this way to turn and run like a little kid. He's the one who's nervous. I walk to the door calmly—well, trying to look calm, just to infuriate him—and step inside.

The store is even darker than the alley, if that's possible. I feel my heart pounding and stand still, afraid to move, but as soon as he closes the door to the alley, Sodum flicks the ceiling panels on. He picks up a thin plastic card from the table his eyecomp is on and hands it to me. As I hold it, it becomes as flexible as a glove and follows the contours of my palm, warming to body temperature. I examine the swirl of tiny wires encased within it. The design is vaguely familiar.

"A palm override," he says. At once I recognize the design—it looks just like the lines in a human hand. He shows me how to adjust the wires delicately with the edge of my thumb, to fool the infra-red sensor and open his office safe. Not surprisingly, it's empty.

"There's no such thing as a private safe," he says, grinning his horrible death's-head grimace at his pun on the word 'safe' as he resets the wires so I can try it. It's trickier than it looks, setting the wires to cover my own palm and fingertip signature in order to fool the lock. When I'm able to open the safe fast enough to satisfy him, he reaches into a lower cupboard and brings out a two-foot square metal box. Each of its sides has a different kind of locking mechanism. He hands me a tiny finger comp and teaches me to break the codes and hack into the two most common types of comp locks. Over and over and over. It's the middle of the night and I've been here a couple of hours at least.

I'm about to remind him I have to get up and go to class in a few more hours, when he nods his head, satisfied.

He hands me a flat piece of metal encased in a light film of moldable plastic. One edge of the metal is serrated, narrowing to a rounded end. I stare at it, too tired to care what it is. Then I recognize it as an antique key.

"Do people still use these?" I touch the silver lock on the third side of the box with the enhanced key.

"Usually just fer show, along with a sensor. They can be lasered off pretty easy, but that leaves evidence." His lip curls with professional distaste. He gives me a tiny pick and shows me how to use both of them to open the ancient, mechanical locking devices on the other two sides of the box. Now I have to practice this over and over until my eyesight goes blurry and my hands shake with fatigue.

"That's the most popular," he says, pointing to the palm override. "And they're hard t'come by." He places the devices in a bag and holds it out to me. "These'll cost yu C30."

"I haven't any money."

His face thrusts suddenly toward me. "Yu have C500!"

"I used it to pay my first year in the College of Translators."

"Yer trainin' t'be a Translator?" Behind the spectacles his eyes gleam. "Embassies, gover'ment offices," he mutters to himself, rubbing his hands. Again his face thrusts forward, this time twisted into the hideous grimace he considers a smile. "Yu can owe me." He drops the bag into my hands. "Take care o' that palm override. I can't get another. And if yer caught with it yu won't be treated as a 'young offender', they'll consider yu a seasoned criminal. Remember that!"

I'm tempted to throw the bag back in his face. I hate the thought of being in debt to this horrible man. And I'm not a criminal! I'm not a thief! ...just one ring, that's not a real thief. I raise my hand—

But how can I explain coming here, spending all this time learning something and then not take the tools to do it? There is no explanation. It would be crazy.

And what if I don't get that scholarship? Owegbé's face fills my mind, taunting me: sneaking home, a failure... I lower my hand.

Sodum grins. He leads me to the back door and opens it a crack, cautiously peering up and down the alley before swinging it wide enough for me to pass through. I'm brushing past him, trying not to touch him at all, when I remember.

I might never see him again. If I want to ask my question it should be now. He's the one most likely to know and least likely to mention it to anyone else.

"Have you ever seen a kind of gem that looks like a diamond but bigger? With colors, all the colors of the rainbow. And a black center." When I say the last phrase his gaze focuses on me so intently I unconsciously take a step back and bump into the door frame.

"A black center? Where did yu see this gem?" He pulls me back inside and shuts the door.

"I..." I'm about to say I don't remember but it won't work. Of course I'd know where I saw a gem I can describe so well. "At an Immigration Investigation. I was translating."

"Translatin'? Yu can't be a translator already."

"I'm not. But I can speak Malemese and they couldn't afford a real translator."

"A Malemese Investigation? Yer lying. The Malemese don't emigrate."

"Well these two were." I'm angry now, mostly at myself for bringing it up at all. "They wanted work on a farm."

"And the stone?" His gaze is piercing.

"His wife..." I falter. Where would a diamond that size be worn? And why did I mention Malem? No one from Malem would have a diamond like that, especially someone who couldn't afford a translator. I expect him to call me on it, but he nods, as though I've confirmed something for him.

"A Malemese diamond." He says it almost reverently.

"A Malemese diamond?" They're only a myth, no one's ever proven their existence. But I can't say that, he'd know I've researched them. And...

And I think he's right. "It's yours," my father said, in Malemese, when I spoke to him in that language. He wasn't speaking to me. He wasn't giving it to me. I feel a pain in my chest, and I look down so Sodum can't see my face.

"I'm s'prised they let it be seen. If yu bring me one of those, little missy, yu'll make both our fortunes."

"If I had one of those I'd never give it to you!" I reach for the door. I just want to get out of there.

Sodum looks at me, his hand on the door, holding it shut. "I don't give advice," he says in a tone so lacking his normal sharpness that I stop trying to open the door, and look at him. "...but I'll say this: if yu ever find yerself in possession of a Malemese diamond, yu'd do best t'get rid of it as soon as possible. They aren't meant for the likes of us. And," his face regains its normal avaricious expression, "it's better t'sell it than throw it away."

He reaches out his hand to touch me. I shrink back and he drops his hand. "I have high hopes for yu," he says, his expression so intent I can't look away, "so I'll tell yu this: if yu can't find a way to sell it, yu'd better throw it away."

"I... I haven't any such thing, anyway." I look aside, breaking the spell of his intense gaze.

"Shame. We coulda both been rich." He opens the door enough for me to slip through. As soon as I hear it close behind me I break into a run and flee through the darkness until I'm panting and exhausted, within blocks of the college.

I palm open the door to my residence room, and find my college roommate going through my dresser drawers.

"What are you doing?"

"I'm looking for that glitdust you borrowed last week." She doesn't even look up or pause in rifling through my clothes. She's dressed in a sleeveless silk tunic which falls from a high neck rill in a suggestive curve down to her mid-thigh. It probably cost more than my family makes in a year. Her hair hangs down in a shimmering black wave, but she's gelled the sides up in a swirl of braided rosebuds. I feel awkward and poor beside her, not to mention the fact that I couldn't wear that dress if I owned it— it'd fall in a puddle at my skinny feet. No wonder Jaro treats me like his kid sister, even though he pays me to tutor him.

My roommate pulls open the second drawer, and my heart lunges into my throat. The leather pouch is in there. I rush forward and give the drawer a hard shove.

She yanks her hands out just in time, with a yelp, and turns to me, outraged.

"If you ever go through my things again, I'll call a pol."

"Where's my glitdust, then?"

I push past her and cross the narrow room, stepping over her things littered across the floor. "On," I say to the comp workstation on my side of our joint desk, and I swipe my card through the side slot.

"Here, buy a new one." I punch in my pass and account and step aside, nodding to her to complete the transfer. I rarely refer to her by name, even in my thoughts. As if to mock my attempt to escape my family, I'm stuck with a roommate who has the same name as my sister.

"I don't need your creds." Even frowning, my roommate is beautiful. She has the same black skin and wide brown eyes as I, and everyone with a long ancestry on Seraffa, have. But she's tall, with high cheek bones and a straight, slender nose. And she's two years older than me, with a shape that makes every guy she passes stop just to watch her walk. Every time I look at her, I hate my round cheeks and short, turned-up nose which make me look even younger than I am. People have asked if I'm her kid sister visiting her at college. Last time someone asked that I said, "no, I'm her illegitimate daughter." When she protested I said, "Oh, sorry, I'm not supposed to tell. She thinks it ages her, but she's so pretty, what does it matter she's twice your age?" The guy left so fast you could feel the wind suck into the space where he'd been. Oghogho didn't speak to me for a week, which was really stretching how long she can remember to be mad.

"Just give me back my glitdust," she says, looking bored. "I'm in a hurry."

"I used it."

"All of it?" Her pouty lips open in surprise.

I feel myself flushing but I can't stop it. I'd intended to add a soft glimmer to my skin, like she does, and ended up looking like radiation in the club's infra beams. Fortunately, no one who knew me was there, including Jaro, who was the point of my using the stuff in the first place.

"It spilled," I lie.

The comp beeps, ejecting my card. "Transaction time exceeded," a regretful feminine voice informs me.

Her lips twitch. "You must have been quite a sight." She's laughing as she palms the door open.

"Go spread your joy," I mutter over my shoulder as she leaves. Her name, 'Oghogho', meaning 'joy,' is a popular Edoan girl's name. The minute she introduced herself I knew she hated the commonness of her name as much as my sister does. I immediately decided to keep my totally uncommon name, and introduced myself as "Kia," knowing an exotic name would be the only advantage I'd ever have over my glamorous roommate. The next day I went to the birth registry and made it official.

She made me pay for that advantage.

"How many languages do you speak?" she asked, as though it was an afterthought.

"Three," I said without thinking and regretted it instantly. I should have realized this was the real status question here, more important than money or clothes or good looks. "Fluently," I added. But I knew it was too late.

"I thought Traders would know more." She smiled.

"I'm on my fourth. I don't count them till I'm perfect." It's the truth but it sounded defensive even to me.

"Perfect?" Oghogho laughed. It was a lovely sound, like a singer hitting a difficult note perfectly. "No one is ever perfect in a second language."

By the end of the week I became "Perfect Three" to half the students in our year, "Three" for short. The other half said I was lying. Apparently, no one's ever been admitted to the College of Translators with only three languages before.

# Chapter Five

"Kia! Kia Ugiagbe!"

I ignore the distant voice. I'm balanced on my tiptoes, trying to see the student compscreen around the heads of the students in front of me. The college concourse is crowded with kids, all taller than me, inching their way toward the wall monitor to see their grades. It's so noisy I'm not even sure I heard my named called, until a hand grabs my shoulder.

"Didn't you hear me, Perfect?" Jaro grins at me when I turn.

I frown, damping down the queasy feeling his grin always gives me, not to mention the way he shortens my nickname to 'Perfect' instead of 'Three'. "I'm trying to see my grades," I say, turning back toward the 'screen before my frown turns into the dopey grin my face wants to wear.

"Like there's any question how you did. I'm the one who should be worried."

What does he want me to say? Despite my tutoring—for which he pays well—he'll be lucky to get a C+. At least he's no longer failing. I'm still trying to think of a response when I feel him lean in close behind me.

"Anytime now, you should smile," he whispers. His warm breath tickles my ear. I feel myself grinning, and hope I don't look as foolish as I feel. He nods and leans in close again. "C+," he whispers.

That makes me laugh. The second time he came for tutoring, he told me he'd decided to pay me in more than creds; he was going to tutor me, too—in social skills. By then it was known I could speak the *three* languages I claimed as well as our professors. Not that I ever said so: I only antagonize my peers. So I told him, "I don't need to be liked."

"It's enough to be admired, is it?" He was close enough to finishing my thought that I blushed. He just waited, let me think it out. Jaro is popular. People want to do what he suggests. Not necessarily me, but other people. It would be useful to learn how to do that.

"Fair enough," I said. "Your skill for mine. You pay me for the first hour, I'll give you an extra half hour each session and in return, you make me popular."

As soon as I said it I thought he was going to make some joke about doing the impossible, but he just grinned and said "Good for you!" Which admittedly was a little patronizing, but the way he said it, and the look on his face, made it hard to be annoyed with him—just what I wanted to learn. He'd kept to his bargain, and he didn't tell anyone, which I hadn't had the sense to make him promise at the time. Since then, every time he sees me, he grades me. It took me a long time to move beyond an F.

So even though I'm sure I look like another idiot girl in love with gorgeous Jaro, I smile at him now. He grabs me and lifts me up high. I'm about to kick him to make him put me down, when I realise I can see the compscreen above the sea of heads. I shut my mouth and look for my courses.

A+ in three of my languages and two of my four cultural linguistics, A in the other two. The two A's are disappointing but I can bring them up. It's the place where my fourth language mark should be that worries me. It should be my best mark, but instead there's no mark at all, just the Dean's office number.

Did they lose my exam? I froze it in time and date and posted it to the prof before leaving the exam room, so there should be a back-up on the exam comp. My login will prove I wrote it. How could he not have got it? Then I think: they don't post failures.

Impossible. I know that language now as well as I know Edoan.

"Hey," Jaro says. "My grades?"

I know his student number from tutoring him. He gives a Whoop! when I tell him, even though they're mostly C+ and two B-'s. He looks like he's going to swing me around but the crowd's too tightly-packed.

"What is it?" he asks as he lets me down and sees my expression. "Missing an A+?"

"Yes," I snap. I push my way through the crowd toward the exit.

"Back to C-," Jaro calls after me.

᠊ᢀ

Dean Harris opens the door on my first knock.

"Kia Ugiagbe, Sir. I've come about my grade."

"I know why you're here." He motions me into a chair in front of his desk, closes the door and returns to his chair across from me. I'm too nervous to sit, but he looks at me until I do. After rummaging through his top drawer he finds a holodisc and tosses it on the desk. "Professor Brecher gave this to me."

I click it on. Across the top of the first page I read: 100%. I look up with a grin that dies under the Dean's stare.

"Professor Brecher tells me no student has ever achieved a perfect score before."

I attempt a winning smile, but he's still frowning. I should have paid more attention to Jaro's lessons.

"How did you do it, Kia?"

"I studied, Sir."

"There are three questions on this exam that weren't covered in the lectures. They're not in the textbook. They're not even on the language disks in the college library. According to Professor Brecher, only a native Salarian could get a perfect score on this test. Are you a native Salarian?"

He knows I'm not, but I shake my head anyway.

"Do you know a native Salarian?"

I shake my head again.

His expression becomes even grimmer. "Cheating is taken very seriously here."

I open my mouth to protest but before I can deny it, he says, "It would be better for you if you confessed." He's switched languages, a common practice of the profs here. Without thinking, I match the one he's speaking.

"I… I didn't think it mattered, Sir. I didn't mean to cheat."

"You didn't *mean* to?"

"I already knew some Salarian before I came here. I chose it as my fourth language because I thought it would make my first year easier." I look down at my lap, ashamed. The word "easier" hangs in the air, condemning me. The silence is terrible.

"You didn't hack into the exam?"

I look up, shocked. "What? No!" It never occurred to me he'd think that. Steal knowledge? I'm furious, until I remember that I *do* steal. But not grades.

"I don't have to," I say coolly.

"Do you remember the questions to which I am referring?"

I nod. They were colloquialisms, very current and meaningless outside the cultural context. They'd been on the most recent Salarian flash at the Trader's Library, which I'd been studying on my own when I applied to the college. I only half-understood the explanations and it bothered me, until two of the lessons in my Salarian culture course suddenly made the meanings clear.

"How did you know the answers?"

For a while after I tell him he just looks at me, then he asks, "What language are we speaking?"

I blink and have to think a moment. "Salarian."

"You must have known it quite well before you came." He glanced at his workstation screen. "You claimed to know three languages: Edoan, Coralese and Malemese. That's a strange choice, Malemese."

That's exactly what he said when I applied to the college: strange choice. Translation: useless. He had to give me a written test on it, because no one on campus could speak it to confirm my claim. I don't want to go into that again, so I just nod. Neither of us mentions Central Ang. Everyone knows it, so it doesn't count.

"Why didn't you include Salarian?"

"I didn't know it then—not perfectly."

"Perfectly? You expect to know every language perfectly?"

I begin to nod, then I stop. "Perhaps not Kandaran."

The Dean smiles. "Not even the Kandarans can speak Kandaran."

It's a well-known expression. I think of Jaro and make myself smile, when what I'm really thinking is whether I'll get my grade in Salarian now.

"You'll get your 100%. I'm satisfied."

My forced smile turns real. I don't want to jinx it though, so I get up to go, but the Dean waves me back into the chair. "What do you know about translators, Kia?"

"They're highly respected, Sir," I say, "but not terribly well-paid."

"Why do you want to become one?"

"Because I tried it once. And I didn't do it very well."

He waits, but I have nothing to add. Like I'm going to tell him about the Immigration Investigation. Bad enough remembering it myself. After treating a Malemese woman for some illness,

Dr. Eldrich gave my name to the couple because they wanted to immigrate. They named me as their translator in court and I was stupid and conceited enough to agree. Who would imagine translating would be so difficult? The longer it went on, the more mistakes I made, and everyone had to wait while I sorted them out. The government translator was laughing at me behind his somber expression, on the first day. On the second day, he stopped listening. On the third day he stopped pretending to listen. The judge's verdict was to allow the Malemese couple to stay, but I'm still convinced that was only because he knew I'd never stop trying to correct my errors until he did. Then I started arguing that the court shouldn't charge the couple their translator's fees because I shouldn't be paid, and the Malemese couple insisted I should be, and I said I wouldn't take it, so he had to rule on that, too. Then I objected to his ruling that I *should* be paid and asked for a lawyer. He threatened to send me to jail if I ever opened my mouth in his court again, so I shut up. And that is something that wasn't on my application to the college.

I realise the Dean is speaking to me and look up.

"...ever wonder why we accepted you early with only three languages? You must know by now that most students have four or five before they come here."

I'm still thinking of the judge and my habit of arguing, and I don't want to lose that 100%, so I try to look interested without saying anything.

"Because you know them so well. You speak each one so fluently it's impossible to determine which is your mother tongue. That is exceedingly rare. Are you aware we're speaking Coralese now?" I have to think a minute before I nod.

"In order to translate, one language must be unconscious— the one you're translating into. The difficulty in translating is remembering what was said."

That was my problem at the Investigation. I recognize it as soon as he puts it into words.

"While the short-term memory is holding onto the foreign words, the mind must be able to speak in another language instinctively, without distracting the short-term memory and losing the train of thought.

"Accuracy of word, nuance, inflection—that's obvious. But most important, a translator must be able to hear in one language and speak in another, simultaneously. Most translators are only able to translate from a foreign language into their mother tongue. When we examined you for entrance here, we found you were able to translate equally well both ways. In three languages."

He looks at me. Am I supposed to respond? "Thank you," I mumble. Then honesty forces me to add, "but I couldn't, not when it mattered."

"I suspect you did much better than you think. Twice now, while we've been speaking, you have switched languages seamlessly: grammar, syntax, idiom, all perfect, without a pause. I know of no other student here who can do that. You have a rare talent, Kia. I hope you will use it wisely and bring honor to this college."

No one's ever praised me like that. I don't know what to say. He sits there, waiting, till finally I get out: "I won't let you down, Sir." Immediately I'm embarrassed at how dumb that sounds.

"I hope you won't. Because a talent like yours also has the potential to bring disgrace to this Institution. If I had found that you cheated I would have expelled you. You wouldn't be given a second chance. A dishonest translator at the highest levels can do great harm. We want no part of that here." He looks across his desk at me sternly.

I swallow. What if he finds out about Sodium? The very thought makes me sick.

"I'm glad I didn't find that to be the case," he says, dismissing me at last. I walk back to residence repeating his words, *rare talent*, to myself, and don't even need Jaro to remind me to smile.

This must be my day, because as soon as I get back to my room, there's a knock at my door. I open it, all unsuspecting, and almost slam it shut again.

"Akhié—"

"My name is Kia."

She stiffens. Her smile is forced when she speaks again.

"Yes, Etin told us. I forgot."

I can feel my roommate, Oghogho, watching us curiously from her desk. I've never told her anything about my past except to introduce Etin as my brother on one of his visits. He understood at once when I told him my new name that I won't talk about the past.

Now here's my sister, dressed in a trader's jumpsuit, with our ship's name—the *Homestar*—emblazoned on her left shoulder. I step into the hall, pulling the door shut behind me.

"What do you want?"

"To talk to you, Ak… Kia."

"You miss our long sisterly conversations, right?" Oghogho barely spoke to me the entire last year I lived at home, even though we shared a room. Who does she think she's fooling now?

"Mother is ill."

I look at her without saying anything. I was ill last semester with flu. Where was 'Mother' when I was feverish and throwing up and terrified because I thought it might be my father's malady? But there's a tight feeling in my chest that keeps me from speaking. Oghogho wouldn't be here unless it was serious.

There's a knock from the other side of the door. I open it.

"I'm going to do some research at the library," my roommate says. As she steps past us, she's examining my sister. "Hello," she says.

It's the opening for an introduction, which I ignore. My sister finally gets it and just says "Hello" politely back.

On impulse, then, I say, "Oghogho, this is also Oghogho." You're as common as the red dirt, I think, smiling coolly at both of them. They both look down on me. But I, at least, am unique. *A rare talent,* the Dean said. I smile sweetly.

Oghogho my roommate nods curtly to Oghogho my sister and leaves, her knees and backbone held so stiffly her sandals slap against the tiles. I watch with satisfaction.

"I see you've made friends."

"Of course. I'm a friendly person." I wave Oghogho into the room, but her comment has ruined the moment for me. I imagine Jaro demoting me to a D. Maybe all the way back to an F. I don't have to be popular with everyone, I argue with him in my mind, but it's no use; he doesn't think like that.

Annoyed, I slap the door shut. At least we have privacy now. I sit on my roommate's chair, tossing the clothes that lie on it onto her bed, and face my sister, who's perched on the edge of my chair.

Oghogho leans over and picks up an earphone lying on the dresser beside my bed. Like many students, I've learned to sleep with language discs plugged into my ears, reinforcing the lessons I study before going to bed. But I do it regularly, test or no test. After a while, Saturday nights, the one night I allowed myself to rest from learning, began to feel strange. The silence was eerie. I'd wake up muttering foreign phrases into the darkness to fill it. Finally I simply started wearing the language headphones every night.

I take the earphone from Oghogho. She's deliberately postponing the news she came to tell me. Either it's very bad—so bad she doesn't want to talk about it—or they want something from me. That's unlikely, but I'm beginning to hope that's it.

We sit for a while without talking.

It must be very bad.

"What do you expect of me after all this time?" The words burst out without me intending to say them.

"It was you who left," Oghogho says. "And you who chose to stay away. Did you want us to run after you and beg you to come back?"

I flush, because I realise I did want that, and she just has to look at me to know how pathetic I am. So I get mad instead. You made me a thief! I want to yell at her. But it isn't true. My father made me a thief by passing on his stolen legacy: the mystery I can't solve despite all the hours I've spent in the library researching diamonds, and can't part with, either, despite Sodum's warning.

"Perhaps we should have," Oghogho says. "Yes, I should have. I'm sorry. But you were so aloof after father died. And, I'll admit it, I was relieved at first. When you left, all the tension left our house. It was like some guilty secret hung over us, and then it was gone."

"Was I so terrible?" I feel my eyes water and blink furiously. After how they treated me, why do I even care?

"No, of course you weren't. It was all of us. I think now it was Father…" She takes one look at my face and says quickly, "I loved him, too, Akhié. As much as you did. Maybe more, because I could remember how he was. But he was *sick*, and now that I'm older, I can see how it affected us all. I was glad you left, Akhié, but it wasn't you, it was him. If he hadn't died, he would have destroyed us all. He almost did."

I jump up so angry I can hardly breathe. "You're wrong!" I scream, not caring who hears. "It was Owegbé! It was never Father! It was… Owegbé!" I can only repeat it. I'm so good at arguments but now I'm too mad to think of any. "And I'm Kia," I shout, "Kia!" I stop for breath. "You should go. You should go now!"

"Mother's very sick, Kia." Oghogho stands up, too, but her voice is quiet. Sad. "She may be dying. I didn't come here to fight with you." She holds out her hand, palm up in peace. I ignore it. "I'm sorry. We should be over this by now. I came because I thought you should know."

"In case I want to see her? Has she asked for me?" I already know the answer—she hasn't called once since I left. I try to laugh sarcastically. It doesn't come out right.

*Does* she want to see me now? I wonder.

Etin never asked what father and I had talked about in Màlemese. I don't think he blames me for Father's death—he said it wasn't my fault, that day when he sent me away. But Owegbé?

"Tell her… Tell her I hope she gets better."

"You'll have to tell her yourself. I'm on my way to the Spaceport. I'm shipping out in two hours."

"But Etin's out with the *Homestar.*"

"No, he's trading for the *Montrealm III.*"

I open my mouth to tell her it isn't true. Etin told me last month he'd been approached by one of the Montcliffs, the family who own the largest trading chain on Seraffa, but he turned them down. He'd never be happy trading for someone else; he likes being his own boss.

But why would she lie? I close my mouth, noticing for the first time how tired Oghogho looks.

"Mother needs a heart transplant."

I shrug. "She's a citizen. Her medical care is free."

"Yes, but Mother can't take a standard lab 'plant. You know how sensitive she is to allergens. It's why she could never go into space with Father."

I hadn't known that. I feel a stab of envy. Oghogho was always so much closer to Owegbé.

"Her body won't accept anything but a human donor's heart," Oghogho says, "and there isn't likely to be one with the right blood type on Seraffa in time. Medical aid is free, but bringing another heart in, on a speedship, with the machines and storage unit to keep it healthy and a specialist to watch it—"

She sounds as though she's ticking off expenses she's calculated many times. I imagine her and Etin sitting with their heads together in front of a screen of figures. I should have been with them. Why am I always excluded?

Oghogho glances for the second time at the digital display on my workstation. "Look, I'm sorry I haven't come before this. And I'm sorry we argued. But I have to go."

"Wait. I have some money." I jump up and run to my workstation. C28. I already know how few creds I have left.

Why did I only take one necklace at the Ossidian Ball, when the whole safe was open to me? Because that's all I needed, I answer myself. If only I hadn't spent most of the money already. I slide my card into the slot, turning toward Oghogho.

"I can get more. ...Translating," I add quickly, hoping Oghogho doesn't know students aren't paid for translating.

"I didn't come here for your money."

"Take it!" I key in my access without a pause in the rush of words. "My tuition and board are paid for the rest of the year now. I don't need it. I want to help you and Etin."

"Not Mother?"

I stand up, waving my sister into the desk chair. "Take it."

"I can't take it. I'm on my way to the Spaceport. You should take it to her yourself. But, Kia... Thank you."

We stand for a moment looking at each other, before she turns and leaves.

# Chapter Six

The Newtarion Embassy is the most impressive embassy on Seraffa. I climb the dozen steps that lead up to the ten-foot-high double doors at the entrance, feeling a cross between excitement and fear. I give my name and registration number to the armed guard as I lean in toward the monitor for a retinal scan. He confirms my ID and palms one of the doors in an unmarked spot. Both doors slide open onto a huge foyer at least two stories high. Cool air rushes out, engulfing me. The waste shocks me, even though it feels wonderful.

Excited as I am to see this embassy, I wish I hadn't been assigned to it. The Newtarions are known for their tight security. But when you put your name down as a student translator you can't specify when and where, and the Newtarions are wealthy. The safes in the guest rooms have to be full of expensive jewelry. I'll take two pieces this time, to buy my mother a heart. It's probably the best use that jewelry will ever be put to. I can already imagine the look on Etin's and Oghogho's faces when I transfer the creds to them.

Oh yes, I have a rare talent, as Dean Harris said: my father's talent.

Two more guards are stationed beside a second set of doors between the foyer. I'm ID'd again before I pass through into the main hallway. It's at least twenty feet wide and three times as long, hung with holo-portraits of famous Newtarions in gilt-edged frames. On the left there are several doors, some of them standing open to reveal huge waiting rooms with real leather armchairs and Earthoak tables. I can't help wondering who they think needs this much impressing on Seraffa.

I checked out the internal layout as well as I could online, so I know the wide spiral staircase that I pass just before the ambassador's reception hall will take me to the upper offices and the guest suites. The ambassador's suites are also upstairs, though the secure stairway to his rooms is separate, past the reception hall.

I ladle myself a glass of fruit punch at the refreshment table. A translator can't accept food or drink in case it's been tampered with, and the best way to keep from being offered something is to have a drink already in hand. There are stories of translators causing far-reaching upheavals after being put under a mild hypnotic inducement before translating. It's hard to prove a translator was drugged and the person who schemed to provoke the conflict is seldom identified. Better to be wary, even at a primarily social event like this one.

As a student, my duties are light. The Newtarions have their own translators on staff, but not enough for a huge reception like this. And not everyone trusts embassy translators, even those wearing the highly respected dark green jumpsuit with its stylized initials, E.T.—Earth Translator—that promises political neutrality. I stroll through the reception room sipping my punch. This is the first time I've worn my E.T. jumpsuit; they had to make a special one for me because I'm too small even for XS. Privately, I think the forest green with blue piping is ugly— the colors are from Old Earth, where the College of Translators originated, and I prefer the reds and yellows of Seraffan scenery—but its effect is exhilarating. The guards and servers treat me with respect and people move aside to let me pass.

I look around for anyone wanting my services. At least half of the people here are wearing electronic devices, most small enough to fit inside an ear. No one important relies on them, though.

# Chapter Six

Only a human interpreter can get the nuances right, the colloqui-alisms and cultural connotations conveyed by word choice, ges-ture, and expression which can change the meaning of a phrase completely. Detecting irony, appreciating humor, are crucial to making political or business contacts. I spend as much time learning the social cultures of different worlds as their languages.

Across the crowded room I notice a certain shade of blue. My excitement drains away as I slip between the people to get a bet-ter look. Yes, I'm right, it's the blue and white habit of a Select of the Order of Universal Benevolence. I turn and walk casually in the opposite direction, swearing under my breath. I don't dare steal anything here now.

I'm so upset I almost miss my first summons. A tall woman is signaling me with an imperious gesture. Her thick white hair is curled and piled on top of her head, making her even taller. Strange that she'd let her years show in her hair while she's ob-viously had every sign of them removed from her face, I think as I hurry toward her. The black on blue of her flowing kaftan identifies her as Coralesian, and she's wearing the small planetary symbol of an ambassador: a very important woman. There's a translation implant above her left ear. As an ambassador, she al-ready speaks several languages herself. But she's surrounded by a triad of Salarians, the most easily offended people in the galaxy. I feel myself start to sweat under my jumpsuit.

A male translator is closer, but she waves him off when he steps forward. He should know better. The Salarian women would be insulted to have a male translate for them. I think of that 100%, and breathe a quick prayer. I'm so nervous I'd claim not to know Salarian if the flags weren't sewn onto my left shoulder.

I lean against the wall just inside the reception hall. I've been translating for three hours now, for five, no six dignitaries, three of them ambassadors. I think they've adopted me as some kind of pet, the way they keep calling me over, even when there are other translators closer to them. At least I haven't started any wars. I may be about to, though.

I've decided to do it, after arguing with myself all afternoon. It might be weeks before I get another chance like this. Owegbé—my mother—could be dead by then. I hate that I'm in my new uniform, that if I'm caught I'll bring shame on it, and even if I'm not caught, every time I wear it I'll remember this. But I can't let her die, knowing I could have prevented it. I can't kill both my parents.

I take a sip of punch, glancing over the rim of my cup to make sure no one's watching, then slip through the door and around the corner out of sight. I make myself walk slowly up the wide stairway. There's no reason to be nervous. No one saw me leave the crowded reception. There's only one Select there and I was never anywhere near her. If someone sees me, I'll say I'm looking for a restroom. But no one will be up here; they're all downstairs enjoying the party.

My arguments convince me; I reach the top ready to do what has to be done. I pass the first guest room—too close to the stairway. The second is double-locked and I don't want to stand outside picking the second lock unless I have to. The third guest room opens at once when I press my palm, covered by the thin, wired-plastic override, against its sensor. Whoever is staying here was in too much of a hurry to join the party, to use the double lock. I hope they made the same mistake with the safe.

It makes me a little nervous when the safe opens to the palm override as easily as the door did, like this is too good to be true. But as Sodum told me, the more well-guarded the premises are, the more lax the guests become. If you can get inside—and a good translator can—the rest is easy. I shrug and reach inside.

I'm admiring a diamond necklace when I hear a soft cough behind me. I freeze. At the corner of my eye I see the Select. She looks at the open safe and then down at the incriminating evidence in my hands.

I don't say a word. I don't move. I can't bear to do anything that will start what I know will happen, happening. I wish it was me with the failing heart, and I could die right now. How did I ever imagine I could get away with this while a Select of the O.U.B. was here? Embassy Security, even the Planetary Police, are nothing compared to them.

"What have you taken?"

Nothing. I haven't taken anything yet. I can still put it back, we can pretend this never happened, because it hasn't yet, not really... I open my mouth—and close it again, because there is the palm override, on the table under the safe, and beside it the little finger comp, and there's nothing I can say. I open my hand to reveal the stunning necklace. Even in the darkened room, its diamonds sparkle.

"Oh no, no. Not that one. Of course, I do admire your taste. It is exquisite, isn't it? But I happen to know it's a family heirloom, and one of the few Lady Khalida owns. You see, she's the youngest daughter, and not her mother's favorite. If it hadn't been for the intercession of her paternal grandmother, who, I might add, has no more affection for the girl than her mother has, but a better sense of propriety... that's beside the point, isn't it? I get sidetracked, you'll have to forgive me. The point is, Lady Khalida has only three pieces of jewelry she really cares about, and that is one of them. You mustn't take it. Put it back, and let me help you choose another."

She lifts the necklace out of my hands and returns it to its velvet box. I'm too stunned to say anything, I just watch her replace the box in the safe and lift out three others, all the while continuing her chatter as I stand there going over everything I ate and drank downstairs. Maybe I'm really lying on the floor in the reception hall and they're trying to revive me and I'm going to get a terrible lecture from the Dean about not drinking anything anyone gives me—I hope so, oh I hope so!

She stops talking and looks at me. "You're not going to faint, are you?" she asks.

I don't think you can faint in a dream, so I shake my head, even though I'm feeling dizzy and my knees are weak. I recognize her now. It's Agatha, the Select I met at my father's funeral. She's still as strange as I thought she was then. When I think that, I really start to shake because if this is Agatha being weird then I'm not hallucinating and I've been caught stealing by a Select.

"Let me see. She's a bit of a magpie, you know. But then, perhaps you understand that better than I?" Agatha chatters on and now I try to listen, to figure out where this is going, because I'm really shaking now and when I grab onto the table to keep from falling it feels very solid and wooden and real, not like a dream at all.

"Look, this one's about the same value as your original choice. The design is less intricate, but the stones are larger and very nice... Ahh, no, she still sees this gentleman occasionally. We don't want to embarrass her, do we? What's in here?" She opens the second box.

"No, this won't do at all. It's not nearly as valuable as the others. I don't want to cheat you. You believe that, don't you?"

She looks at me earnestly. I nod. The whole episode has taken on a surreal quality. I risk a glance at the open bedroom door and clear my throat. "Perhaps…" It comes out a squeak. I clear my throat again and try for something more like a human voice. "Perhaps we should just forget this?"

"Here's just the thing!" From the third box, Agatha takes a heavy gold bracelet, studded with diamonds.

"The stones are quite nice. I think you like diamonds, don't you?" She pauses till I give an embarrassed nod. "It's about the same value, and the work is so plain it's almost a crime *not* to melt it down and see if someone else could do better." She lifts one of my hands from its grip on the table and puts the bracelet into it. "Best of all, Lady Khalida no longer sees this suitor. Perhaps because she doesn't like bracelet. She won't even notice it missing for quite a while."

She closes the empty box and puts it at the back of the safe with a pleased smile.

"That's enough, isn't it? You aren't greedy, are you?"

I shake my head vigorously.

"Good, I thought not. You must watch out for that. You don't want to end up like Lady Khalida. I shouldn't say it, but I've never liked her very much."

Suddenly I get it. She's testing me. The O.U.B. are known for that. I should have caught on sooner. I drop the bracelet onto the table. "I don't want it."

Agatha looks at me sadly. "I can't give you the necklace," she says. "I really can't."

"I don't want either of them. I don't want them." I wish I could be more eloquent, tell her I've learned my lesson, I didn't know what I was doing, whatever she needs to hear from me. But I'm better with other people's words, not making up my own. All I can do is repeat, "I don't want it."

"Of course you do. You're not the kind of person who would take something for no reason."

What can I say? Yes I am? I don't know what to say so I just blurt out, "My mother's dying." And for no reason I can imagine, I start crying. I don't want her to die and I don't want to disgrace my uniform and most of all I don't want to cry *again* in front of Agatha. This is the second time I've cried to keep something from her and I don't want to be someone who uses tears to gain pity, so I make myself stop *right now*.

She leans her eye toward the small seal at the side of the door, and murmurs something into the tiny retinal-voice scanner. The door of the safe slides shut.

"It's very complicated, isn't it dear?" She says. "Now, wouldn't you like to hide that bracelet and get back to the party before either of us is missed?"

# Chapter Seven

Messer Sodum stands in the doorway. He doesn't move aside to let me in, which is odd. Usually he can't wait to pull me out of sight. Finally I squeeze in past him.

"What are you waiting for?" I ask. He closes the door slowly and turns to face me with none of his usual abruptness. He doesn't activate the ceiling panels.

"Show me what yu have." His voice is lifeless, as though he doesn't care. I feel a prickle of fear at the back of my neck. Last time he was so eager to examine the glittering prize he snatched it from my hands. I stand still, looking at him, trying to guess the reason for his strange behavior.

He holds out his hand. "What've yu got?"

"What's wrong?" I glance at the door.

"Nothing's wrong." His voice trembles, betraying him.

I should leave. Sodum sees me look toward the door and says, with a return of his customary sharpness, "Don't question me, Missy. Show me what yu've brought. We don't have all night."

He's right. Whatever's bothering him is no concern of mine. I reach into my pocket and pull out the bracelet. He makes no move to take it.

"Who's is it?"

"Lady Khalida's." Even as I answer I'm wondering, *is?* Not *was?* He always asks who owned a piece in order to sell it discreetly elsewhere, but this time the question sounds different.

"And how'd yu come by it?"

I stare at him.

"Out with it, girl. Did she give it t'yu?"

"No." I step back, toward the door.

Sodum looks exasperated. "Did yu find it lying on a table, p'rhaps? See it in passing and take it on impulse? Regretting it already, aren't yu?"

There are beads of sweat on his brow. Messer Sodum never sweats. For a man who's always nervous, this is remarkable. I think of him as a lizard: quick metabolism, cool skin. But now he's sweating. I take another step toward the door.

The lights go on. Blinking in the sudden brightness, I don't at first understand what's happening. Then the blue and white robe registers.

I drop the bracelet. It hits the clay tile floor with a harsh, accusatory report, clattering angrily for a moment as it settles. I'm reminded of Owegbé in one of her rages.

Then the silence is absolute.

Is it too late to run?

"Kia Ugiagbe," the Select says calmly, destroying any thought of escape. He bends down and lifts the bracelet from the floor. "I believe you were bringing this stolen jewelry to Messer Sodum?"

"I want none o' this!" Sodum cries shrilly. "I've done my bit. Yu said it would clear the past an' I'd be done."

The Select doesn't even glance at Sodum. "You may go now, Kia Ugiagbe," he says. "You will come to Number One Prophet's Avenue in two days at ten hundred hours. Please be punctual. An Adept's time is precious."

I turn and open the door, too numb to do anything but obey. Behind me, I hear the Select addressing Sodum. "You will no longer accept stolen property. We will know if you do."

"No, no! Never again! I was tempted but I see the error now—"

I close the door on his pathetic protests and stand there, frozen in the dark street. I've been ordered to appear before an Adept—I alternate between disbelief and utter terror. Why didn't they just turn me over to the pols? What will the Adept say, what will he do to me?

I start to run. When I reach the transit strip I leap on without waiting for it to slow, and race down the middle of it despite the rush of wind caused by the strip's speed. You're not allowed to walk, let alone run, in the accelerated center of the transit strips, but I tear down it, risking my life and anybody else's who might be on it. I have to get away, that's all I can think: Get away!

The strip turns into a curve. The force of the wind, suddenly hitting me sideways, knocks me into a pole. I grab it going down and hold on, banging my legs against the seat I should have been in as I fall. My hands, slick with sweat, slip on the pole, and for a second I think I'm going to be thrown off. Clinging desperately to the pole, I manage to brace my battered leg against the bottom of the seat where it meets the strip, until the transit straightens out and the wind dies down. I crawl up the pole and fall into the seat.

I sit there gasping for breath. My hands are sore and my right shoulder is on fire, I can barely move that arm. My left ankle screams with pain, I must have twisted it going down, and my right knee throbs; both legs feel sore and bruised, but nothing feels broken.

The near-catastrophe clears my head. What was I thinking? That I could run away from an O.U.B. summons? Where did I think I could hide from them? They're on every settled planet, with an information network that rivals any government's. Not that there's any rivalry; they work harmoniously with every world's pol force. I'll stand in front of an Adept one way or another; trying to run will only make it worse. I get up and hobble to the edge of the strip, holding the poles with my left hand and trying to put as little weight as possible on my left ankle as I reach for the pull that will slow the strip. I grit my teeth to keep from crying out as I swing off the strip and hobble across to the one going the opposite way, back to my dorm at the college.

I spend the first day at the college library listening to every flash I can find on the O.U.B. Most of them are about religion. I skim the explanation that the O.U.B. was created in the 23rd century as an amalgamation of the six major Earth religions at the time, that their goal was to bring order, faith and peace to the planets being colonized by a mishmash of cultures from over-populated Earth. Yada, yada, yada, basic history. I fast forward in nervous jerks, searching for something on punishments. When I exhaust the college library, I go to the Trader's library, but there's even less on the O.U.B. there, and next to nothing about their judiciary role. There's only one flash on which Adept hearings are even mentioned. They're referred to as a "rumor"; yet they're on an authorized learning flash, which means that they can neither be doubted nor proved. I run it again.

"Rumor has it," the disinterested voice on the flash states, "that the O.U.B. might, on occasion, approach a person and ask him or her to appear before an Adept. The Adept will hear the evidence, examine the accused, and possibly offer a "path of atonement" as an alternative to civil justice. These judgments, if they occur, do not appear on any public record." That's it. I play it until I've memorized it. It's no use at all.

I widen my search and find a few people who mention in their memoirs being approached by the Order. They all played some role in the history of a world by accepting an Adept's request. Perhaps they'd been caught in some wrong-doing, perhaps not: they don't mention that. And there's no one like me—an ordinary person, a nobody. But then, ordinary people don't write memoirs.

# Chapter Seven

A few convicted criminals claim to have been approached by the O.U.B. before their court appearance, but they have only the haziest memory of their interrogations and don't mention refusing any 'atonement'. If it's true, what must they have been asked to do, for them to choose public disgrace and internment instead? They knew they'd be found guilty. When the Select hand someone over to the pols there's no doubt of his culpability; the proof is delivered along with the culprit.

Or maybe they didn't get a choice. Maybe the Adept examined them and they failed whatever test was put to them?

What an idiot I was to take that bracelet from Select Agatha. Of course a Select wouldn't help me steal—and let me get away with it. But I'd been so sure of her sincerity. Dumb, dumb, dumb! What made me imagine I could read a Select? I shouldn't be tried for theft, I should be tried for stupidity!

I give up my search and go to bed, but I can't sleep. Oghogho snores across the room while I consider my options. Could I make use of Agatha's complicity, even if it was fabricated to trap me? They wouldn't want one of their own exposed as an accomplice to theft. Imagine the newsreels: Select jailed for theft. But the thought of Agatha in jail doesn't give me any comfort, it makes me feel worse. Owegbé raised me to revere the O.U.B.; my father to distrust them. Neither would give me a good reason why, so I settled on indifference. Indifference is a little hard to maintain in my current circumstances. Owegbé would be pleased by that, at least.

Owegbé! She's going to die of shame when she hears about this. I sit up suddenly in my bed. I will cause both their deaths. And Etin, he's going to despise me.

This is too painful to think about, so I lie down again and revert back to Agatha. It doesn't make sense that she'd make me trade the necklace for the bracelet if she knew they were going to catch me at Messer Sodum's and get it back. For that matter, why didn't she just tell me to report to the Adept when she saw me standing before the open safe with the necklace in my hands?

Nothing makes sense.

I get up early the next morning and take a long, hot bath followed by a shower. There may not be such luxuries in prison. I spend some time debating whether to take my father's leather pouch with me or not, but in the end I hide it under my mattress, along with the tools Sodum sold me. Then the whole way there on the slowstrip I berate myself for choosing such an obvious hiding place. At least it takes my mind off what I'm heading toward.

There's a Prophet's Avenue in the capital city on every world, and Number One always houses the O.U.B.'s planetary administrative offices. The rest of Prophet's Avenue is lined with residences for the Select stationed on the planet. Even those working in distant cities have a unit here. The Adepts live in residential wings in Number One.

As I limp down Prophet's Avenue, still favoring my left ankle, I have the sensation of being watched. I imagine a Select at every window staring at me, knowing why I'm here. When I find Number One I go straight up to the door, even though I'm early. I won't give anyone the satisfaction of seeing me hesitate, as though I'm afraid. Which I am, terribly, but that's my business.

The porter leads me to a waiting room and asks whether I'd like something to eat or drink. She's middle-aged, dressed in a blue and white jumpsuit, with her hair knotted tightly at the back. Her voice is pleasant but she doesn't smile; in fact she shows as little expression as a Select. Agatha excepted.

I take a drink, as though I'm here on a social visit. My stomach's in such knots I have to work at not gagging when I sip it, but I don't let her see that. When she leaves I look around. That plant in the corner wouldn't mind absorbing some liquid. I sit down beside it casually.

At precisely ten hundred hours the porter reappears and escorts me to an inner room. There's a high desk on a raised platform at the far end, and two smaller tables in the middle of the room facing it, each one with a Select sitting at it, their backs to me. The table on the right has a second, empty chair beside the Select. It all looks very plain and unimposing—until the Adept walks in.

She is wearing the blue and white robes of the Order, but all I notice are her eyes. She glances round the room and settles on me with an intense, unwavering attention that makes me feel like a bird caught in the stare of a snake. I freeze in the doorway. I can't move, can't even think straight, although there's nothing overtly sinister about her. She doesn't look angry or cruel or judgmental. She's just so focused that everything and everyone else dims by comparison.

"Kia Ugiagbe," she says. Her voice is calm, but it resonates in the room, which seems too small to contain her. I take a nervous step forward. Should I bow? Approach her? I dip my head quickly.

"Face your accuser." The Select on the left rises. He bows to her and turns to face me. It's the Select I saw at Messer Sodum's two days ago.

"And the companion who will advise you." The second Select stands, bows, and turns around.

It's Select Agatha.

# Chapter Eight

"I know this person, Adept." Agatha has turned back toward the Adept so I can't see her expression, but her voice is calm, emotionless.

"Tell us."

I force myself to breathe evenly, and wait for the damning evidence to come out.

"I met her at her father's funeral."

"Is that all?"

"No. She is training to be a translator. I met her again at an embassy reception."

"Did you speak together?"

"Yes."

The Adept and I both wait (me more anxiously than her) but Agatha volunteers nothing further. I avoid the Adept's eyes when she looks at me, trying to keep my face as blank as possible.

"Do you want another advisor?" she asks me.

Yes! I want Agatha—and the testimony she can give, assuming she hasn't already—as far away as possible. But if I say yes, the Adept will know there's more to the story than Agatha admitted. She'll read it in my face. No, I correct myself, she already has. And Agatha won't lie if the Adept asks her outright, which she's probably planning to do.

Why didn't Agatha tell her the whole story? Is it part of the role of advisor, Agatha has to do her best to help me? If that's it, and I say I don't want her as my advisor, I might be releasing her to testify against me. I have a headache already, and the interrogation hasn't even started yet.

Whose decision was it to make her my advisor? Is she trying to protect me, or—I remember her strange behavior at the embassy—is she trying to protect herself? To keep that from coming out? Or did she already confess, and this is the O.U.B.'s way of making sure it doesn't come out?

I don't know enough about this process. Enough? I don't know anything! But if I ask questions they'll know at once why I'm asking them. I look at Agatha. All I can see is the back of her head, and the blue habit. She doesn't sit like the other Select and the Adept. She slouches a little. Not really—you have to know her to see it. It's that intangible slouch that decides me.

"I don't care," I say. Wait. Wouldn't an innocent person want someone she knew?

"She was kind to me at my father's funeral." I let my voice tremble and wipe my eye. It's dry with fear. I'm not dumb enough to imagine this will get me any sympathy, but a little dab might explain why I don't look the Adept in the eye. She'll see right through me if I let her look in my eyes.

"I take it then that you accept your present advisor?"

I nod without looking up, and dab again for good measure.

"There is nothing wrong with your eye. You may be seated."

I walk forward and sit beside Agatha. Drop into the seat, more like, my legs giving out. Well, anyone would be nervous here—it would look more suspicious not to be.

At a nod from the Adept the male Select gets up and walks around his table. He bows to the Adept, nods to Agatha and me, and then recounts everything that happened at Messer Sodum's shop two nights ago, word for word.

There's no point questioning his story. Even in civil court, if a Select proves he or she was in a position to hear a conversation, not a single word of the exchange can be in question. If their enhanced memory slips—and that's unlikely—their video-audio scan implant won't.

Listening to the Adept recreate my conversation with Sodum, I recognize Sodum's attempts to downplay my actions. I didn't pick up on them at the time, but how could I have known? Protecting himself, no doubt, making our joint enterprise look a little less shady—hah!—but maybe I can still use his suggestion that the bracelet was lying on a table and I picked it up on impulse. I didn't answer Sodum, so the Select can't record a denial. As soon as he finishes speaking I stand up, glancing quickly at the Adept for permission.

I should never have looked at her. The concentrated focus of the Adept's gaze turns on me. I'm caught, half-way between sitting and standing, immobile. *I do not want to lie to this woman. It's essential to tell the full truth. I'll feel so relieved when I do...*

Agatha's hand is on my arm. I can see it but I can't feel it. "Sit down until the Adept addresses you," she says. Her calm voice cuts through my trance. I gasp, only realizing now that I haven't been breathing, and sink back into my chair.

What happened? I peek through my lashes and see the Adept is contemplating Agatha now. Agatha returns her look blandly. Maybe she doesn't know what she interrupted? Her expression and posture give nothing away.

They all give nothing. I'm totally out of my depth here: a blind girl taking on the sighted. They can read every thought on my face and I can see nothing on theirs. I look down at my hands folded in my lap, feeling utterly helpless. Beside me, Agatha doesn't move or say anything, but I can feel her, and I know she deliberately broke the Adept's hold on me.

The Adept must know it, too. The silence is so thick I feel like I'm breathing it in, choking on it. I won't look up. I won't, no matter how much I want to. My hands are clenched so hard in my lap my knuckles are white, but even an Adept can't see through a table.

Like that matters. She can see the tension in my face, whether I look at her or not. Well, who wouldn't be tense? It doesn't prove anything, as long as I don't look up.

"How did you come by the bracelet, child?" she asks.

I look down at my lap. *Ashamed,* I think, trying to infuse myself with the emotion for them to read. That's got to be what they want, they already know I did it.

"Stand up," Agatha says quietly.

I get up slowly, giving myself time to formulate the story and convince myself of it. To mix in an equal measure of the truth so the false parts can slip by. I'll only look up when I tell the true parts.

"I believed Lady Khalida wouldn't mind if I took the bracelet."

"Why would you think that? Look at me, child."

"I'm so ashamed." Good. I think I actually felt that. Now the truth: "I'm very sorry I did it." Perhaps a little too vehement, but I look up quickly as I say it so the Adept can see truth in my eyes.

She doesn't speak. She doesn't have to, she understands everything. Everyone is sorry when they're caught. She sees right through me, and now I *am* ashamed. I have to tell her the truth.

"I took the bracelet." Some part of my mind screams at me, *shut up!* but it's too distant to matter. I'm overwhelmed by a realization of the futility of lying, by a compulsion to confess.

"How?"

"I stole it." No, my mind cries, don't answer. But I can't stop myself.

"Tell me."

Trapped in the Adept's gaze, I can only obey. "I picked the lock of the safe."

"How is it that it was closed with no sign of tampering?"

I'm silent. I want to tell the Adept, and the longer the silence lasts the more desperate I become to say it, tell it all. But Agatha didn't tell on me. I grit my teeth against the longing to speak…

The room begins to spin. I start to feel sick, exhausted by the effort of not speaking...

Agatha stands up beside me. "I closed it."

# Chapter Nine

"You were there?" The Adept's voice is mild, and yet I wouldn't want to be Agatha at this moment for anything in the universe.

"What is done to her must be done to me also."

I'd considered making that point myself, but I was going for the opposite twist: let us both go.

"You participated in a theft?" The Adept looks only at Agatha. There's no difference in her expression that I can see, but Agatha's face turns white. I feel like I'm witnessing something brutal, as though the Adept is beating Agatha and Agatha's barely holding up under the onslaught. And yet there's no sound, no movement; only the quiet look between them which is so charged it leaves me faint and shaken.

"It seemed the right thing at the time," Agatha says finally. Her face is still rigidly inexpressive, but now it's chalky-gray. Her pale blue eyes are full of that miserable expression that makes me want to slap her and defend her at the same time.

The tension eases, as though the Adept has pulled it back.

"Then it must have been." She turns to me. "You have still committed a crime. With or without an accomplice." She says the last as if she knows what I considered earlier. As if. Of course she knows; she's an Adept. Why bother talking at all?

"It is worth your while to answer my questions. You might still surprise me."

I blink. It's a very small movement, but I might as well shout out loud that she's guessing my every thought. Agatha, standing

73

beside me, is caught in the same intense scrutiny. Somehow she's ended up on trial with me.

"I stole it. She—" I almost use Agatha's name "—came in and found me in front of the open safe. The Select is innocent."

"You must tell the whole truth," Agatha says softly beside me. "If I had told you not to steal, you wouldn't have."

"I would have gone back later." The truth is being drawn out of me against my will. I even want to tell the Adept about my father's stolen diamond. No, not that!

"You're holding something back."

"It isn't mine to tell." I will *not* shame my father's memory.

"But it's eating at you, child. It's hurting you."

"It isn't mine to tell."

The Adept looks at me a moment longer, then glances at Agatha. "Sit down, both of you. I've seen enough." She nods at the male Select, my accuser. "Thank you. You have fulfilled your role."

Agatha sits down carefully. Her face is still gray. The other Select stands up to leave. "She is a common thief," he says distinctly.

I hate the way it sounds, dripping out of his judgmental mouth.

"No." Agatha's voice is firm despite the weary expression she cannot hide.

The Adept looks at me.

"Not, like, full-time," I mumble. "…Maybe occasionally…"

Her face doesn't change, but something in her eyes looks like if she wasn't an Adept, she might laugh.

For one insane second I almost grin at her, but Agatha touches my arm discreetly and I swallow it. Cocky wouldn't go down well here.

"You are going to Malem," the Adept tells Agatha when the door has closed behind my accuser. "You will relieve the Select who is there now."

# Chapter Nine

"Thank you, Adept." Agatha's voice is as calm as though she's been offered a post on Earth, not been sent to obscurity on a horrible, disease-ridden, backwater planet further out than even Seraffa. I look sideways at her with a mixture of horror and pity.

"You may accompany her if you'd like."

I'm not sure I've heard right until I look up and see the Adept looking at me. There's no pressure or command in her look this time, just a calm neutrality. I want to laugh but my throat has closed so tightly I can't even pull air into my lungs. "I should accompany her?" I croak.

"You may if you choose to."

"To Malem?"

"I believe you speak the language?"

I want to say no, but there's no sense denying it.

"The Select will need an interpreter at—" it sounds like she's about to say 'at first' until she looks at Agatha. "—for a while."

"What's the alternative?" my voice comes out high-pitched, desperate.

"Alternative? The alternative is that you don't go."

"My punishment. How will you punish me?"

"Where did you hear such a thing? We do not administer punishment. Weren't you raised in the Order?"

"You'll just let me go?"

"Of course we will."

"And the bracelet?"

"It will be handed over to the pols. We do not keep stolen goods."

"So… So I'll just go free?"

She allows herself an expression. It is pained. "Surely you can work that out for yourself. The bracelet will be returned to Lady Khalida. She may press charges. The Select who accused you may be asked to testify. You have already heard his testimony.

75

You are young, and this is the first time you've been caught stealing. I expect they will go easy on you."

Easy on me. I close my eyes. It will be the end of translating; the Dean made that clear. And then Owegbé will hear of it. Even if she wasn't already sick, this would kill her. Etin and Oghogho will never forgive me. Why should they? I'm a monster, killing both my parents.

"Don't torture yourself, child. It is self-indulgent. If you were irredeemable, you wouldn't be here."

I consider telling her about my mother, that I took the bracelet to pay her medical costs. But the Adept must know it wasn't my first theft; they knew that when they waited for me in the back of Sodum's shop.

"And if I go? What testimony will the Select give then?"

"The Select will have to say the thief is no longer on this world. He will not be told where you have gone. He will not give your name unless he can accuse you to your face; that is our way. Lady Khalida will have her bracelet back, but she will have no one to press charges against."

She isn't smiling, but I've been so aware of every clue my face and body send, I can't help being more aware of hers. She isn't smiling. But she is.

"Why me?" They could afford to hire any translator they wanted; surely they could find *someone* who speaks Malemese and Edoan. Why choose a 16-year-old student?

"You have become… available," she says.

That does it. That *arrogance!* I open my mouth to refuse, but before I can speak she adds, "There has been a vision placing you on Malem."

I sit there with my mouth open. The O.U.B. never lie. I know it, but right now I can't believe it. They do have visions, and usually their visions come true—but a vision about me? I just look at her, not knowing how to respond to such a ridiculous statement.

"The vision occurred two years after your birth."

"What was it?" I play along. "What amazing thing will I do on Malem?"

"That is not for you to ask," she says coolly.

I flush. They never reveal a vision to the subject, I know that. A person cannot know her future. But this is crazy, a vision about me. She must be mistaken.

"We hope, while you're doing it, you'll teach our Select to speak the language." The Adept glances at Agatha, "and translate for her until she is proficient."

"I have school…" It's useless to argue. If they've had a vision, they'll get me there whatever it takes. I *am* going to Malem. I picture my father's face before he died. What if I come home crazy and sick with fevers, too? I want to throw up. I swallow hard.

"Dean Harris will be told we have contracted your services and you'll resume your studies when you return. Perhaps you will only accompany our Select there and return with the ship." The Adept's voice is calm, soothing. I immediately feel reassured. I look away from her, fighting the false emotion, and catch Agatha watching me.

"Did they see us both? In the vision?" Why wasn't Agatha taught Malemese if they knew she'd be going?

"Only you. We hoped the choice of Select would become clear. And it has. The Select herself said we must ask of her what is asked of you."

"I can't go. My mother's sick!"

"Our fee for your services will cover her medical expenses. A priority will be placed on finding her a compatible heart. When you return, your tuition and residence at the college will be covered until you graduate. You will have no further need to steal.

And you will never do so again." The last sentence is said in the same calm tone, but with a firmness that hits me like a whiplash. The Adept is done with my delays. She is accustomed to being obeyed.

For this reason alone I want to refuse her. If only there was some way I could. But they have me trapped. My family, my education, my future: nothing will be left if I refuse.

"Come with me to Malem, Kia," Agatha says softly. "It will be alright. It is God's plan, not ours."

I close my eyes. I am beaten.

"It is settled, then," the Adept says. She rises to leave. As if it is an afterthought, she adds, "That secret you are keeping, child. You must carry it with you to Malem. It will be important there, I think."

# Chapter Ten

The clay tiles of the footpath are warm against my bare feet as I walk through the flowers and redgrass toward the mansion. Imported marble columns rise at regular intervals from the front of the verandah, which is made of burnished Earthoak to match the huge double doors. The roof is tiled in a soft beige with gold inlays that catch the sun and carry the rich look of the marble onto the roof.

I approach slowly, squinting as the sun blazes off the gold embellishments on the doors. The windows flanking them are opaque and glitter golden even in the shaded recess of the porch. The door opens easily to my touch; I enter with the confidence of a proprietor.

The interior is full of light and utterly empty. No ornaments, paintings or furniture mar its impersonal beauty. I breathe in the clean smell of fresh-cut wood, of new paint and sunlight through glass. My bare feet slap lightly on the warm, blond hardwood floor as I pass from room to room through frosted doors which open by themselves ahead of me.

In the third room I hear the faint sound of laughter. I pause. Am I trespassing upon another occupant?

With every step I take the laughter increases in volume, intentional now, directed at me.

It echoes from wall to wall in the barren house. I turn slowly, trying to determine which direction it's coming from. I dread meeting the source of that sardonic laugh, yet I'm compelled to move forward. As I approach each frosted door I hold my breath, waiting in horror as it opens before me.

A second voice joins the first, this one crying. It frightens me more than the laughter, though I don't know why either sound should frighten me. I should have expected it, I think. The two are inseparable; how did I forget that? My own thoughts make no sense to me. I move on.

The house with all its opulence no longer holds any allure. The white sunlight that filled it minutes ago as though the sun itself were trapped inside has faded away, leaving only a weary dullness to the air. Menacing shadows reach from the walls toward the centers of the rooms as I walk through them. Gloomy, I think. Gloaming: that other word for dusk. The time of tricks of sight. The time of thieves.

The two sounds, laughter and weeping, echo from every wall, seeking me, willing me onward. The last pair of frosted doors opens and there they are, as I knew they would be.

My father lies sobbing in his bed, his dark, emaciated arms reaching out to me.

"Give it back, Akhié. Give it back!" he weeps, his outstretched arms imploring. His eyes are vacant. He stares right through me, seeing someone else even as he cries my name. I am not real to him; I have never been real to him.

Owegbé's laughter increases, drowning out Itohan's weeping. "Everything in this house is yours!" she cries, contemptuous and amused, sweeping out her arm to encompass the empty rooms. "Nothing! Nothing is yours. You have earned nothing!" She throws back her head and laughs, the sound bouncing off the bare walls, louder and louder, deafening...

❧

I wake with a gasp, my heart pounding. There's a dry, hot feeling behind my eyes like I want to cry. The cool recycled air of the ship, with its bitter, metallic musk, fills my nose and mouth and lies cold and heavy in my chest.

I sit up, hugging my knees, and pull the blanket around me. "Not real," I whisper to myself. The dream is not, but this is real: I am on my way to the planet that killed my father.

"I won't stay on Malem," I mumble under the covers. "I'm going back with the ship." My mother's dream-laugh taunts me even as I say it.

To drive it from my head, I think of Etin. The last time I saw him, he was coming off the *Homestar* after a run. I was waiting there, to tell him the O.U.B. had hired me to translate for them and I'd be going off-planet.

"Where?" he asked.

"Various places." I made a vague circular gesture with my hand as we walked toward the transport offices where he had to check in. I had just come from there, checking out. The ship was waiting for me, but I'd insisted on talking to Etin before leaving.

"They're going to pay for Owegbé's transplant."

He stopped. "Kia, that's not your—" I could see it in his face, his concern for me, and it warmed me. But I couldn't let him try to argue with me. He didn't know everything, and I hoped he never would, so I cut him short. "They're paying the rest of my university fees when I get back, too."

He put his hand on my shoulder. "I know that's not why you're doing it," he said. "You should tell her, Kia."

"I can't." I waved toward a ship across the 'strip. Agatha stood in the open door, waiting for me. "We're leaving now."

"So soon?" He bent and hugged me tightly. "Thank you," he whispered into my ear. "Come home safe."

That was a good moment. It carried me through boarding and liftoff. I thought of it while I held my ears to deaden the terrible scream of the drives just before my first leap, and in the hours of vomiting afterward. It even made up for the pilot's surly refusal to speak to me after I threw up on his boots.

*Thank you. Come home safe.* I have done something right at last. Etin is proud of me.

The memory barely has time to cheer me before the sardonic laugh from my dream returns, carrying another memory, of Agatha knocking on the door to my room to tell me I'd received an incoming 'cast. One look at her face and I didn't want to hear it, but I followed her to the comset anyway. The Adept, her face as expressionless over the 'net as when she handed out my sentence, informed me that my mother's body had rejected her new heart. She is dead.

I never said goodbye. We never got the chance to…I don't know…stop being angry at each other? I was so sure the O.U.B.'s money would solve everything, I decided to wait to see her till I got back.

I get up and wash my face, determined to set aside both the dream and the memory. A glance at my workstation tells me it's the middle of the night. I shrug. It's always the middle of the night in space. I order the comp on, choose one of my language programs and plug the 'phones in my ears. When I return I'll get an implant. I can afford one now.

The ship is quiet except for the subliminal vibration and the low, persistent hum of its drive, which has begun to sound like the murmur of unpleasant voices. It's no bigger than the *Homestar*: a two-man operation—captain and engineer—with a cargo bay, rooms for a couple of passengers, the caf, the cockpit, the com room, and the drive. It makes me feel claustrophobic, this tiny shell we're hurtling through space in. I focus on the voice in my ears, speaking Kandaran. I intend to learn it on this trip. Perfectly.

Three hours later my head is spinning, but I've learned the regular verbs. That's because there are so few of them. I yank the 'phones from my ears and head to the caf, a cramped little room with cold metal walls on all six sides. I hate the place. It makes me feel like a worm, a small black slug caught inside a tin can, living off the contents. But it's time for Agatha's morning language lesson, and the caf is the only eat and meet space on this ship. My head aches from lack of sleep, but Agatha can't afford to miss another lesson. It took two weeks after I learned of my mother's death before I resumed her language lessons, and only because she tried to wish me good morning and instead asked me to dance.

Agatha's already there, sitting on a metal bench at the metal table, her head bowed over a bowl of hot porridge. When she looks up I say, meanly, "You can pray all you want, it'll still be porridge."

"I like porridge." Agatha picks up her spoon and smiles through the steam rising from the bowl. She's been sickeningly nice to me since the day of the transcast.

"If you spent as much time studying…" I let the sentence hang while I give my order to the wall dispenser. She knows how hopeless she still is in Malemese.

I drink my juice, trying to decide what fruit it's supposed to taste like, and carry the rest of my meal to the table. "Describe what we're eating," I suggest as I sit down.

Agatha gets a cornered look on her face, which annoys me. I push my protein patty around on my plate as she stumbles through two sentences. I don't know which is worse, the food on ship or having to listen to Agatha mangle Malemese grammar. I'm losing a semester of education for this? I want to scream.

"It doesn't make any sense," Agatha complains the third time I correct her grammar.

"It will, when you know it well enough to think in it," I tell her with a confidence I no longer feel. "Languages only make sense from the inside."

"Oh! Like people."

"People don't make sense at all."

Agatha smiles. "They do from the inside."

I grind the patty into my plate. She's changed the subject again. All she has to do is learn one language. That's all. One. And if she doesn't learn it by the time we get there, I'm stuck by my agreement to stay with her and translate till she does.

"You," I snap.

Agatha groans.

"Tell me."

"There are four separate words all meaning 'you'. One is used between spouses," she ticks them off on her fingers. "Another is for family members and close friends. The third is for everyone else who is Malemese and the last is for non-Malemese. I wonder why they have that distinction? They don't see many off-worlders."

"Languages change. Their ancestors used the fourth 'you' for strangers, people from other villages. But there's so little habitable land on Malem that eventually the villages merged into one city. The fourth 'you' almost disappeared from the language, until off-worlders began to come."

"How do you know all that?"

I did some research, I think. Didn't it occur to her to learn something about the place she's going? Like that it's a cold, wet world, the opposite of Seraffa's semi-arid desert. I packed my warmest jumpsuits but I only have two—it seldom gets cool enough on Seraffa for long sleeves. And that there's only one continent surrounded by water, and no natural life-forms on the land. Everything—plants, animals, birds—was brought there with the colonists over a century ago. She could have learned that much, at least, but there's no use saying it now.

"I helped a couple of Malemese at an Immigration Investigation. They went to work on a farm and I visited them a couple times."

"They emigrated? I thought the Malemese never emigrated?"

"They wouldn't talk about it. Not even at the Investigation. They were almost turned down because they wouldn't give a reason for wanting to emigrate, but in the end there were no real grounds to refuse them."

"What were they like?"

"Reserved. Very religious."

Agatha smiled.

"It isn't the same religion as the O.U.B.," I warn her.

"It's all the same God."

"Is that what the Adept thinks?"

For the first time Agatha brings the subject back to language lessons. "Each of the four 'yous' has three declensions plus singular or plural, and can be masculine or feminine depending on the final letter. You forgot to ask me that."

"And?"

"And?"

"And each one must be said with the proper inflection to indicate the power differential."

"The power differential?" Agatha's little frown appears.

"It's about respect. Who's due it from whom. Older from younger, say, or royalty from commoner. It's very important."

"What if I get it wrong?"

"Don't. It's an FTA—a face threatening act." Even without linguistics, Agatha should understand that concept. It must be part of their training in reading expressions. "The rules of courtesy are very strict on Malem. For example, in order to request something of someone else, the speaker must have more authority than the person he or she asks."

"Will I be able to ask questions?"

"Questions, yes. Favors, no. Until you establish your own authority."

"How would I do that?"

"I don't know. Very carefully, I think."

Agatha is quiet, considering it.

"How many languages do you know?" Maybe I can show her similarities between the grammatical structures. I only half listen for her answer. What I'm really waiting for is an opportunity to ask about Malemese diamonds. But it has to come naturally.

"Two."

"Two?" It takes me a moment to remember my question. "Two? I thought the Select were taught languages?"

"I had so much trouble with Central Ang they didn't give me another."

"You had trouble with Central Ang?" I stare at her, till I realize my mouth is open, and shut it.

Central Ang was developed for interplanetary use. It's stripped of all complexity in order to make it accessible to everyone. There are no irregularities in its verbs, its nouns, its formation of plurals and possessives; no declensions; no synonyms; no multiple spellings or pronunciations. Its vocabulary is limited to the essentials necessary for tongue-tied tourists and cybermail—and that's all it's good for. It doesn't have the complexity needed to exchange ideas, or the subtlety required in negotiations, or the warmth and humor that create friendship. But at some fundamental human level where the fear of not being understood touches us all, Central Ang ties the human universe together.

"You *can* speak Central Ang?" I ask, in Central Ang.

"Yes I can," Agatha replies in the same language.

"And Edoan." I revert back to the language we've always spoken together.

"Edoan is my mother tongue. I was brought to Seraffa as a child."

"What about your parents' language?"

"I never knew my parents. They died when I was very young. My father was an Adept, so I was raised in the Order."

"That's it? Edoan and Central Ang?"

She looks at me without blinking. The O.U.B. do not repeat themselves; they expect you to listen the first time.

"Why didn't you tell me you couldn't learn languages before I agreed to teach you?"

"Because I can. I did learn Central Ang," she says, breaking their rule about repeating.

She means it. At least she appears to—she *is* a Select.

I stand up, avoiding her eyes. "Work on your vocab. I'm going to work on my...my Kandaran...I brought it with me..." I'm babbling, and Agatha can't help seeing it. Just get out, I think. Out of here, now. "We'll meet later. After supper...."

The door slides shut behind me. No one can see me but still I hold myself back, the sound of my footfalls on the metal floor even and casual, all the way to my room. Agatha might not know the extent of her linguistic incompetence—hard as that is to believe—but the Adept did. She had to have.

I'm not here to teach Agatha Malemese.

Why am I here?

# Chapter Eleven

Balancing my fork on one prong, I give it a quick twist. It twirls in a brief moment of gracefulness then wobbles and falls noisily onto the table. I lift it, balance and spin it again.

Where is Agatha? She was supposed to meet me here an hour ago for her language lesson. In a week we'll reach Malem, and she still can't say a single sentence without making some cultural-linguistic gaffe.

We've kept up the pretense—at least I have, because the alternative terrifies me—that I'm here to teach her Malemese. And that's what I mean to do, as best I can. That's *all* I mean to do. Whatever else the Adept has in mind, whatever was in that dream she mentioned, she can forget it.

But teaching Agatha is impossible. "They'll know what I mean," she says when I correct her, as if language isn't even necessary.

I give the fork a savage twist. It spins wildly to the edge of the table and clatters onto the floor. Where is she? I grab my plate and cup, retrieve the fork, slam them all into the slot for used dishes, and stomp down the narrow, claustrophobic corridor to find her.

The vibration of the ship has seeped into me; I can feel my blood vibrating in time to the engines' beat as it cycles through my body. I can't wait to get out of this spaceship! I'm desperate to feel the sun on my face and the wind in my hair again. I curl my toes, imagining the warmth of living soil under them, solid and *still*. But it's Seraffa I'm imagining and Malem I'll be stepping out onto in one week's time.

She isn't in her room, so I head for the com room, and there she is, standing in front of the portal, her eyes shining and her hands clasped together in prayer. Her lips are moving, murmuring something too low for me to catch. It reminds me of the time just before I left home when I came upon my mother talking to a holo of my father. As if the dead could be reached through their effects. Only the living are reachable, until it's too late.

I clear my throat. Agatha gives no sign of hearing me. I cough. It's a little forced but unmistakably audible. No response. I think of the Adept's stare and throw myself into it...

Apparently, I haven't mastered that trick.

"Select Agatha, I was hired to teach you Malemese." I pronounce each word distinctly. "By your Adept," I add desperately. Is she aware, as I am, that she will not learn Malemese in the next week? Does she think I've failed, or... or does she know I've been sent here for some other reason? I think of my father's fever, and then of his diamond in its leather pouch, hidden under the mattress in my room, and I feel myself sweating.

"Come to the portal," Agatha says. "You can see Iterria."

Iterria, viewed through the portal, looks huge. It's the only other habitable planet around Malem's sun, and it blocks them both out, casting a reddish glow in the dark of space.

"What's it like?" I should have researched Malem's solar system as well.

"It's very hot, a desert planet. They harvest the few precious clouds that form over the mountains at night, for water. It's not enough, though, to support the present population. Without another water supply, their civilization could die."

At least we have water on Seraffa. I look at her, reevaluating. She has done some research. "Why don't they take hydrogen from the stars?"

"Iterria's oxygen is very thin, not up to the task of converting the hydrogen into water. Besides, there aren't any large stars close enough to make that practical."

"What about a comet?"

"There's no oort cloud near this solar system."

I'm beginning to get the picture. "Malem is mostly water."

Agatha nods. "Iterria wants to buy enough of Malem's water to create a closed, self-replenishing system on Iterria. Malem could easily spare it."

The cost of lifting that much water off a planet staggers me. "How would they do it?"

"Iterria and Malem are small, low-g planets with stable orbits. They're both suitable for skyhook towers. Iterria already has one; they want to build another on Malem."

"And send water up and down the elevators. The only transport they'd need would be between the satellites, in space."

Agatha nods again.

"Iterria must be rich." I look out at the glowing planet.

"Rich, and desperate."

"Why not just land on an uninhabited part of Malem and take the water they need?" As soon as I say it, I wish I could take it back. There is no uninhabited part of Malem. With only one continent, every bit of land is precious. Agatha doesn't answer. She's probably stuck on the "just take what you need" part. I look out the portal.

That's that, then. Inter-planetary strife is left up to each world to settle on its own, but intra-planetary aggression is forbidden. If Iterria attacks Malem for water, they'll be fighting the entire Alliance.

"They need a trade agreement," Agatha says. "It would be a good solution. Iterria's a technological world, they have a lot to offer Malem."

"But Malem doesn't want it."

"No."

"And you're supposed to make them want Iterria's technology?"

"I'm supposed to try to bring them into the Alliance."

"They don't want that either." I'm guessing, but it fits what I saw of the couple I translated for: reserved and self-sufficient. "How are you supposed to get them to join?"

Agatha's anxious frown reappears. "I don't know. I only know the problem, not the solution. This is my first posting."

"You haven't been given instructions?"

"Not yet." Agatha looks out at Iterria. Her face clears. "I will be told in time."

"Aren't they cutting it a little close? Malem isn't on the cyber link."

"God doesn't need the cyber link."

I let that one lie. If God decides to talk to her, I'm pretty sure I won't be asked to translate.

"Why won't Malem just give it to them?" I ask, looking out the portal. "Malem has more water than they'll ever use."

"I don't know. There must be a reason."

Iterria hangs red-hot outside the portal, a dying planet surrounded by cold space. All those people having to leave their homes, and the O.U.B. sends a novice Select with a sixteen-year-old language teacher.

"Chalk one up for space," I murmur; "One down for humans."

"Not yet," Agatha says.

But after an hour of language lessons I'm certain Iterria is toast if it's depending on Agatha.

"How did you pass your examinations to become a Select?" I finally ask her.

She looks at me, and I know she's got the seeing-right-through-you part down. But there had to be some studying involved, too, and if she could do it then, she can do it now. So I stare right back at her.

"I prayed," she says. "I closed my eyes and prayed. I don't even know who examined me. I never saw them."

"And you passed?"

"They told me my explanations were incoherent but all my answers were right. The wrong words but the right ideas." She smiles. "Maybe on Malem—"

"On Malem," I say "the right words matter very much."

꿍

I check my spacebags one last time before leaving my room. The pouch containing my father's gem is tucked among my clothes near the bottom of the second bag. Somehow, in the short time I'll be here, I have to find out if it is a Malemese diamond. Sodum never actually saw it, after all. For all I know, Malemese diamonds are just a myth. The ship's engineer seemed to think so. The one time I broached the topic with him, he just laughed at me.

I drop the flash on Malem and the two on Kandaran into my spacebag, along with my travel-tab. According to it, the original Malem settlers took a vow of poverty. If they still keep to it, that may explain why they won't sell their water.

The idea of intentional poverty gives me the creeps, to tell the truth. The Select and the Adepts don't own anything individually, but they have the entire wealth of the O.U.B. behind them. That's not poor. Poor is when nothing stands between you and disaster. If that's the Malemese's choice, they *are* crazy. And it probably means there aren't any diamonds here.

While my bags are inflating, I pull on the full-length woolen tunic I've been told to wear over my jumpsuit. It's hot and heavy and it itches where it touches my skin at the neck and wrists—I have to stop myself from taking it off again. I leave the heavy black boots I've also been given beside my bags and go to find Agatha. After three months in space I can't wait to go outside, even on Malem.

There's no response when I touch the door to her room. She's not in the caf. I go to the com room and find her standing in front of the portal again. As politely as possible, I ask her whether she's packed up yet.

"Have you seen them?" She gives a quick little nod toward the portal.

I walk over and look out. It's early afternoon but the sun I have longed for is hidden by dark clouds. I can hardly see through the heavy precipitation that falls in torrents onto the gray soil—and bounces back up! Hail? I've heard of frozen rain, but never seen it. Several figures hurry from a small stone building across the open landing field, stooped over to protect themselves from the stinging onslaught. I watch, fascinated, until I remember I'm about to go out in that.

Two Malemese men are close enough to the ship for me to see. Their dark hair clings dripping to their scalps under light brown arms lifted to shield their heads from the hail. One of them looks up at the ship, his open mouth revealing a missing tooth as he yells something to the other over the wind. They both wear plain dark robes, several layers by the bulky look of them, similar to the itchy woolen thing I've been given to wear on Malem. The wind buffets them roughly as they fight their way to the ship. They look cold, dirty and underfed.

"Beautiful," Agatha whispers. "They're beautiful, and I can't even speak to them."

Maybe they look better when they're not sopping wet, but beautiful? I stare at her. Her face is tense and pale. She must have meant something else.

"You've learned a lot of words," I say. "And you'll get better." I hope so, anyway.

"I don't know what to do. They didn't tell me anything. They never do." Agatha's voice is close to breaking. It takes me a moment to realize she's talking about the Order now, not the Malemese people. "I don't think they trust me," she says.

"I'm sure they know you're loyal." "I don't mean that. I mean, I don't think they believe I'm very competent."

I understood what she meant and had hoped to sidetrack it. What can I say? She's probably right. "They made you a Select."

"I passed the tests. I don't think they were happy about it."

"You *are* a Select," I tell her. "They sent you here, didn't they?" I wait until Agatha nods. "You'll know what to do. You always do, better than them."

I remember Agatha at my trial saying, "It seemed the right thing at the time," and the Adept replying, after a pause, "Then it must have been."

"They trust you," I say, certain I'm right. "They just don't understand you."

Gradually the strain in Agatha's face eases. She opens her eyes. I remember Jaro's instructions on social skills and give her a cheery, confident smile.

# Chapter Twelve

"There's a decontamination unit at the station," the captain says to Agatha, not even looking at me. "Take all your things. The Malemese shoot anyone who brings something into the city, hasn't been checked and buzzed. Building's to the left." He steps aside and opens the hatch.

A fierce gust of wind and hail howls in through the opening. Agatha staggers back, falling against the captain. He grins and helps her regain her footing. She opens her mouth to say something, apparently thinks better of it, and reaches for her spacebags. I follow her out of the ship.

My first step launches me straight into the gale, which blows me backward, slamming me into the side of the ship hard enough to expel the air from my lungs. A bark of laughter comes from the hatch before it closes. I struggle up carefully. The captain could have warned us about gravity being lighter here. Too bad I hadn't vomited all over him, not just on his boots.

The pounding hail and the wind make it impossible to see more than a few feet ahead. We shuffle along the ground holding hands against the ballast. My spacebags whip about crazily, threatening my tenuous balance until I stop and deflate them half-way. Then I'm forced to carry them above the ground—they aren't made to withstand the tear of twigs and stones. I've never been so cold in my life. My cheeks sting, my eyes are running and I can barely feel my fingers, let alone move them. By the time we reach the spaceport we're breathless and shuddering with cold. I'm wondering whether the ship, with its life-support turned off, can be worse than this.

The port is small and dark inside. It keeps out the wind and hail, but other than that it's not much warmer than outside. There's a desk and a chair just inside the door, with a man sitting at it and a woman standing beside him. He gestures for us to leave our bags beside the single standard decontam unit in the middle of the building.

Decontamination procedures are thorough to the point of paranoia. I have to strip to my underwear before entering the unit. Once inside, I'm ordered to rotate slowly, like a piece of meat on a skewer. The woman gives me a blanket while I wait for my clothes to be buzzed at a higher intensity. One thin blanket. I shiver in the damp, unheated building with the wind and hail pounding against it. I watch the man go for my bags, terrified he'll empty them, but he only deflates them and throws them into the unit. None of my tools are large enough to show up on a scan as a weapon, so I breathe easier.

They treat Select Agatha with a little more consideration, but not much more. When she and her things are deemed 'clean', the man tells her to report to the hospital within two days to have her aud-vid implant removed. I'm so shocked I can barely translate his demand, but Agatha receives the news calmly.

"It's standard practice here," she tells me as we dress quickly behind a flimsy curtain. "They'll reinsert it when I leave." The curtain blows aside as I hear the door to the building open; I barely catch it in time to preserve our modesty.

The captain is talking to the two Malemese officials when we pick up our bags. He turns and calls out, "I depart in two standard weeks. At noon. If you're coming, don't be late."

Agatha pulls open the door. A gust of freezing wind makes me gasp. My woolen robe is still cold and damp from making my way to the station, but I hug it tight around me. When I look back, the captain's talking to the two Malemese again, so I leave without answering him.

The hail is abating. By the time we fight our way across the landing field it's stopped. The wind, however, is still fierce. It batters our spacebags, slowing us down as we struggle to hold on to them. I keep close to Agatha, letting her break the wind somewhat for me. This is her mission, not mine; I'm only here till the ship leaves. At last we reach the grain elevators we were directed towards and huddle against them, shielded from the wind, catching our breath.

Agatha leads us down the narrow dirt streets of the city. The buildings are close on either side, and tall, most of them six or seven stories high. They're all stone or gray brick, with small windows and not many of those. At least they block the force of the wind, but its coldness stings my cheeks and I have to clap my hands to keep them from freezing. There are people out in this weather, women and children as well as men, all dressed in dark, ankle-length robes, the women's a little looser than the men's but otherwise the same. Don't they have the sense to stay inside on a day like this?

No one approaches us, or smiles at us, or lets on that they've even seen us. When we stop to ask directions, however, we re-ceive a polite reply expressed in terms as close to friendliness as the Malemese language permits between strangers.

Prophet's Lane is no more than an alley leading to a small, gray, single-story stone cottage crouched on a narrow plot of land between the tall apartment buildings, like a nervous toad surrounded by cranes. Even the groundcover around it is gray, dull and flattened under the beating of the wind. We hurry up to the metal door, eager to get inside.

There's no infra sensor. We wave our hands all over the front of the door and its frame but the door doesn't slide open, nor do we hear the echo of a chime inside announcing our presence. Finally I kick the door in frustration, despite Agatha's frown, but it's more solid than it looks. If I wasn't wearing heavy Malemese boots I'd have broken my toe. As it is, I lose my balance and fall in the low g.

Agatha taps on the window. The tapping, like my kick, is drowned by the howling wind. We walk all around the house. Every window is dark.

"We have to find someplace to stay!" I shout over the gale. Agatha tries the door and the windows again before agreeing to go to an inn for the night and find the Select in the morning.

"There's only one inn, the Brief Sojourner," we're told when we finally find someone still out on the streets to ask. He gives us directions which I have to strain to hear over the wind whistling down the narrow streets. Naturally it's on the other side of the city.

I lean against a doorway, half-protected from the wind. I won't make it. I will freeze to death right here. The thought is almost tempting, till Agatha gives me a look.

There's none of that sympathy I got when my parents died, in this look. Nope. This is an if-you-are-stupid-enough-to-die-here-don't-expect-me-to-stand-in-this-wind-praying-over-your-body look. Despite the allure of freezing to death, I am impressed. I didn't know she had it in her. I push myself out of the doorway with a shrug, as if she was totally mistaken about me.

This walk seems even longer than the trek into the city. I promise myself I'll never take transit strips for granted again. I wind the cords of my spacebags around my wrists to prevent them from being pulled from my stiff fingers by the wind. At least my tunic has a hood that ties in place; the hood of Agatha's Select cape keeps being blown off. I watch her bare neck go from scarlet to white as I follow her.

# Chapter Twelve

Three months on that cramped little spaceship for this? *Come with me to Malem,* Agatha begged me. All I wanted today was a little sunshine. My disappointment turns into a bitter pleasure at the thought of leaving Agatha on this horrible planet while I head back to beautiful, warm Seraffa—really beautiful, not some weird, warped concept of the word that only Agatha understands. I imagine waving farewell at the door of the ship, grinning down at her as it closes.

I pull at the neck of the woolen tunic. It's frozen stiff from the hail. At least it's warmer than Agatha's blue and white habit, meant for Seraffa's climate. Even so, I'm shivering and she's not. I glare at her back ahead of me. It's probably a Select thing. She could freeze to death and never show it.

Agatha turns and smiles at me.

She'll probably have to wear two of those outfits at a time, or get some of this wool for underclothes. Yes, this nice, rough, itchy wool right against her skin. She didn't throw up once on the spaceship. The Captain didn't refuse to talk to her. But I'm the one who'll get to go home with him.

I smile back at her.

There's no sensor on the door to the Brief Sojourner's Inn, either, but the door swings open after Agatha taps on the window. The Innkeeper cuts off her embarrassed apology and shows us how to turn the handle of the door and push it open to let ourselves into the small interior porch, where we can call out our names and wait to be admitted.

The room at the B. S. Inn is small and sparse but scrubbed clean enough to lick. It has a bed large enough for two and a small table, both made of the same metal as the doors, and an electric lamp operated by pressing one's thumb against a button on its base. The inside walls, like the outside ones, are gray brick.

I can still hear the wind howling outside. The innkeeper thumbs on a small machine he calls an electric heater, which looks inadequate to the task of warming even this small space. At least there are plenty of blankets on the bed. He shows us how to operate the facilities, all of them strange and awkward, requiring physical manipulation. I look at Agatha, wondering if our voyage here has included time-travel.

Agatha offers three of the local coins she's been supplied with to the skinny, hollow-eyed innkeeper. He returns one of them.

"We need dinner," she says, offering the extra coin again, "and breakfast tomorrow morning."

"Included," the innkeeper says, pocketing the two coins.

❧

We're finishing our breakfast in a little room set with tables at the front of the inn when a man wearing the robes of the Order walks in. The first thing I notice is that he's brown, like the Malemese. He fits in, blue robes or not. I look at Agatha's milky complexion, and down at my own black skin. What are we doing here? We're piano keys in a coffee bar.

"There you are," he says in Malemese, taking us in without a flicker of expression.

"Yes, here we are," Agatha replies serenely, in Edoan.

"You're speaking Edoan," he says, in Edoan.

"Yes."

"No one here can speak it."

"Then it is convenient that you are not no one."

He pauses a moment, but then continues smoothly, "I was not home last night."

"No. But then, you weren't expecting us."

"You were not in orbit long enough for the news to reach me before you landed. I would have met your ship if I had known."

"That wasn't necessary. As you can see, we have had no trouble finding our way."

"When you're ready we can move you over to the Order's lodgings."

Agatha finishes her breakfast serenely as he waits.

"What was that about?" I demand, as soon as we're back in our room.

"What?"

"That verbal dance the two of you just did."

"You know very well what it is, Kia. You play it yourself often enough."

I concentrate on packing the few things I took out of my bag for the night.

"He'll get over this soon enough," Agatha says. "We've surprised him, and the Select are not accustomed to being surprised." Her eyes twinkle.

So that was why the Select was so cool and formal after Agatha's comment about him not expecting us. She held her own, although he did his best to put her at a disadvantage with his comment about her not speaking Malemese. I seal my bags and grin at her.

"Perhaps we could keep the surprises to a minimum while we're here?" she suggests.

My grin fades. Is she just guessing, or does she know my secrets?

# Chapter Thirteen

The stone house on Prophet's Lane is as sparsely furnished as the rooms at the inn.

"The Malemese stand to talk, or sit on cushions on the floor," the Select explains, noticing my expression as I stare at the table and two metal chairs in the main living area. "There is little wood on Malem and no petroleum for plastics. Furniture is an expensive luxury. We will move your bedroom chair into the dining room in order to eat together."

I shake the excess water from my hair, staring around glumly, and hang my dripping robe on a hook beside the door. The floor slopes slightly toward a drain beneath the row of hooks.

Only two of the bedrooms are furnished. Apparently they don't expect many guests here—I wonder why? I'm willing to sleep on the floor in order to have my own room, but Agatha vetoes that, probably afraid I'll freeze to death. She could be right.

"The Malemese have few resources," the Select says. "But there is water, and hydro energy. Just not much modern technology to go with it."

"Why not?" I don't know how I'll survive two weeks without the 'net. At least I have my travel-tab and some language flashes. How can they live like this?

"It's partly due to their limited resources and partly it's philosophical. They prefer their isolation and independence. They have a city-wide com system but no interstellar communications.

They don't need automated transportation, they live so close to-gether it's not necessary."

"Obviously the Malemese diamonds are a myth," I say in dis-gust, staring around the bare, cold rooms.

"They're real," our host says. "I've seen them. But they can't be taken off-world, or holo'd, so there's no proof of their existence outside of Malem. The Malemese guard their secret. But those diamonds…You've never seen anything like them."

"What makes them different from any other diamond?" I ask, trying to sound like it's not that important.

I feel Agatha looking at me and pretend not to notice.

"Some geological occurrence millions of years ago caused "phantom" growth layers—interruptions in the growth of the crystals—which caused inclusions of another mineral. The dia-mond crystals continued to form around it. They mine them with the inclusion at the center, a type of melanite shot with silver peculiar to this planet, and use an enhanced "brilliant cut", only possible because the stones are so large. The effect is beauti-ful beyond imagination."

He's described my father's diamond exactly! If you translate the geological stuff into plain words, that is. There's a pause while I feel him staring at me. I dare not look up for fear he'll see my excitement. Instead, I hug myself and shiver. It's not a hard act to put on. "Why don't they sell them and warm up this planet? It's a dump here. Or aren't they valuable?"

"Valuable? The Malemese could be rich, selling those gems. But they have a cultural taboo on trade. Besides, Terra-forming is risky, especially on a low-g planet with a thin atmosphere. It's also illegal if the planet is already habitable."

I give a snort and mutter, "habitable?"

There's another pause. "What are you not telling us?" he asks quietly.

I have to look up now. To continue looking away is as good as a confession. Either way, he'll know he's right.

"Don't be so disdainful of the way others choose to live," Agatha interrupts. She looks at him as if to say, *teenagers*, and I can look at her instead, and frown as though I'm ticked. Which I am, because who likes having their *attitude* commented on?

"I just don't buy it," I say. "If the diamonds are real, and are valuable, who'd choose to live like this? I'll bet someone's selling them."

"Why would you think that?" he asks. I realize I've gone too far. I should have let it go, let him think me "disdainful" as Agatha put it. She saves me again.

"She comes from a trader family. I imagine she was raised to be interested in buying and selling."

"Don't get interested in these," he warns. "The gems are part of their religion. The priests themselves mine and cut them. They bless them in a sacred ceremony and give them where they are needed. It would be the highest sacrilege for a foreigner to own one."

I shrug, trying not to look as sick as I feel. There's no doubt, then: my father stole it.

We eat lunch prepared by the Malemese woman who cleans and cooks for the Select. She answers our questions in soft monosyllables and offers no comments herself. After lunch Agatha gives the Select a letter from the Adept. He'll only be nastier after he reads that he's dismissed, so I excuse myself to go unpack the few things I'll need while I'm here.

"You have not come as my assistant," I overhear him say from the bedroom where I'm setting out my toiletries on the small table. There's no expression in his voice at all. "You are my replacement. They need me elsewhere."

He must be dying to get away from here, I think. No cyber-mail; no outside news at all, except every year or so when a ship comes in. But still, he doesn't want to have failed, which obviously he has, since Malem isn't in the Alliance. I'm glad I'm not in the same room as them.

"Have you arranged for me to meet their Majesties, the King and Queen?" I hear Agatha ask Select Hamza—she's told me his name, though I'm not allowed to call him by it.

There's a pause that's heavy with whatever opinion Hamza isn't offering, then his calm voice: "I'll send word. The King might grant you an audience in a month or two. That will give you time to learn enough Malemese to speak to him."

"But not the Queen?"

"She'll be there, but she won't speak to you. She despises the O.U.B. It has to do with the death of her child, fifteen years ago."

Fifteen years ago? When my father was here? I dump the clothes I've unpacked on the bed and move to the door to hear better.

"How did the child die?" Agatha asks.

"The plague. In four years it cut the population in half. I assume you know of it? Yes, well the Queen blames the Order for bringing the virus. She had the Select who was here at the time thrown in jail. Of course she was exonerated later, and left as soon as a ship could be sent to get her. That was fifteen years ago, at the height of the plague. The Order sent in doctors, medicine, sterilization units, disinfectants—but it was too late for the little princess."

"Poor woman," Agatha murmurs. "Has she had any children since then?"

"You won't say 'poor woman' after you meet her. But no, the Queen hasn't conceived again. There will be no heir to the throne until she does, and perhaps that's why the King indulges her humors."

"Have they cured it?"

I grip the door, waiting for his answer.

"The plague? There is no cure. It was a new strain of coronavirus—a viral respiratory illness which spreads by person-to-person contact. In this damp climate where everyone lives close together it spread rapidly. A vaccine was developed but the virus underwent mutation—"

"It's over, then," Agatha says, louder than necessary.

"Yes, of course. The people are still terrified of it, however. When someone comes down with it they completely isolate him, and quarantine the entire family for double the incubation period."

"But there's no danger? They can cure the patient in the hospital?" she says clearly. She knows I'm listening.

"The hospital? No, they take the infected person to an old pavilion at the edge of the swamp. When it was first built dozens of people were sent there at a time and left to die. Now, as I said, the disease is rare. It may no longer, in itself, be fatal. But they still leave them there to die or get well on their own. That's the theory. I've never heard of anyone surviving a stay in what they call 'the fever house'."

"They just leave them there?" She has forgotten her reassuring tone.

I have a grisly image of a house full of skeletons and rotting bodies. I run into the room.

"We have to get away from here!" I can't believe he's discussing it so calmly. Does he have some kind of death wish?

"It is under control," he says. Unlike you, his eyes say.

"I'm leaving." I turn to get my things and get out, but he says, "Where will you go?" as if it's simply an interesting question. I don't have an answer.

"Kia—" Agatha says.

I glare her to silence. For all I know, that vision the Adept mentioned showed me dying of the plague down here. They'd still send me, if they thought I'd further their plan before dying.

Hamza looks from me to Agatha and back to me. He says, with infuriating calm, "You have nothing to fear. They brought it under control over a decade ago through isolation and sterilization, and the strain has since weakened. There hasn't been a new case in nearly a year."

"How horrible, sending them away like that," Agatha murmurs.

"Yes. And these people are not cruel—not when you know them. When the victim is a child there is a pall over the entire city. Sometimes the mother goes with the child—and usually dies with him, too, after living in the fever house for six days. It's one of the worst things I've lived through. Yet they still do it."

I'm so angry my voice goes quiet. "I guess the Adept forgot to mention this," I say, looking at Agatha.

"It's not something anyone would know unless they lived here a while," Hamza says, defending his Order. "You have nothing to fear. The virus has stopped mutating now."

"Kia's father was here during the plague," Agatha says. "He died years later from a recurring fever."

"I am sorry to hear that. This must be hard for you, then. It was brave of you to come." His tone makes it sound more like an assessment than praise. Or a re-assessment.

"I've heard of that," he continues. "The fevers are not a recurrence of the illness, but a rare side effect. They are not contagious. That is what I have heard. I have never seen it myself."

*I have.* I look away. Did my father come down with the virus while he was on the planet, or did he make it to his ship and suffer alone on the long trip through space? Maybe his fevers were because he hadn't had medicine or proper care. Because he had stolen the diamond and had to get away quickly?

"Why does the Queen blame us for the epidemic?" Agatha asks.

"Coronavirus was eliminated centuries ago on Earth, yet a new strain mysteriously arrived here. The Malemese believe it came on an O.U.B. ship from Iterria. The Queen insists they were deliberately infected to force them to join the Alliance in order to get the cure."

"But there is no cure," I say.

"That can't be true!" Agatha cries at the same time.

"I have never seen any evidence to prove it," Hamza says to Agatha. "But the Iterrian captain was tried and beheaded and his ship was burned. Another ship had to be sent all the way from Seraffa to retrieve the Select. They would not let a ship from Iterria land. They still won't."

He turns to me. "There was an antidote. It worked on the first strain of the virus, until it mutated. Now there is an injection which alleviates the symptoms and enhances our natural immune system to fight the virus."

"What is the King's attitude toward the Order?" Agatha asks.

"He is grateful for our intervention and assistance during the plague. But he loves the Queen and humors her in most things, including her desire to have as little as possible to do with us. She may be influenced by the High Priest in this, but I have no clear evidence."

It's a strange thing for a Select to say: *no clear evidence*. I wonder what he means, until I remember the aud-vid implant Agatha had removed this morning. They must feel lost without it.

"Which of them still refuses to join the Alliance and supply Iterria with water?" Agatha asks.

"The King and Queen hold court together. It is forbidden to mention Iterria in front of them."

His words swirl in my mind: *forbidden to mention Iterria in front of them... forbidden to mention Malem in front of Owegbé...*

*forbidden to speak Malemese in front of Father...* 'Forgiveness is the least reliable virtue,' my mother used to say.

"I wonder if the Iterrians would dare drink water sent by the Malemese?"

They both turn and stare at me. I shrug. Surely someone has thought of that.

"The Malemese are more direct," Hamza says. "It is enough for them to deny the water."

"How are we ever going to convince them to help the Iterrians?" Agatha asks.

"That is your problem now."

Agatha looks at me. I look away.

Her problem, I tell myself. I'll be leaving with the ship, too. I feel guilty, as though I'm abandoning her, but there's no way I'm staying a single minute longer than I have to, not with even a 'rare' chance of catching CoVir.

# Chapter Fourteen

The day is cold and overcast again, raining off and on in short, angry bursts. In the three days we've been here there's been as much precipitation as we get in a year on Seraffa. I go out anyway, hoping to walk off the bad feeling I have, and trudge down the muddy road, flapping my arms to keep warm.

I stop when I realize I must look like a duck in the rain. Too late. I've already emerged from Prophet's Lane onto the cobblestone street, and a guy about my age is staring at me as he walks past, his lips curved in a mocking half-smile. I stare back, partly because he's being rude, and partly because he's worth staring at: tall and slim, with high cheekbones and dark eyes framed with long, black lashes my college roommate would kill for.

"Quack," he says, laughs, and keeps walking. I stand there, trying to think of a clever reply to shout after him, but all my four-and-a-half languages fail me. I turn and walk in the opposite direction, feeling exactly like I must look: not just normal stupid, but major moronic.

The sky matches my mood. Dark, brooding clouds lie over the city like the folds of a scowl. I'm getting used to the lower gravity, but I'll never get used to these dull, dark days. The city is as dismal as its weather. It smells of dampness and of fish, which so far has been served at every meal I've eaten here. Everything is gray: the sky, the dirt, the cobble-stones, the bricks of the buildings huddled together in seamless rows as though clutching each other against the cold; even the groundcover and shrubs, gray on gray on gray.

The clothes the people wear are gray. Perhaps they think color is frivolous, or else dye is hard to come by with so little natural color on Malem to make it from. The city and its people look washed-out, survivors of a tragedy that has left no joy or color in their world.

The plague must have been terrifying, people dying all around. My father was never able to exorcise it, physically and emotionally. Now I understand why so many buildings are boarded up. Did some of these people take years to die, with each recurrence of the fever weakening them more, like my father? I imagine ghosts everywhere: in the boarded-up apartments, in the cold streets, in the way the people rarely smile and avoid touching one another. How am I to find one ghost amid so many?

Itohan—his name means 'mercy'. My father was Itohan Ugiagbe, I want to say to the Malemese hurrying about their business, ignoring me, a foreigner in their midst. He came here and suffered like you. I watched him die all the years of my childhood and I didn't understand.

Every time I pass another death house, empty and boarded-up, I understand a little better my father's long despair. What would he have been like if he hadn't come to Malem? I never really knew him. Already his image is fading in my memory. I look around the dirty streets as I walk. They stole him from me, but they might also be able to give a little of him back. If I can find out what happened to him here, I'll know him in a way I never did. The Malemese diamond must be mixed up in it somehow.

"Tell me," I whisper to the cold, gray streets. "Tell me who my father was."

Agatha's interest in learning Malemese has increased, perhaps because Select Hamza has impressed on her the importance of choosing her words carefully when she meets their Majesties. I overheard him mention she should have had a "more experienced" language teacher, as though Agatha's inadequacy is my fault.

"The Select do not find fault," Agatha replied, neatly defending me without belittling herself. Now I only speak in Malemese, and every minute we're together is a language lesson.

"What's this?" I ask Hamza at lunch, pointing to a long slice of purple. I've made a habit of asking Hamza questions about everything, on the pretext of learning local words that weren't on the language discs. But really, I'm hoping the topic will stray onto diamonds or the fever, and give me more insight into my father's time here. Hamza's talk the first day just brought up more questions than it answered.

"A parza," Hamza says. "It's a local fruit, a type of melon. Very sweet."

"And last night's vegetable?" I reach for a slice of parza and take a bite. It's the best thing I've eaten since I left home.

"A tuber. They call it 'swamp potato'."

"Why haven't we had these before?" I wave the rind of the parza, reaching for another.

"The first spring crop is just coming into season. You'll be tasting a lot of new foods soon."

"We should go to the market." I finish the second slice of parza in three gulps and consider licking my fingers, but Hamza would disapprove.

"It's Friday," Hamza says.

"Isn't the market open on Fridays?" Agatha asks.

"Yes, in the afternoon. The farmers bring their produce in early, spend the morning in worship and the afternoon at the market." He hesitates as though considering adding something.

"The Select," I avoid referring to Agatha by name in front of Hamza—why irritate him needlessly?—"and I need to learn the words for produce unique to Malem. We could go by ourselves and ask the market sellers, though."

"Don't go alone," Hamza says. "I'll come with you. It will probably be alright."

Agatha looks at Hamza. I suspect his reluctance is only pride: he doesn't want to be seen in public with us while we exclaim over fruits and vegetables and Agatha mispronounces the new words. He'd probably refuse if he didn't feel it his duty to acclimatize Agatha before he leaves.

The market is along a wide cobbled street not far from the city square. I don't know why they don't just have it in the square, a natural gathering place, but maybe that's reserved for special events or announcements. It's always empty, anyway.

The street smells of fish, for sale in big carts, but there are also stalls with brightly-colored fruits and vegetables. It's noisy and cheerful and full of people. I notice that while they talk animatedly to one another, they never touch, and I remind Agatha not to brush against anyone. Hamza grows more and more ill-humored as we load him up with each new fruit or vegetable we find. Every time we add something to our basket I make Agatha repeat the name of each product we already have while Hamza stares stoically off into the distance ignoring the amused glances of the Malemese. The sun is shining for a change, and I'm determined not to let Hamza's moodiness spoil it for me.

"Quack."

I look up and there is the boy who laughed at me the other day. He crosses the street and leans against the wall of a building, facing me with the same conceitedly amused look in his eyes. I want to say something insulting but he's far enough away now that I'd have to raise my voice for everyone to hear, so I just glare at him. He laughs, pushes himself off the building and strolls away.

Agatha's still reciting the names of the produce in our basket when I feel Hamza stiffen beside me. The crowd has suddenly gone quiet, except for the market vendors, who are throwing tarps over their stalls. But it's barely mid-afternoon.

I turn to ask Hamza why they're closing so early. He's staring down the street. Agatha has stopped talking, too, and when I look where they're looking, I see guards coming toward us. They march in uniform, their faces grim, their right hands resting lightly on the handle of some heavy and probably deadly weapon which I don't want to see any closer, strapped to their sides.

"What is going on?" Agatha asks quietly.

"On Fridays," Hamza says slowly, "they distribute justice."

"Justice?"

The people around us look grim as they turn and walk in the direction the guards seem to be herding us. Vendors wipe their hands on their aprons and hang the aprons beside their stalls then briskly move into the throng. Hamza grabs Agatha's arm and mine and urges us forward with everyone else.

"I'm sorry," he murmurs to us as we walk. "It doesn't happen every Friday. Usually I stay home on Fridays, but I was not aware of…"

"Aware of what?" Agatha says with the deliberate control of the Select. It's a sure sign she's upset.

"Of any recent convictions."

"Select Hamza." Agatha stops abruptly, forcing the Malemese behind her to stumble as they veer sideways around her, "tell me exactly what is about to occur or I will not take another step."

Hamza tightens his hold on Agatha's arm and forcibly propels her forward. "Don't stop," he whispers harshly. "Do you want to be shot for refusing to be a witness to justice? Those lead-arms they're wearing are crude but effective weapons."

I'd been about to rebel also; instead, I look quickly around. One of the guards is staring straight at us, his hand half-lifted to signal another guard, but he relaxes when Agatha resumes walking.

"Where are we going?" I whisper.

"To the public square in the center of town."

"And what will happen there?" Agatha asks, not bothering to lower her voice.

"Most likely we will witness a beheading. If there has been a theft, we will watch the culprit's hand being cut off."

I stumble and would have fallen if Hamza wasn't holding my arm. Is he serious? He must be, he's always deadly serious. I nearly choke on that—*deadly serious*—and feel my throat close. I swallow, and breathe in and out quickly. I can't be sick here.

"I wish you did not have to see this," Hamza says. "But the guards make no exceptions. Everyone on the streets is gathered to the square to serve witness. Justice must not only be done but must be seen to be done."

"You call that justice?" I ask, switching to Edoan.

"They call that justice," Hamza replies. "We are not here to interfere."

We're at the square now. There's a raised wooden platform in the middle, which I want to look away from but can't. Hamza points to the far end where the King and the High Priest stand on a raised dais. They're dressed in long dark robes, more elaborately designed and probably lined with something soft, but otherwise no different from their people's attire.

A half-dozen guards surround the platform looking out into the crowd. Another dozen or so patrol the parameters of the square and still others stroll through the crowd watching for... What? Defiance? A rescue attempt? The whole thing seems unreal to me—the silent crowd, the watchful guards, even the unusual brightness of the sky which casts the wooden platform into stark clarity amid the dark robes and glum brown faces that surround it like shadows. Shadow people, I think, all standing as still as the barbaric past they appear to have just stepped out of.

A priest climbs onto the platform. He looks to be in his late thirties, and would be handsome except for his stern expression. I recognize the impassive control of a Select in his face and bearing, but don't mention that to Hamza and Agatha.

A guard climbs up behind the priest. He's heavily built, at least 5'10 or 5'11—tall, by Malemese standards. His thick, black eyebrows join above his nose in a permanent scowl and his nose is crooked, as though it has been broken. I shiver just looking at him.

A third man follows the guard.

"Is that the condemned man?" I really want to be sick now.

"That is a doctor."

I look at Hamza. Is he developing a sense of humor now when it's completely inappropriate? "There's a cure for beheading?" I ask.

"I expect we're about to see a thief punished." He gives me a long look.

Two more guards climb the steps to the platform with a third person between them. They reach the top and turn. Beside me, Agatha utters a cry of horror. The figure between the guards is a boy no more than ten or twelve years old.

His eyes are wide with terror and his chest heaves. The muscles of his face are clenched as though he's afraid that if he relaxes for a moment he'll shame himself even more by crying. His left hand moves convulsively, stretching and curling back into a tight fist at his side. He seems unaware of its movement.

One of the guards leads him to a block in the center of the platform. He kneels down and puts his left hand on it, fingers spread wide. He stares at his hand as though he's never seen it before.

"Don't look, Kia," Agatha whispers. Her lips move in a silent prayer. Her face is so white that even her lips are a pale ivory color.

"You must look, both of you" Hamza says quickly. "The guards are watching to see that we do. Try to look without seeing. Stare straight ahead but focus inward. If you can't do that, watch the priest, not the boy. Under the law he's still a child; they'll only take off two of his fingers, not the whole hand."

I swallow, hard.

In a loud voice that carries across the square, the priest cries out the name of the boy and his crime: theft. The priest's face is impassive but in the sunlight I can see beads of sweat on his forehead. He grasps an axe which is leaning against the wooden block, and raises it. He holds it aloft for one terrible moment while he takes aim. He won't do it, I think, staring at the axe as it trembles in the air. It flashes down so quickly I don't believe it's really happening until I hear it *thunk* deep into the block of wood.

The doctor springs forward and raises the boy's hand for all to see. The boy is staring at his hand, the thumb and first two fingers spread wide and the blood gushing from two small stumps where the other fingers were. The doctor holds it up for only a moment before pouring an ointment over it. The boy screams then, short, high bleats of terror and shock as the doctor wraps his hand in a cloth and helps him down from the platform.

My legs are trembling. I need to sit down but I can't, the guards are watching. Hamza's arm under my elbow holds me up.

A man is led onto the platform. The priest calls out his name and offense: treason.

Treason? What constitutes treason on this sick planet? Not watching an execution?

The man steps forward and kneels in front of the block.

"Where's the doctor?" I whisper.

"Don't look at him," Hamza says. "Watch the priest's face, only the priest."

Agatha's prayers are audible now, a rushed, urgent whisper of sound rising through the silent crowd. A steady line of tears tracks down her cheeks.

I look at the priest. His mouth has tightened into a thin line of distaste. At the crime? The criminal? Or at his own role in this draconian form of justice?

His arms rise, holding a larger axe this time. As he raises it above his head his sleeves fall down, revealing his arms to the elbows. The muscles in his forearms stand out in tight cords and his fingers on the axe handle are stiff with tension. The sun flashes off the blade as it hangs in the sky like an ancient sundial marking the last moment of a human life. The axe descends.

I hear the soft slicing, the solid *thunk* as the blade digs into the wood. My own still-beating heart is loud in the unbearable, acquiescent silence of the crowd. I lean forward and throw up.

I am barely aware of the long walk back to Prophet's Lane. The smell of the crowd, a rank scent of fear and excitement, clings to me. In my room, I pull off my Malemese robe and fling it away. I want to bathe, but I'd have to leave the room and pass Agatha and Hamza to get to the wash room, and I can't bear to look into the face of anyone who watched the execution with me. I lie across the bed. The sound of the axe digging into the wood block echoes in my mind. I crawl under the covers, close my eyes, and recite verb declensions in Kandaran...

I wake hours later, still dressed in my jumpsuit. It is pitch dark. My left arm, minus the hand, lies heavy across my chest. I can feel the stump of my wrist above my breast. I cannot breathe, cannot move. I lie there paralyzed with terror. A strangled whimper gurgles in my throat, and I am breathing, sweating, but still too afraid to move, my every sense focused on the arm across my chest. Is there a hand or not? As nightmare and sleep recede, I gather the courage to raise my right hand, to feel along my forearm… and grasp my left hand with a relief so great it leaves me dizzy. I become aware of Agatha lying beside me in our bed, her breathing deep and regular. I am safe in the house on Prophet's Lane.

Not safe. None of us are safe, stranded here at the mercy of barbarians.

I think of my bags and what's in them, and close my eyes. My left hand is still cradled in my right, but I'm no longer reassured. I listen intently: all is quiet. I get up and grope by touch in the darkness through my spacebags until I feel the smooth, hard surface of the little box of thieves' tools Sodum gave me.

Opening the bedroom door soundlessly, I peer out. Hamza's bedroom door is closed. I tiptoe into the kitchen, find a large steel spoon in the cupboard, and quietly let myself out the back door.

The clouds have returned to Malem's sky, obscuring even the dim starlight. Nevertheless I keep close to the house, a shadow figure against the dark walls.

What's that? If I should be discovered now—

A night bird repeats its call. I breathe out slowly.

At the back corner of the house I crouch and dig into the dirt until I have a hole almost as deep as my elbow. I put the plastic box inside it and refill the hole, replacing on top the square of groundcover I carefully set aside. Groping in the darkness, I find a large stone which I place just to the left of the sod as a marker. The wind and rain will soon erase all sign of my digging.

Agatha half-wakes and mumbles something when I return to the room.

"I'm just getting undressed," I whisper. "Go back to sleep."

# Chapter Fifteen

A reply to Hamza's request for a royal audience arrives three days later. As abruptly as is possible in official Malemese, the royal courier welcomes Select Agatha and bids Select Hamza farewell. There is no invitation to attend the palace. He turns to leave.

"I wish their Majesties good health and happiness and thank them for allowing my presence in their city," Hamza says quickly. "Please convey my gratitude."

The courier bows. "I will inform the Queen. The King left this morning on a tour of the farms and will be away for several weeks."

"That explains Friday," Hamza says when the courier has gone. "The King pushed those convictions through before he left. It was the only way to get the boy out of jail. The order must be signed by two of the Triumvirate and the Queen won't sign against a child."

"She's a kind woman, then," Agatha says.

"Do not delude yourself. The Queen has no compassion. She cannot abide the sound of a child screaming, and those who sign off must watch their commands carried out."

"What is it that concerns you?" Agatha asks.

Hamza looks up slowly. "If I had known the King was leaving, I would not have brought you to their attention."

"They know we are here."

"But not that you are staying." Hamza forgets himself so far that even I notice the small furrow between his eyebrows.

"What are you afraid of?" Agatha's voice is mild but she is watching Hamza intently.

The little crease disappears. "Nothing."

"Tell me."

"Nothing, I said."

I pull the woolen robe over my jumpsuit and go outside. Hamza's always gloomy, I tell myself. He's been here ten years and nothing has happened to him. I walk slowly, looking down at the road and kicking up dirt. I'll be leaving on the ship; it's no concern of mine. The thought makes me feel worse instead of better.

It's just as well Agatha won't be meeting their Majesties yet. Her Malemese is hardly presentable. She's reached a plateau of semi-intelligibility and seems to be stuck there. I kick a stone from the dirt with such force it clatters to the end of the lane. How could the Adept have sent her here? How could she order Hamza to return, leaving Agatha alone?

I cross the cobbled road at the end of the lane and turn down another dirt side street, preferring the earth under my feet even though I can't feel it in these clunky Malemese boots. It'll be months before I can walk in light, open sandals on the warm soil of Seraffa. I glance up at the tall, drab buildings. My time on Malem is slipping away and I haven't learned anything more about my father or how he got the diamond. Knowing more about the diamonds might tell me something, but I don't dare ask. This cold, dark city guards its secrets close.

I hear laughter, a rare sound here, and turn onto a wider street. A group of ten or twelve Malemese about my age are kicking around a ball. I stop to watch. They're in teams, one group with their backs to me, guarding two stones a few feet apart, the other group facing them. They control the ball with their feet, never touching it with their hands.

Kickball, I think, or something close to it. The teams are mixed, girls and guys playing together, hiking the heavy woolen robes they wear up high enough to kick the ball.

I tried to join a kickball team at school when I was a kid, but everyone knew my father and the fevers that made his mind wander. Every mistake I made, they asked if he taught me that move. I quit after the second game. I practiced on my own, though, till I got every move down perfect, better than anyone playing on the school team—then I tossed my ball in the recycler.

I start to back up before they see me, but as I do a girl kicks the ball so awkwardly it wobbles straight to a guy on the opposite team, and nobody laughs or groans or hoots. Some people, I think. They can do anything and everyone likes them. But that's not me, so I turn to leave.

Something bumps into the back of my boot. I look down at the ball they've been playing with. "Kick it!" someone yells.

They just want a laugh; they're expecting me to fumble it. I'm tempted to prove them wrong, but they won't care. If I was an outsider at home, I'm a million times more of one here, a foreigner on this isolated planet where no one looks even remotely like me.

Jaro's image pops into my mind, shaking his head. So fail me, I think—then, Okay, what the hell, because I don't like to fail, and I'm good at kickball. I'm already imagining the surprise on their faces as I turn and aim for the goal stones, and kick it…

The surprise is on me because it's made of leather or something, and even in the lower g it's like a dead weight with no bounce at all when it hits the dirt. It kind of flops before it reaches a girl at the edge of the group, and I brace myself for laughter—but she just flashes me a quick grin and gives it a really hard *whack!* and scores.

I figure I'm out of the game after a dismal play like that, but someone yells, "We're a player short"—I don't see who—and the ball comes flying toward me again. Now I'm stuck. I'll look dumb if I play, and even dumber if I leave. Well, I can't make a worse kick than I just did, but I can make a better one, so I hook the ball. I play with it a minute between my feet, trying to get the feel of it. What a crappy ball.

I throw myself into the kick this time, putting all my higher g muscle behind it, and send it flying right through the goal and on down the street, into a wall at the far end. Everyone stares at it, even me. Then, as if nothing happened, someone runs and gets it and the game continues.

It's harder than I thought, controlling the heavy leather ball with my feet, holding up the skirts of my robe, and remembering to compensate for the lower g and not send the stupid thing into space again. I think I'm doing pretty well, though, not embarrassing myself any more, when someone from my team comes up behind me and says, just loud enough for me to hear, "Quack."

I don't have to turn around to know who it is. I consider taking off, but that would look dumber than staying and taking the ribbing I'll get when they hear about me walking down the street flapping my arms. He'll tell it worse if I'm not here. Besides, if I can get to know these teens, they're my best chance of learning about Malemese diamonds.

The game ends at dusk, which falls pretty fast here, the sun being as inadequate for its task as this stupid leather ball is for its. He saunters up, heart-stoppingly gorgeous except for the wicked gleam in his eye. "Not bad," he says, and smirks, just so I know he's thinking, *for a duck*, but he doesn't say it.

"You, too," I say without smiling.

Two guys and a girl from the other team come up then. "Hey, Jumal," one of them says to my tormentor. He's a little shorter than Jumal, about my height, with curly hair. He nods to me. "You could be on our team," he offers. "Micah," he adds.

I'm tempted, but I figure it's better to have Jumal as a team-mate than an opponent. "Thanks, Micah." I smile. "Might as well stay with the one I started on, if that's okay." I glance at Jumal.

Jaro would definitely not give me a pass for that glance. It's not a let's-be-friends kind of look. More of a no-more-of-that-duck-crap look.

Jumal shrugs, but it's a friendly shrug, more or less. The others come over and introduce themselves, now that the team leaders have accepted me.

I catch myself grinning on the walk back to Prophet's Lane. I wonder if they play every evening. I kick a stone between my feet down the street, then send it flying into an alley. Two girls on my team looked friendly, they might talk to me. I'm going to clear up some of the mystery of the diamonds before I leave, after all.

I open the door to our house quietly. Hamza and Agatha often go to sleep early, but tonight I hear them talking in the dining room. I'm about to call out when Hamza mentions my name. I stand still, half inside the door, listening.

"She is hiding something from us."

"I know," Agatha answers.

"Why haven't you learned her secret?"

There's silence for a minute, then Agatha's voice again. "She'll tell me if I need to know. It can't be anything important to our task."

"She thinks it's important. It's got to do with Malemese diamonds, and they are very important here."

"I trust her."

"Malem is a dangerous place for foreigners. Neither of you realize yet just how dangerous. We have to know what she's hiding from us."

I step back outside and very slowly close the door. How had I forgotten you can't keep something from a Select? I consider

going to the inn where the pilot and the engineer are staying, but all my things, including the secret diamond Hamza
and Agatha are on the verge of guessing about, are inside this
house. I count to twenty and noisily open the door, kicking
off my heavy boots. I head straight for the room I share with
Agatha and close the door. I pull off my robe, reach quickly
into my bag till I find the leather pouch, and seal it in my
jumpsuit pocket.

It's too precious to bury, so I carry it with me all the next day,
but that's even worse. I don't want to think about what will happen to me if I'm found with it. It lies like a bomb in my pocket.
No wonder my father hid it so well and never told anyone.

I'm sure everyone will see the bulge in my jumpsuit pocket,
which isn't actually there but I pat it so often to make sure there's
no bulge, there might as well be one. When Hamza and Agatha
are out—he's finally taking her to meet people he knows here—I
sew the pouch into the hem of my robe.

The kickball gang isn't there the next evening, and the day
after that is Friday. Hamza insists we stay home all day. I don't
see them Saturday, either. I wonder if it was a one-off, or if they
decided to play somewhere else and not tell me. But then, why
did they ask me which team I wanted to be on? Sunday Hamza
and Agatha expect me to stay in after dinner for the O.U.B.
tradition of prayers and meditation. Well, Agatha doesn't expect
it, but Hamza obviously does, and I don't want him getting even
more suspicious of me than he already is.

By Monday I'm sure there's no regular game, or if there is,
they've given up on me. I'm almost surprised when I find them
there, kicking the ball around, limbering up while they wait for
everyone to arrive. I ask Mehda, a girl on our team, if Jumal's
coming, not sure whether I'm disappointed or relieved that he
isn't here.

"He usually comes," she says. "He lives with his uncle, who's a priest. Sometimes he has to help with a ceremony. It's part of his training." She looks like this is a really big deal, like Jumal is someone special. I think of his sardonic smile and the way he says "quack," just to get to me, and I can't imagine him as a priest, or helping with holy observances. Mehda obviously can, though, so I keep my thoughts to myself.

Mehda's older sister, Kaline, comes over with the ball. She's shy, so she doesn't talk, but kicks the ball around a bit, trying to control it, before passing it to Mehda. Kaline could use the practice, but Mehda's good, she's fast and always in control of the ball. She passes it to me, and I practice, trying to forget the rubber balls I'm used to and get a feel for this one. I haven't quite got it but I'm improving when Mehda moves in, hooks the ball and passes it to Kaline, who stumbles a bit, leaving herself wide open, before she gets control of it.

I look up and see Jumal watching us. How long has he been there? Kaline notices him then and kicks the ball in his direction so we can start. He moves to intercept it with no indication that she sent it sideways. Am I the only one he mocks?

Kaline's and Mehda's brother, Emilian, is on Micah's team. Once, during the game, Kaline runs with the ball into Emilian's area, and he lets her get a shot in even though he could easily have checked it. No one on either team comments.

They'd probably let me play even if I was a handicap, like Kaline and a few others, but just playing isn't what I want. I have to impress them so they'll stay and talk to me afterwards. Besides, I like to win.

I watch the other players, especially those on Micah's team. Salua runs fast but she can't kick. Emilian makes good kicks but he's slow. Hamil is as much of a handicap for them as Kaline is on our team. Micah, like Jumal, is a natural athlete, good at all the moves in the game. That's probably why they're the team captains. I'll avoid him when I get the ball.

The fourth time I play with them, I'm confident enough to move into serious competitive action. I hook the ball away from Hamil three times—why in the universe do his team-mates ever send it to him?—and twice I intercept Salua's kicks. I score three goals by myself and pass the ball twice to Jumal. Near the end of the game, he turns aside when I'm ready to send it to him, so I pass it to Pica, instead, the other good player on our team. We win by a lightyear.

No one congratulates me. Instead of gathering to cheer over winning the game, my team-mates drift away without speaking. I stare after them until they've all turned down other streets.

The next morning Agatha cuts short her language lesson, saying she'll practice on her own till my mood improves. I pull on my robe to go out after lunch, but a dense fog has rolled over the city. It envelopes me immediately on stepping outside. There's no point walking the streets blindly. We all stay cooped up inside.

I arrive late the next evening, after arguing with myself about coming at all. The game has already started. I approach, my expression neutral, but Jumal nods me into the play without comment. His face is as expressionless as a Select's. I brace myself, expecting to be checked hard now that they know I'm good. Instead, I'm not checked at all. Every shot is an easy shot. After four scores I begin deliberately avoiding the ball in a way that makes my anger clear. Then I think, what the hell, and I rack up every goal I can, in a fury. If they want to lose, let them. Micah's team congratulates us afterwards with excessive humility.

"Hey," Jumal says to me. He waits till everyone else has cleared out, then says, "You're messing up here."

"I'm not the one messing up. I'm the only one *playing*!"

"Making bad choices."

Bad choices? What is that, priest-in-training talk? "Who gave you the right to comment on my choices?"

"I brought you in," he says. "I vouched for you. You're making me look bad."

I stare at him.

"I passed you the ball," he says, as though talking to an idiot. "I accepted you on my team." He emphasizes the word 'team'.

I'm getting it now, but I'm too mad to care. "Guess you made a *bad choice*," I snap.

Jumal's face is as stiff as mine when we turn our backs on each other and leave.

I don't need their friendship.

I don't need anyone.

But I was one of them. Not like at trader school, where I was an outcast because my father was weird and he only owned one ship. Not like the college where everyone competes and the other students only talk to me because I know some language better than they do. (Except maybe Jaro, a part of me thinks.) But here, they just accepted me for no reason at all.

And now they've rejected me for no reason at all.

I shrug. I don't care.

So why do I go back the next night? I tell myself on the walk there, I just want to pick their brains. I won't even look at Jumal. I don't care if I don't make friends, or help my 'team' win the game. I'm going to get Kaline and Mehda to talk to me about Malemese diamonds after the game and then I won't need to see any of them again.

As soon as I get the ball I pass it to Kaline and block the better players until she finally makes a score. I do this twice more, till Kaline becomes so flustered she can barely play at all, so I ease off and stay on the sidelines—not quite out of the game, not really in it.

Our teams are tied, and it's already dusk. I look up to find Jumal watching me. He nods quickly, then moves in and hooks the ball, and passes it to me.

Is this some kind of a test? What does he expect me to do? Win the game for them, or lose it? No one's guarding me. I have a clear shot anywhere I want to send it.

As the ball shoots toward me, I look for Kaline. Forget their stupid approval, just get her to like me and answer my questions. They were mad when I won for them, let them deal with me losing the game for them. But Kaline's on the far side of the street, blocked by better players and not even looking my way.

I have a clear shot to Mehda, but Mehda's well guarded. She probably won't be able to make a hit even if she's able to hook the ball.

If I send the ball to Mehda or Kaline, Jumal will know I deliberately lost the game, even after his nod to me. I push the thought aside, and the funny feeling it gives me. Because I know Mehda will be grateful to have her chance even if she can't score; she hasn't had the ball once this game. And then I can talk to Kaline and Mehda, who always walk home together, and that will be the end of it. Jumal won't want me on his team any more, but I won't give him the satisfaction of turning me away.

I hook the ball, kick it from foot to foot a moment and shoot it toward Mehda. Mehda leaps in front of the kid guarding her and hooks it, and kicks it hard toward the goal. But there are too many others nearby. Micah stops it, turns it and kicks it back. Jumal dives sideways, but the ball is already past him and through the goal, and Micah's team has won.

Jumal goes over to Mehda and says something that makes her smile, before he turns toward me. He's probably telling her I knew she couldn't score, that it's my fault we lost, not hers. He knows I threw the game.

I turn to leave. There's no point trying to talk to Medha or Kaline now that Jumal's got to them first.

"Hey, duckling." His nickname for me since I've been playing with them. I really want to hate it, now more than ever, but I can't stop myself from looking back.

"Good play," he says.

I'm as lost for words as the first time he said "Quack," and just as frustrated.

Kaline and Mehda wave at me, smiling. Go with it, I tell myself, and wave back. It's too late tonight, but next week when we play I'll find a chance to talk to them. None of it makes sense at all, they're all backwards here, but as I walk home I keep hearing him say, *good play*, and I can't help grinning.

The next morning, Hamza's housekeeper answers a knock at the door and calls us to receive a royal message. Select Hamza translates so Agatha can follow the Malemese, "On the third day of the seventh month—that's tomorrow—" he says, "your presence is requested in Her Majesty's reception chamber, at ten o'clock in the morning."

The tiny line between his eyebrows reappears.

# Chapter Sixteen

The three-story stone palace sprawls across several acres of land at the southern edge of the city. It isn't the Newtarion Embassy, but after the cramped confines of the city, it looks almost as luxurious to me. The groundcover shines silver in the rare sunlight, and up against the walls of the palace is a line of shrubbery with purple and white blossoms, the first flowers I've seen here. Behind the palace is a thick woods and at the edge, where the trees thin out, I can see the ocean, dark gray waves tossing against a white and gray sky lit up with sunshine.

A guard lets us through the gate and escorts us to the palace door, where another guard ushers us into a large waiting room. A number of Malemese stand quietly about the room.

I'm becoming accustomed to rooms with sparse furnishings. It makes them seem more spacious on this planet where every inch of land is precious. This room is huge by Malemese standards—at least fifteen feet square, with a ceiling that must be nine feet high.

I've never been presented to a Queen before. My stomach's doing flip flops as I wait. I don't look at Hamza because even though it doesn't show on his face I know how he feels about us being here, and I don't want this spoiled by his constant gloominess. I glance around at the Malemese in the room, wondering if any of them are related to the King and Queen. Hamza told us the Royal couple and their children—if they have any, which these don't—are the only ones considered royalty. The Queen was a commoner until the King married her, and the King's own brother will live his life as a commoner unless something happens to the King and he has to assume the throne. Apparently he's a lot younger than the King; three siblings between them died in the plague.

The door to the reception chamber opens. I catch a glimpse of walls hung with tapestries depicting land- and sea-scapes of Malem. Along the far wall a row of tall, narrow windows lets in the bright daylight. The guard signals us to enter. On a raised platform at the far end of the room are three high-backed, elaborately-carved wood armchairs—the most profligate use of wood I've seen on Malem. The Queen is seated on the middle chair, her back regally straight.

Our footsteps echo on the stone floor as we approach, our heads bowed. Out of the corner of my eye I see her tap her fingers lightly on the arm of her chair. A huge Malemese diamond sparkles on one of those fingers.

Agatha and I curtsey low in front of her, Hamza bowing beside us. Coming up, I glance quickly at the Queen. She is wearing a dark blue robe that follows the lines of her willowy figure, the wool fine and soft and embroidered at neck and bodice with intricate designs in gold thread. Her raven hair is tightly bound behind her head, revealing a heart-shaped face. Her dark eyes are large and wide-set, rimmed by long black lashes that make a striking contrast against her sand-brown skin. She looks only a little older than Agatha—early thirties, maybe—and I remember Hamza telling us the King assumed the throne at age sixteen, when his parents died in the plague, and married the Queen that year. She turns her head slightly, catches me looking at her and returns a gaze so cold and imperious I quickly look back down.

"Select," the Queen nods stiffly to Hamza. "And this must be the new Select." She looks at Agatha with even more disdain than she turned on Hamza.

"And your servant."

Not sure what to do, I bob my head nervously and glance up again. The Queen is staring at me with an expression of animosity.

I can barely swallow. Now, too late, I believe everything Hamza said about this woman. Why has she called us here? And why did she include me, whom she believes to be a mere servant, in the invitation?

"The new Select's language teacher, your Majesty, not a servant," Hamza murmurs with another bow.

The Queen waves her hand, as though an insect has irritated her.

"Your name?"

I open my mouth, but nothing comes out. I swallow. "Kia, your Majesty." Why is she interested in me? A feeling of dread settles in my gut.

She taps her fingers once against the arm of her chair. "Your full name."

"Kia… Ugiagbe."

"As I thought. Seize her!"

I freeze in a half-curtsey, disbelieving, while two guards hurry forward and grab my arms.

"What's happening?" Agatha cries in Edoan.

"Select!" I cry. Hamza does not move or speak but his eyes dart between the Queen and me.

"Take her to prison," the Queen orders.

"No!" Agatha cries in Malemese. Then, in Edoan, "What are they doing—"

"Quiet!" Hamza hisses in Edoan.

"We can't just let her be taken away!" Agatha appears about to throw herself in front of the guards as they start to drag me out, but Hamza grabs her and pulls her back.

"You are here to help the people of Malem, to bring them into the Alliance. Don't sacrifice that for one insignificant girl." They're both speaking Edoan in tense undertones. A third guard stations himself beside them, his hand on his lead-arm.

They stand there watching as I'm dragged out of the room.

"Your Majesty, please allow us to know the girl's crime," I hear Hamza say formally in Malemese as the door closes behind me.

The guards march me out of the palace at a brisk pace. I stumble trying to keep up, clumsy with fear. People avert their eyes as we march through the city. We pass the center square and stop at a building adjacent to the square. Its windows are high up and tiny, with iron grid work instead of glass. The door opens at a sharp knock by one of my captors, and they hustle me inside. I trip on the stone step, banging my shin against it, sending a sharp stab of pain up my left leg. They ignore my cry.

There are three more men inside, dressed in the same long, dark robes everyone on Malem wears, but with stylized gray and yellow insignias sewn onto their shoulders. They all wear wide belts with leather holsters holding their lead-arms on their right hips.

The guard stationed at a door in the back of the office opens it at a barked command from one of my captors. They pull me across the room and through this door to a dark stone hallway with narrow iron doors at regular intervals on each side.

Voices call out to us along the hallway. Behind the grid work in one or two of the doors I see dirty faces peering out at me. A low moaning comes from one of the cells and from another, a monotonous, hopeless weeping. I can barely take it all in as I stumble between the two guards, terrified. One of the guards opens a door and they shove me into a small stone cell. The door clangs shut.

I am alone in the cell. There's a narrow metal cot bolted to the far wall with a tiny barred window above it, a stained washbasin and an equally grubby toilet. I take two unsteady steps and sink down onto the cot.

Why am I here? Even as I ask the question, I know the answer: because of my name. My father's name. That's all the Queen wanted to know. I no longer have any doubt he stole the diamond. Either he got away before they discovered the theft or there wasn't enough proof at the time to convict him. But now they have me. The Queen clearly thinks that's just as good.

A plate of food is delivered through the slot in my door at dinnertime. I hear a clamor of questions and pleas from other prisoners as their food is delivered, but no response from the guard, so I don't try to speak to him. I eat the fish and fried bean mash in silence, concentrating on the taste and the sensation of warmth filling me from the inside. Briefly, as I eat, I stop shaking.

And then I am back to sitting on my cot staring at the metal door, waiting. Where are Agatha and Hamza? Why don't they come? The gray at my window turns to black. Finally, I lie down, pull the blanket around me and fall into a fitful sleep.

I wake in the night shivering so hard the cot shakes beneath me. The wind howls outside my barred window. The wall is thick and the window is cut into it at an angle, so neither the wind nor the rain actually reach into my cell, but a steady cold draft keeps the room clammy and freezing, and the sound of the wind howling and moaning unnerves me. Tomorrow Agatha and Hamza will come and get me out, I tell myself. Surely tomorrow they'll come.

They don't. Nor do they come the next day. I try to remember whether it's a holy day, and tell myself they have to get permission, but all I can think about is Hamza reminding Agatha of the importance of their mission while I was being dragged away, and of my comparative unimportance. Will they just leave me here?

There's nothing to do in this bare little cell but think, and worry. If only I knew what happened when my father was here. How can I defend myself when I don't know anything? I go over every word of our audience at the palace. There's got to be some clue there, if I can uncover it. *What is your name? Your full name?* That's all the Queen said. And when I told her my name, she wasn't surprised. So she already suspected I was related to him, which means she knew him personally, knew what he looked like.

I stand up and pace the floor of my cell, trying to puzzle it out. Why would the Queen know a ship's captain, a foreigner delivering supplies and picking up the Select?

Supplies that came too late to save the princess. What if this isn't about the diamond at all? Maybe she hates my father because he came too late?

I imagine my father arriving at the palace with the needed medicine, and the Queen meeting him there with her dead daughter in her arms. A bit melodramatic, but wouldn't a mother—a normal mother, not mine—hate forever the man who could have saved her child if he hadn't arrived too late?

The more I think about it, the more this seems possible. She looked disdainful when she greeted the Select, but she looked angry when she looked at me, like she despised me. How many black people come here? Agatha's white, and Hamza's brown-skinned like the Malemese and the Iterrians. But I'm black, like my father. She just needed to hear the name to be sure.

If she blames him for her daughter's death, will *his* daughter's death seem justified to her? I stop pacing, horrified at the thought. A cold gust of wind from the window starts me shivering and once I start I can't stop. I sit on the cot and wrap the blanket tightly around me.

It seems to me there's something else I should remember. I go over the brief audience again and again. I'm missing something...

but I can't recall it. If only I could talk to Agatha or Hamza, they might remember. Where *are* Hamza and Agatha?

On the third day I break down and ask the guard whether anyone will be allowed to see me. I'm so desperate I ask a favor— would he get a note to Agatha?—even though he's my superior in position here. He ignores me, silently shoving my plate of food through the slot and moving on to the next cell.

I eat, although I'm not hungry. The low moaning I've heard since I arrived pauses long enough to eat, then resumes. Across from me the weeping is intermittent now. Is the prisoner dying?

There's no message the next day, or the next. I sit in my cell, silent and cold, looking up at the tiny window. I eat my meals.

One morning a female guard lets me out of my cell and takes me to a small room with a tub full of water. The water is cold and I have to undress and bathe in front of her but it's worth it to feel clean again. When I'm escorted back to my cell a Malemese man is standing in it. I think he's another prisoner at first. My eyes dart to the blanket.

"I am Prad Gaelig," he says. "Is there anything you need?"

I stare at him. I need to get out of here. I don't bother to say it. He wouldn't have asked if that was a possible answer.

"Are you being fed? Have you been beaten?"

"No. Yes. I'm fed, I haven't been hurt." Why are you here, I want to ask. I've read about prisoners receiving a final meal of their own choosing before being executed. I feel my legs get shaky and sit down on the edge of the cot before he notices.

"Do you know why you're here?"

"No." I can barely get the word out. I'm not sure I want him to tell me.

He frowns. "You were told your crime before you were brought here."

"No."

"What was said in the court?"

"Court?" I sound like an idiot, but what is he talking about?

"How did you come here?"

"The Queen ordered her guards to bring me." There's something familiar about him, but I can't place it. Where have I seen him before?

His eyes narrow. He calls for the guard.

"Why are you here?" I ask.

But the guard has arrived and is opening the door. Prad Gaelig, whoever he is, leaves without answering me.

I replay his face, his expression when he spoke to me... Suddenly I straighten. I know why he looked familiar. I *have* seen him before: he stood on the platform in the square, wielding the axe of punishment.

And now I know why he came.

I don't cry. It's too late for crying. I lie awake staring into the darkness. For once the chill of the room doesn't bother me. For once, I do not want to see the sun.

I wait for them to come for me the next morning. Every step in the hallway fills me with dread, but the day passes and no guards come. I lie awake again the next night wondering about death, and trying not to think of what punishment Prad Gaelig might be practicing for.

The next day I'm allowed another bath. I hold myself rigid, trying not to let the guard see me shaking with fear. The Malemese dislike public displays of emotion, and I'm too proud to let her see my weakness. All I can think is: what day of the week is it? Is it Friday? I am afraid to ask. The soap falls from my hands several times before I give up. I'm clean enough for them to murder. When I'm dressed, the guard escorts me to the front room. I walk with my back straight and my head erect. Itohan Ugiagbe's daughter will not cringe.

Two palace guards are waiting for me. "Hold out your hands," one of them orders, and when I do, he ties my hands together. Looping the end of the rope over his arm, he leads me out the door. The second guard falls into step behind me.

They march me to the square.

And across it. It's empty. No crowds, no platform, no executioner-priest waiting for me. I am so numb with relief I can barely walk. The guard behind moves up and grabs my arm, supporting me, until I regain my strength.

Suddenly I know what it is I've been trying to remember from my audience with the Queen. It's the last thing I heard before the door closed and I was dragged away. Hamza asked to know what my crime was. She had me arrested, but she never accused me of anything. Even if it was my father's crime, she should have said what it was. I should have remembered that when Prad Gaelig asked what my crime was, but then he talked about court and confused me.

She didn't accuse me of anything. Is it something she can't prove? Something she isn't sure of? I feel a surge of hope. Then I think: is it something so awful she doesn't want anyone else to know? Would she have me murdered in secret?

"Where—" I swallow, forcing the quiver out of my voice, and raise my chin. "Where are we going?"

"To the palace."

The palace? She wouldn't have me murdered in the palace. Would she? Or perhaps the king has returned? Hamza spoke well of the king.

They don't take me to the audience chamber, but up a flight of stairs and down several corridors to a medium-sized sitting room. One of the guards remains with me while the other stations himself at the door. I breathe deeply. Whether or not the King has returned, I will need to be very careful in what I say. If only I knew what my father did here!

The Queen enters and orders the guards to wait outside the door.

I am again at the mercy of this merciless Queen. I drop to my knees. "Whatever I have done to offend you, I am sorry for it, Your Majesty," I say with my head bowed.

"Get up."

The Queen watches me coldly as I stand. "What is Ugiagbe to you?" she demands, dispensing with the elaborate hedging and apostasy that's integral to formal Malemese.

I consider lying, but if she asks the Select they will not lie. "Itohan Ugiagbe was my father."

"Was?"

"He caught the Malemese fever. He is dead."

"Was he buried with all his possessions?"

I try not to look startled by her question. "We don't do that on Seraffa, Your Majesty."

"What do you do?"

"We gave his clothes to the poor."

"His clothes? What do I care about his clothes?"

It *is* about the diamond. Why is she dancing around the question this way? She isn't sure he had it, I think. He wasn't ever convicted. If I can convince her I don't know anything about it...

"My guards have searched your possessions. What do you think they found?" She sits back, watching me. "It is treason to lie to me."

She has the diamond. I have to confess. It isn't like *I* stole it—I could just give it to her... *'It is a sacrilege for a foreigner to own one,'* Hamza's comment comes back to me. It won't matter who took it, if it's found in my bags.

Is sacrilege worse, or treason? I think of the man on the scaffold. My stomach lurches. I grit my teeth: I can't throw up on the Queen's shoes!

"Answer me!"

I feel sweat forming on my brow. Why does she need a confession at all, if they found the diamond? And why is she questioning me alone in this room deep inside the palace, without even a guard present? I look up, filled with indecision—

—And fall to my knees, bowing my head again at once. The Queen isn't angry; she's terrified. Oh God, I should never have looked up. And then to react so strongly! The Queen must know I saw her fear. An off-worlder has seen the Queen of Malem afraid.

The silence in the room is unbearable. I can barely breathe. I fight to hold back tears, until I realize that they might save me. I let them fall then, let my breath become audibly ragged, my shoulders shake.

"Majesty," I sob, "I'm afraid." Am I overdoing this? "I don't know what you want, I don't understand your questions," I sob. This is it, I think. I'm committed to defending my ignorance now. If they found the diamond in the hem of my robe, I'm lost.

"Stop that." The Queen's voice is cold, filled with disgust. I am a distasteful, pathetic foreigner, lacking the dignity to control my emotions. I've never been so happy to be the recipient of someone's scorn. I wipe my tear-streaked face with my sleeve: another gaffe. See how ignorant I am, Your Majesty? Nothing for you to be afraid of.

Should I plea for mercy? I open my mouth, hesitating in indecision…

The door to the chamber flies open. I feel the Queen's start of surprise although I dare not look up again. Light footsteps rapidly approach.

I know those footsteps. I risk a quick glance over my shoulder.

Agatha is rushing across the room toward me.

# Chapter Seventeen

Agatha's appearance dries my tears at once. I have no intention of crying in front of her a third time. Fortunately, the Queen is too startled to notice.

"Your Majesty—" Agatha reaches my side and drops into a low curtsey.

I groan inwardly. She used the familiar 'you', between friends. At least she got the inflection indicating the power differential correct. Don't speak! I think fiercely to her. You'll just make things worse.

"This my..." Agatha hesitates, obviously trying to come up with the right word, and gives up. "...girl," she continues, blithely unaware of her atrocious pronunciation. "If she offends, I have the blame. Sit on me."

Sit on me? She means 'punish me'. She forgot the diphthong! But I hold my silence. The Queen is silent also. Probably no one has ever asked her to sit on them before. I bite down an urge to giggle.

"Sit on me," Agatha repeats earnestly, "And let her go pee."

Free! I think. It's a long, hard middle consonant, not a soft, quick one. I'm going to laugh. I can't help it. My nerves are stretched too thin; it'll come out hysterical. The Queen will be furious.

"I wasn't aware she had to," the Queen observes.

I give a little gasp and bite the inside of my cheek hard, until I taste blood. My eyes water.

Agatha hesitates. But Agatha can't be held back for long. "I understand Malemese no well, Your Majesty..." This time she uses the intimate 'you' for lovers.

"Shut up!" I whisper, not looking up. Out of the corner of my eye I see Agatha glance at me uncertainly. But she's already committed to the sentence.

"...but I learn to understand your people. They are beautiful,"—I feel a momentary relief when she gets the word out right—"and squishy."

"Squishy?" the Queen asks. Agatha beams at her.

"I think she means 'kind', Your Majesty," I murmur, turning my escaping giggle into a hiccup. The Queen is silent. I want very much to see her face, but when she orders me to look at her, my urge to laugh freezes in my throat.

"Kind?" She gives me a hard look. "Do not expect that from me. I buried my kindness long ago."

I've chosen to feign ignorance, so I can't say anything to show I know what she means. Apparently she doesn't expect me to, because she continues, in formal high Malemese: "Malem does not actively seek conflict, but is intent upon maintaining its solitude. The Select of the Order must respect our choices if they are to come here." There's bitterness in her voice as she says this last; she's still thinking of her daughter. She continues coldly: "My people appreciate the help they have offered in the past. I cannot send this Select away. You, however, are merely a foreigner. No one cares what happens to you. Do you understand?"

"Yes, Your Majesty."

"We will talk again." She pauses, letting the comment—a threat? a command?—sink home. "Meanwhile, try to teach the

Select not to proposition people. Preferably before she meets the beautiful, squishy King."

We bow our way across the room, careful not to turn our backs to her. The few minutes it takes seem like forever. I can hardly believe I'm being released.

Outside the door a priest is waiting. He nods to Agatha and leaves before I have a chance to look at his face. All I can think of is getting back to Prophet's Lane and checking my other robe, the one I sewed the diamond into. I walk as quickly as I can without breaking into a run. Agatha walks beside me calmly.

Why didn't Hamza come? It was pure, stupid luck Agatha didn't say something truly awful, and get us both thrown into jail. But underneath that thought, I know she saved me. She rescued me from something worse that might have happened, but didn't because of her presence, just as she did when I stood accused by the Adept.

But I'm still frightened, and I need to be angry at someone, so I also remember that both times she got me into the trouble in the first place: she helped me steal the bracelet, and she's the reason I'm here on Malem at all. What if she can't save me from the next problem she creates?

"You can barely speak Malemese," I fume. "You could have got us both killed!"

"But I didn't," Agatha says.

"Don't you get it?" I yell in Edoan, all my pent up frustration and fear coming out. "She's cruel and malicious and she can do anything she wants to us!" I remember Agatha beaming up at her, like she was as good and kind as Agatha thinks everyone is. "You can't trust her!"

"Kia," Agatha puts her hands on my shoulders, facing me. "Always expect the best of people, even when it requires a leap of faith. They may not live up to your expectations, but I assure you, if you expect the worst of them, they will always live up to that expectation."

I shrug off her hands. It's pointless arguing with her. Agatha will never be thrown into a cold, black cell and forgotten. Her blue and white habit protects her; the Queen admitted as much. But nothing protects me. I'm dead if they found the box Sodum gave me, never mind my father's diamond. I have to get off Malem as soon as possible. At least the Queen didn't order me to stay here.

"Slow down, Kia. You don't need to run. They haven't found it."

I keep walking. "Found what?" I ask without looking at her.

"Whatever it is you're trying so hard to hide. I'm not prying, I just want you to calm down."

"I don't know what you're talking about."

"Your secret's safe with me, Kia," Agatha says softly.

How many times did I wish Owegbe understood me? And now Agatha does, always, and it's infuriating. I stalk down the dirt street in silence, stirring up little clouds of dust that make Agatha cough.

As soon as we reach the house I say, "I need to get out of these clothes," and hurry into our room. My bags are both there. I grab my second robe out of the bag and feel along the hem. It's there! A small, hard lump, barely discernable between the thick folds of wool. I toss the robe on the bed with a sigh. Tears of relief brim in my eyes. I blink them away fiercely, and pull off the clothes I've been wearing. Getting clean ones from my bag, I head for the shower. Tomorrow I'll go straight to the spaceship and wait there till it's time to leave.

"Where's Select Hamza?" I ask when I emerge in clean clothes and dripping hair.

"He's gone," Agatha says quietly.

"He's gone to the ship?"

"The ship? Kia, I'm sorry... The Captain had to leave. The ship's two weeks in port were up yesterday."

"But... he's coming back?" I try to keep my voice calm.

"In two years."

"Two years?" My voice rises. "TWO YEARS?!"

"Maybe something will come by sooner. But—"

I race to the door and pull it open, rushing outside without bothering to close it behind me. They can't have left without me! Hamza knew I was going back with the ship!

When I'm too winded to run I walk, pacing myself, thirty steps walking, thirty running, dodging people on the streets, ignoring their stares. Was it this far? Have I turned the wrong way on the narrow streets? By the time I reach the granaries I'm limping, breathing in labored gasps. I keep going, onto the landing field, before I allow myself to believe what I see: nothing. The ship is gone. I keep walking anyway, across the field of stiff gray weeds, across the darker slate-gray where the groundcover has been scorched by the heat of the burners, until I reach the bowl of churned-up mud where the ship sat. It's that that convinces me: the dark circle of mud lying in the field like the leavings of some monstrous creature that paused here and moved on.

There's nothing to see, nowhere to go. I sink down onto the scorched weeds at the edge of the mud.

The raw wind pummels me, wild in the open field. I didn't stop to grab my woolen robe, and I shiver in my jumpsuit. As cold as prison. The thought jolts me. No wonder the Queen didn't order me to stay on Malem: she kept me in prison until the spaceship left.

After a while I get up and start back to Prophet's Lane. I walk slowly, shivering with the cold and with exhaustion. I've had too little sleep over too many days, and have to stop to rest several times. The shadows in the street lengthen. Rounding a corner I hear voices laughing and calling. I stop walking. It's the group playing kickball. I'll have to detour to avoid them.

"Hello," I mutter to myself, turning wearily aside down another street, "I'm out of jail and ready to play again." I can just imagine their faces. I probably won't go back. The thought of playing kickball has lost its appeal. Was I really once upset because they wouldn't check me?

"Kia, is that you?" Agatha calls when I enter the house.

I close the door, shivering even in the relative warmth of the house.

"Where have you been? I've been worried," she says, coming to the front hall.

I stoop to unlace my boots and pull them off. She follows me to the bedroom. My robe is there, lying across the bed, with my father's diamond sewn into its hem. I'm trapped here with it. It isn't only the key to my father any more. My life might depend on finding out his secret, as quickly as possible.

"Kia, two guards came while you were in jail. They searched through your bags, your room, they overturned the whole house. They didn't find anything." But they'll come again. She doesn't say it, but they will and we both know it. She doesn't ask what they were looking for, either.

"I need to sleep."

She does something strange then: she hugs me.

I'm too tired and surprised to respond before she lets go just as quickly, and leaves. I lie down and pull the blankets over me. Warm. I close my eyes and feel my body relax after way too long.

I wake in the middle of the night from a dream of being back in jail and lie in the dark shaking until I recognize where I am.

"Come with me," Agatha says in the morning as she prepares to visit a Malemese family she's come to know. "You need some sun…" She peers out the window. It's raining again. "…Exercise."

I shake my head. When she leaves, I conjugate verbs in Kandaran as though I will someday be a student again. The precise grammatical rules soothe me.

"I'm going to visit Naevah," she says the next day. "Her husband spoke to the High Priest on your behalf. When he learned you'd been taken to the Queen he brought me to the palace and convinced the guard to let me in. Come with me, Kia. They're good people."

"I'll come next time."

Agatha assigns me chores, since I won't go out. The girl hired by Select Hamza left to get married during my absence and Agatha won't hire another. "We didn't come to employ them," she says when I complain. "We'll live like they do, on their terms, as long as we're here."

"They don't even have dust-bots," I reply. "It's like being part of an historical re-creation society." But Agatha is unmovable on this.

I get up from dinner and run water into the sink to wash the dishes. Through the window over the sink I see evening coming on, the shadows lengthening. Two years.

"Select Hamza should have gone to the High Priest." I frown down at my hands in the soapy water. "He could have got me out of jail in time to leave with him."

Agatha stands still. I look up. She's staring out the window into the gathering twilight.

"What is it?"

"Select Hamza isn't on the ship. He disappeared the day after you were put in jail."

"He's missing?" My breath catches. Is anyone safe here? "Did you speak to the High Priest?"

"Yes I spoke to the High Priest. He told me the Select often journeyed to the farms to talk with the people outside the city."

"He wouldn't go without telling you."

"No," she agrees. She turns abruptly and leaves the room.

I look down at the sink. Soap bubbles glisten under the ceiling light, tiny rainbows trembling inside them. They remind me of my father's diamond. Gently, I try to lift one out of the water.

It bursts apart in my hand.

# Chapter Eighteen

I can't hide in the O.U.B. house forever. My best defense is knowledge. Stealing information will be harder than stealing jewelry, but there must be a way. I decide to go back to playing kickball. I couldn't care less who wins, now. They'll probably love that.

I'm afraid there'll be awkward questions when I show up, or they won't let me join them, but Jumal says, "Hey, duckling," and waves me over. I frown when he says it, remembering how he reamed me out. I'd tell him not to call me that, but he'd probably just do it all the more.

"Welcome back," Micah says, and he drops the ball to signal the game's begun.

I know what they want now. Whenever I get the ball, I cycle through our team of five, making sure I pass it to everyone at least once. Except Jumal. He can get it for himself.

When the game's over I go over to Mehda and congratulate her on the score she made. But then Kaline comes up and they leave quickly. I didn't do anything wrong! I want to yell after them. I think of the boy with the missing fingers for everyone to see, and the choice the Adept offered me, and for the first time, I'm grateful to her. If I get out of here alive, that is.

Everyone leaves but Jumal. When I head home, he falls into step with me.

"You don't talk much," he says after three streets of silence.

"My name is Kia."

He lets it go for a beat. "Okay," he says. "Kia." He doesn't look at me but he smiles, as though he thinks I'm funny. I want to tell him, I know four languages, how many do you know? But he'd probably ask if one of them is duck.

We walk for a while without talking. It's getting dark. The streets are full of shadows. I haven't been out in the dark since… A door slams across the road. I gasp and jump back.

Jumal clasps my elbow, steadying me. "It's alright," he says. "It's just the wind blowing a door closed."

I stand there, shaking, catching my breath. He must think I'm an idiot. Again. But he waits beside me quietly, his hand cupping my elbow.

The Malemese never touch anyone in public. I feel his hand through my robe and the sleeve of my jumpsuit, warm and strong. I've caught my breath, but I don't want to move.

"It'll be summer soon…" We hear a man's voice and the quiet response of a woman, coming from a side street.

Jumal lets go of my arm. We start walking again. When we reach Prophet's Lane, he walks me to the door and stops.

I look at him and smile, like Jaro said, but I have to look away again, because of the way his lashes look against his skin and how that lock of hair curls on his forehead, never mind his eyes looking straight back into mine…

"Kia," he says, "Don't be afraid. I won't let anything happen to you."

I look up at him then, wondering how he knows and how much he knows, and not really comfortable with him knowing anything. But when he smiles I believe him, and I'm not afraid.

Until I get inside, and he's gone, and I remember Hamza holding my elbow at the square, holding me from falling, just like

Jumal. And if a Select of the O.U.B. can't keep me safe—can't keep himself safe, because where is he?—then how can an eighteen-year-old apprentice priest?

I begin going with Agatha on her visits so people will see me with her. The Queen said she couldn't get rid of Agatha. If the Malemese associate me with the Select, the Queen might find it hard to dispose of me, too.

Unless she does it secretly. Lying alone in my bed—Agatha has moved into Hamza's old room—I wonder what happened to him. Agatha says the city police are searching for him now. The ones who put me in jail? I said. Agatha goes to their office every few days to enquire if there's any news, a not-so-subtle reminder. There's nothing more we can do.

Going visiting with Agatha is like growing your hair. All it takes is time. The Malemese women talk about their housework, their children, the things that make up their daily lives. I listen politely and try not to fall asleep. Agatha gives them her full attention, as though everything they have to say is fascinating. They don't seem to mind repeating themselves with gestures and extravagant expressions to make their meaning clear to her, or waiting while she composes her thoughts into the limited Malemese at her command. She won't let me interpret for her unless it's absolutely necessary. After a while I understand why. I would be a barrier between them, a wall cutting them off from Agatha's intense brand of listening. Their conversation would hinge on interpretation instead of understanding. That's Agatha's gift: understanding. My gift is only language. Even Agatha's lack of language endears her to them; they laugh together at her malapropisms and the shared humor erases their differences. She's winning them over one mistake at a time.

"Let's visit Naevah and her husband," I suggest one morning over breakfast. "I want to thank him for helping me." Also, who knows if I might need his intervention again?

# Chapter Eighteen

Agatha gets up from the table, leaving a mug of hot coffee. Coffee is how the O.U.B. pay for their property on Prophet's Lane. It's too frivolous a product for the Malemese to waste their limited farm land on, but coveted enough that it's worth sacrificing the little thirty-by-thirty-foot lot for a regular supply every two years. Agatha only kept two containers for our use, and one is reserved for guests, so it's a rare treat.

I watch her cut a slice of rice bread and apply a thin spread of jam to it. Her delay in answering wouldn't mean anything to anyone else, but I'm getting nervous.

I cut myself a slice of bread as I wait, carefully spreading the jam as thinly as possible over every inch of it. I'm barely aware of the scrimping—that's the way things are on Malem.

"We can visit Naevah," Agatha says when she sits down again. "But her husband's not at home. He's been sent to administer to the farmers. He'll be gone four months."

"I thought only younger priests do that, those without wives and families?"

"Not this time," Agatha says, biting into her bread.

"He's been sent away for helping me."

"There's no reason to think that."

"Or else to prevent him from helping me again."

"The High Priest doesn't explain his directives. That doesn't mean they're suspect."

We finish our bread and coffee in silence. As I get up to clear the table, there's a knock at the door. I drop the plate, catching it just before it smashes.

"It's a light hand," Agatha says, going to open the door.

"Jumal. Come," I hear her say in Malemese.

I walk into the room feeling foolish. I need to get a grip here. "Hey, Jumal." I smile.

"Kia." He nods as though he hardly knows me and turns back to Agatha. "My aunt asks you to visit her. As soon as possible."

"Naevah asks me? Now?" Agatha says in her atrocious Malemese.

Naevah? Jumal's uncle is the man who helped me?

"Before you come to my home I have to explain something." He's speaking slowly so Agatha can understand, but he's looking at me.

"Come, sit," Agatha says. "Anything you say… we'll be silent of it."

Jumal looks at me. I nod. My throat's too dry to speak.

"My cousin Tira is sick." Jumal's hands clench at his side. He has large hands, strong hands. They look helpless now.

"Tira has CoVir." Agatha guesses, when Jumal doesn't continue. Jumal shuts his eyes. "Yes."

I gasp, and can't help myself—I shrink back, away from him. Agatha leans forward. "When?"

"This morning."

"No one knows?"

"Me. My Aunt." He looks at us. "You."

"We come."

Is she crazy? His cousin has CoVir!

"We can't go," I say in Edoan, so Jumal won't understand. "Tira's mother can nurse her."

They both just look at me. "I… I'll go for a doctor," I say, this time in Malemese, since apparently Jumal's a good guesser.

"When the doctor comes," Agatha says in Edoan, "Tira will be sent to the fever house in the swamp. She is two years old. Her family will be quarantined in their home. I am going to visit Naevah before the doctor is sent for. You can come or stay here."

No way in the universe am I going to… I catch Jumal watching me. Agatha's already headed for the door. I take a step, and stop. It's lunacy! Agatha's never seen those fevers, that vacant look in the eyes of someone who's supposed to love you... And what can we do, anyway?

Jumal's uncle put himself in jeopardy to come to my aid. That's why he isn't here, taking care of his family. That's why Jumal's here, asking us for help.

Suddenly I'm angry. How can he ask this of me? *Don't be afraid, I won't let anything happen to you,* he says, and then asks me to go catch CoVir, when there's nothing I can do for his cousin, anyway. And if I don't go I'll look terrible and selfish, and he'll hate me, and God knows what Agatha might offer to do to help them when I'm not there to stop her. And if she dies, where will I be?

"I'm coming," I say, but I'm furious. And Jumal knows it, because he looks at me, and it's the same look Jaro gives me just before he says, "F-."

꿀

Naevah comes to greet us as soon as Jumal opens the door to their apartment. The relief on her face when she sees Agatha confirms my suspicions. She's going to ask her to do something awful, and Agatha will do it, unless I can stop her.

A thin, fretful wail comes from somewhere in the apartment. A little girl runs toward us and throws her arms around Jumal's legs, brushing against me. I jump back into the hall.

"This is Liat," Agatha says, "Tira's twin sister."

I let my breath out and step into the apartment again. Jumal shuts the door. He picks up his cousin and looks at me above the little girl's dark curls. His eyes look worried. I look aside. Jumal's right to be worried, no matter what Select Hamza said about the CoVir strain being weaker now.

The tiny background cry continues. Jumal puts Liat down and starts toward the back bedroom but Naevah stops him and goes herself. Agatha and Jumal and I stand there in silence listening to the soft murmur of Naevah's voice in the next room. The crying eases, but when Naevah returns it starts up again. I try to ignore it, and find myself staring at Liat, who has crept up against her mother's leg.

Naevah picks Liat up. One of her hands brushes through Liat's hair, easing the tangles free, cradling the little head against her shoulder. She holds Liat tightly, as though memorizing the feel of the child in her arms. Agatha takes a step toward them. I grab her arm, stopping her.

"I'm going with Tira into the fever house," Naevah says. She buries her face in Liat's hair.

"You can't!" Jumal says. "The swamp is full of diseases. No one ever comes back." His voice breaks.

"Tira cannot go alone," Naevah says gently.

"Aunt Naevah—"

"I'll go," Agatha says. "You have Liat and Jumal to think of, as well as Tira."

"No!" They all look at me. I don't care, she can't die! She's all that stands between me and the Queen's fury. It's selfish. I know I'm being selfish, but so are they.

Jumal looks wretched. "I didn't mean for this…"

I glare at him. What did he think, when he came for her?

"You can't go," Naevah says to Agatha. "You wouldn't be allowed. You're a foreigner."

"Why does Tira have to go? They have medicine for it now, don't they?" I ask.

"And they'll give it to her, before they leave her there." Naevah's voice is patient, explaining something obvious to a foreigner. "Tira has to be isolated so she won't infect anyone else. And we have to be quarantined, in case the strain has mutated. We cannot let the plague begin again." She sits down, holding Liat in her lap. Her hands continue to stroke the solemn-faced toddler.

Will this be the last time Liat feels her mother's caress? Is that what Naevah's thinking as she cradles one daughter and prepares herself to follow the other into death?

"Select, will you stay with Liat and Jumal while I am gone? You will be quarantined here with them. I know it's a lot to ask…"

"She doesn't need to. I'll be here. I'll take care of Liat," Jumal says.

"And if you get sick? You know nothing must happen to you, Jumal. The Select will know what to do to keep you safe here." She turns to Agatha, a question in her eyes.

No! I open my mouth to remind Agatha that she has a mission here, but I can't say that in front of them. I close my mouth and settle on a Meaningful Look.

"No," Agatha says.

Naevah's shoulders slump but she nods at once. "I'm sorry—" she begins.

"I take Tira Prophet's Lane. It is isolated, not like apartment. No one comes. Tira get well there."

What?!

"We can't disobey the law," Jumal objects before I can. "I can never let myself think I'm above the law."

At the same time, Naevah shakes her head and says, "We have to notify a doctor and go into quarantine. The city cannot be put at risk for one child. The rest of Malem's children are precious too. And the High Priest would never agree to let Tira go with you. The guards will take her to the fever house themselves if I don't."

"I go after, when they gone. I take care of Tira. You stay here."

I know at once that Agatha's planning something. She won't outright lie, but she isn't sharing, either. They don't notice, because they don't know her, but she's drawn that Select lack-of-expression over her face, and she's done it for a reason.

"You won't be able to get in," Naevah says. "They'll lock the door to prevent her from wandering out, and they keep the keys at the jail."

At the word 'jail,' I shiver. As though she fears it too, the pitiful wail of a sick baby comes from the bedroom. I catch myself looking at Liat again. She has taken one of her mother's hands between her smaller ones. She spreads Naevah's fingers wide and sticks her chubby, baby fingers between them. When Naevah closes her fingers around them Liat gives a gleeful chuckle that shakes her whole body.

Looking up, I see Jumal staring toward the back of the apartment where Tira's weak crying can still be heard. His face is twisted as though he's in pain.

"Locks are no problem," I say.

# Chapter Nineteen

We don't speak all the way home. I already know what Agatha intends to do. It's obvious by what she didn't say. She never actually lied to Naevah and Jumal—she only told them she'd take care of Tira, not where she intended to do it.

"You mean to shut yourself in this house with a contagious CoVir patient!" I accuse her as soon as we get inside.

"I intend to nurse Tira until she's well, yes."

"If you die, what will that do to your mission? Or don't you care about that anymore?"

"I won't die, Kia."

"You don't know that!" She's going to risk her life on Hamza's assurance that the CoVir strain is too weak now to be a threat to healthy adults. He better be right, that's all. Because if she dies and he shows up, I'll murder him myself!

If he isn't already dead.

I hate this place.

I stomp into Agatha's bedroom, grab a blanket from her bed and take it to one of the empty rooms. "She has to sleep in there."

"Alright," Agatha agrees.

"And we're burning that blanket afterwards."

She nods. Before I can think of another demand, she asks, "What did you mean, 'locks are no problem'?"

I've been regretting that comment since I made it. But clearly Agatha's going to do this anyway, whether I help her or not. So I tell her.

"You brought what?" Her voice and her expression are completely controlled. I've never seen her so angry.

"The Order made me leave Seraffa. I had to bring everything I owned. What should I have done with them?"

"Given them back to Sodum. Thrown them away."

"Good thing I didn't."

"You aren't a thief any more, Kia!"

"You do know you're about to break the law?" I ask, angry now myself. "Do Select do that?"

"All the time," she says. "When there's an ethical reason to: 'If the potential benefit is greater than the potential risk of harm, and that risk is very slight,'" she quotes in a textbook voice.

"You should have said that at my trial. We might not be here."

"I thought ethics was a required subject for translators. Why didn't you say it?"

"It's a second year course. I won't be taking it for *quite a while*."

She pretends not to notice my emphasis on the last three words. "We're saving a child's life. It is God's work."

"But He's using a thief's tools." And I go outside to get them for Him.

Rain and cold have erased all signs of the hole, and the rock I placed near the spot has shifted. I dig five holes, shoving the spade into the damp soil repeatedly. I'm ticked at the way she called me a thief. Sure, on occasion, I made use of things someone else had set aside or didn't want, but they—the O.U.B.— are making use of me, aren't they? And no one's called them on it. The analogy hurts, like I, too, have been set aside, not wanted. I ram the spade fiercely into the soil again, and feel it hit resistance, slide sideways over the smooth top of the tool box. I dig it out and tamp the soil down again.

"They'll throw you in jail if they catch you with this," I warn her, setting it on the table. "And I won't be able to get you out." I don't mean that. I don't know how I'd do it, but I would.

"I'm not going to be caught."

Of course she'll get caught. She has no idea how to do this; she isn't the least bit sneaky. But I can see that argument isn't going to convince her.

I explain how each device works, but we don't have anything to practice on except the lock on the front door. Nobody puts their belongings in safes on Malem, and I have no idea what kind of lock there'll be on the door to the fever hut. I can tell, though, that she isn't getting it. She has no idea how to arrange the wires of the palm override so they lie close to, but not quite along the lines of her own palm and fingers, where they'll override her personal hand print. She says she'll hear the tumblers in the old-fashioned padlocks, but she doesn't know what she should listen for, and when she practices picking the simple front door lock, she twists the pick too quickly.

"Smooth," I tell her. She gives it another jerk.

"I just need to practice," she says. I remember how long it took her to learn to open the door with a key, and I'm about to remind her of it when she tells me the rest of her plan: I'm supposed to storm off to the inn pretending we've had an argument, and stay there till Tira's well and home again. I take a breath. We're about to have that argument for real.

"I'll go get Tira and bring her here," I say. God knows I don't want to. I'm almost relieved when Agatha refuses to consider letting me, why should we both put ourselves at risk? But that's not the point. Agatha's going to fail; or worse, get caught.

"I have more experience at this sort of thing."

"That's not something to boast about. Anyway, you're not going, I am."

"I'm not boasting, I'm stating a fact."

"Kia," she says, and her voice says: *Enough*. "You're not going to have anything to do with this. You are going to the inn, and you're staying there, where the innkeeper can see you. So pack your bag." She doesn't quite say *'now'* but it's in her voice, and she is a Select. I go to pack my bag. But I'm still steaming. How can she not see I'm the best one to go get Tira?

When I come out with my bag, she takes one look at my face and holds up her hand to stop me from starting again. "It's time for you to go," she says.

Okay, it's your funeral, I think. The cliché makes me wince. I turn back to face her at the door. "Tira has CoVir. Even if you nurse her, she probably won't live. It'll be all for nothing."

"Do you believe that, Kia?"

Yes. I don't say it out loud but Agatha sees it on my face.

"You wanted to save your mother," she says softly. "And then she died anyway."

"You can't save anyone."

"But you tried. Nothing can take that away from you. Your brother and sister know it, too."

"Do you think they told her? Before…"

"I'm sure of it."

I nod. And stand there with my hand on the doorknob, trying to leave. Don't do it, I want to beg her. But I can still hear that little cry from the bedroom, and see Jumal's and Naevah's faces, and okay, I get it. I don't like it, but I get it.

"Even if Tira dies," I say, "I'll know why you did it."

&

*I can feel the hard block under my hand, my fingers spread wide across it. I try to pull my hand back but someone is holding it there. Above me I hear the swish of a descending axe—*

I open my eyes, gasping. Darkness presses in around me with the weight of layered woolen blankets, its voice the pounding of my heart. Where am I?

I sit up in bed. As my eyes adjust to the dark, I make out the lump that must be my bag and the clothes I wore yesterday draped over the back of the chair… in my room at the inn.

I'm safe here, I tell myself.

I arrived at the inn in time for lunch, and sat around the dining room all afternoon and evening, listening to my travel-tab and offering dark hints about Agatha making me do too much work. I managed to act surprised when the innkeeper's wife told me a little girl had come down with CoVir that morning.

I lie down and try to go back to sleep, but I can't help thinking of Tira crying in her bedroom. I try not to imagine her all alone in the fever house. Has she been there all day? She's only two, she won't understand why she's been left there.

I pull the covers down, then quickly back up again. The room is freezing. At Prophet's Lane we keep the temperature raised to merely cold. I close my eyes. There's nothing I can do. But I see Jumal's anguished face and Naevah's bent head as she held Liat, and I wonder where Agatha is right now.

Standing outside the fever house praying, I bet. She couldn't pick a lock if her life depended on it. But she insisted she could do it in that stubborn tone of voice that it's useless to argue against. I roll over. Not my problem.

It's useless. I'm wide awake. I throw off the covers and go to the window. A solid wall of black presses up against the glass. My eyes have adjusted as much as they're going to, but the narrow alley on the other side of the window is only a memory. There's no way of knowing whether the night is just beginning or half over. I hurry back to the bed and grope along the bottom till I find my woolen robe.

Risky or not, I'm going to the fever house. I'll watch from a distance, just to make sure.

I feel my way back to the window, glad that the inn and its guest rooms are all on the ground floor. Opening the window, I lean out. As always, the sky is hidden by cloud cover. I can only hope the alley is as empty as it is silent. I climb through the small casement and let myself down onto the street, pulling the window shut behind me.

The darkness is so dense I have trouble finding and putting on the Malemese robe I tossed out ahead of me. I shiver in the cold until the heavy wool slides down around me, and tug the hood over my head.

I walk quickly, keeping close against the buildings. This is too easy, I think: the window, the pitch-black night, the city so silent and empty it might as well be unpopulated. It was that way earlier, too, when I went to check into the inn. The whole city is gripped in the pall Hamza described as it waits for one of its children to die.

Ahead I see the last buildings that mark the edge of the city. Even the dim and infrequent streetlights have ended now. There's no one around. I pull off my hood to see the way more clearly. I'm about to step out onto the road that leads into the country when I hear someone behind me.

"What are you doing out here?" a gruff male voice demands.

My heart nearly stops. I look around quickly. A woman has come into sight. Even from here I recognize the white on her habit. Didn't she have the sense to wear one of the dark Malemese robes? The man whose voice I heard is nowhere in sight but Agatha has stopped and is looking behind, down the street she came from. I slip sideways into the deeper shadow of a building.

It's too dark to see Agatha's face. Has she noticed me, too? Would she recognize me in the dark? I pull the hood back over my head, hiding my face once again in its folds. Agatha won't be expecting me here; she thinks I'm asleep at the inn. But Agatha is a Select—she's trained to notice everything and understand what she's seeing. Could she do that even in the dark with the distraction of someone speaking to her?

"I am walking and also I pray," Agatha answers the man in her broken Malemese.

I creep around behind the row of buildings to the corner where the voices are coming from.

"You're up praying in the middle of the night?"

"Tonight I pray," Agatha says.

"Aren't you afraid out here alone?"

"For me, I have not fear."

It's true, I think. She worries about everyone but herself.

"Whether you're afraid or not, it isn't a night to be outside."

"It is a night to pray."

I can make them out now, under the dim light on the corner, just down the street from the building I'm standing behind. The city watchman has his back to me and Agatha's facing him. I hope he won't ask any more questions. Agatha will never lie directly to anyone. And what if he searches her?

The watchman gestures to Agatha, pointing down the street ahead of him. "You can pray inside tonight. I'll escort you home."

Agatha turns to leave with him. I watch in an agony of indecision. Should I create a diversion? Would he leave Agatha and follow me? Would he shoot me?

I'm still trying to decide what to do when Agatha gives a little cry and stumbles sideways against the building beside her.

The watchman reaches out to prevent her from falling but she's already going down. She flings her hand out to steady herself against the side of the building, touching the ground, and reaches her other hand up to catch the man's arm. She never looks at the ground but to the watchman for his assistance, which saves her from falling further, and keeps his eyes on her. As he helps her back to her feet, I hear her say, somewhat louder than necessary, "You are true, this very dark night. Anyone out should take much care."

I wait a while after they've turned out of sight, then I go to the spot where Agatha stumbled. After feeling around in the darkness for a few moments, my hand slides over something hard and smooth.

My little black tool kit is lying on the ground against the building.

# Chapter Twenty

I stare at the tool box in my hands. Agatha wants me to rescue Tira. All I expected to do was unlock the door and let Tira out for her. Now I have to do it all, on my own. And what if she's aroused the city watchman's suspicions and he keeps a watch on her house? He'd catch me not only sneaking Tira in to Agatha, but with a thief's tools in my hands!

I was paid to come here. I was paid to teach Agatha Malemese. I wasn't paid to die here. I look around in the darkness, as though someone's going to magically appear and say, "I'll do it!" But no one's that stupid, so I shove the tool kit into my pocket and start walking.

It can't be too far to the fever house, if people suffering from CoVir made it there. I walk quickly past the last buildings of the city. The street turns into a country road, surrounded by crop land. It's a relief when the city lights disappear behind me, because only the darkness hides me now, and no one will think I'm out praying. But Naevah said there wouldn't be any guards aside from the regular city patrols. No one's ever disobeyed the CoVir regulations—Naevah and Jumal, for all they love Tira, would never have agreed with Agatha's real plan.

What if Naevah's wrong? I try to walk quietly on the dirt and gravel road, and listen hard. I wish Naevah had said how far it was when she gave us directions, thinking Agatha only intended to go and console Tira.

Where is that fork in the road Naevah described? Surely it can't be this far? What if I've missed it? I stop and peer anxiously up and down the dark road. Should I go back, or is it just ahead? I decide to keep walking, and finally there it is, no more than a narrow dirt path between the fields.

The path, too, is longer than I expected. I pass rice paddies stretching on either side of me into the night. The pathway is now built up as a dry route through marshland. Tendrils of fog creep up from the ground. I walk into them. It's eerie, rather than frightening, as though I'm moving in a bubble, the land solid and visible under my feet but disappearing all around me into vapor.

It feels like I've been walking for hours. How do the sick make it this far? I've left the rice paddies behind and entered what I guess must be the swamp: deeper water between clumps of land. I have to be close now.

Trees surround me, their roots anchoring the tiny islands. They lean toward me in the darkness, weeping icy teardrops from each leaf. Some of the islands are larger than others, but none is big enough to be the one I'm looking for. Finally, up ahead, I see an island as big as the plot on Prophet's Lane. A stone hut stands in the center. As I get closer, I smell a rank and fetid odor.

It's smaller than the Select's house, a grim square-shaped building, low and malevolent, squatting in the swamp like a poisonous toad. I don't even want to go near it. Tira's two, I tell myself, stopping a few feet away to stare at it. She can walk back beside me. I'll let her out, that's all. Just go and unlock the door.

I force myself forward.

There's a small rectangle cut into the stone near the ground, to push a plate of food through, and one small window on the side, but it's so dirty and the interior is so dark I can't see anything through it. The stones are covered with moss and lichen, damp and cold to the touch. When I find it, the metal door is as filthy as the walls, but the lock's clean and has obviously been maintained. It's a simple antique lock, the kind that opens with a key. It takes me two seconds to pick it.

"Tira," I call softly through the open door. Agh, it stinks in there. I cover my nose and take shallow breaths, trying not to draw the pestilent air into my lungs. The darkness inside is so thick even the walls near the door are invisible.

"Tira?" Why doesn't she come?

"Tira!" I call again, louder. What if she's already dead? I will not go into this hut to find a dead body.

She couldn't die in one day. They gave her the medicine, Naevah said. My father took years to die. I lean a little way in and yell, "Tira, come here right now! This isn't a game!"

Silence. I peer into the darkness for any sign of movement. Nothing. I have come too late, like my father. The thought settles in my gut, as cold and fetid as the air in the hut.

"TIRA!"

A thin little cry comes from inside the shack, a beautiful sound.

"COME HERE!"

The cry dwindles to a whimper and trails off into silence.

"TIRA, COME OUT HERE!"

Silence. The back of my hand brushes the door frame and comes away slimy. I'll have to go in there and get her. I curse, using every bad word I know, which takes some time because I know four languages and those are the first words every student learns.

Tira whimpers again. Taking a breath, I plug my nose and step inside. I shuffle forward carefully, waving my arms ahead of me in the pitch dark. The smell of vomit and diarrhea is overpowering, even while holding my breath. My foot touches something soft. I nudge it again and hear a small whimper in response. Bending down, I feel a little bundle lying on the floor. It's wet and sticky. I pull my hands back in disgust. Vomit! I gag and barely prevent myself from adding to it. I expel the breath I'm holding but close my mouth tight before I breathe in.

"Get up," I choke out without breathing. Tira doesn't move. Despite the cold night, she radiates heat; I can feel it without even touching her.

My lungs ache for air. I begin to see points of light in the darkness, and still I can't bring myself to touch Tira. What if I faint? Then I would breathe in the fetid air. I'd lie here with my face in Tira's vomit…

I race out of the hut, gasping for air. My ears are ringing and my heart's pounding so loud they might even hear it in the city. I lean forward with my hands on my knees, breathing. The gaping black hole of the open door mocks me.

Tira's going to die anyway. If you could save people, my mother would still be alive, and my father, too.

But I saw her little chest rising and falling as she labored to breathe in that stinking air. There isn't any way around that. I'm going to have to touch her, pick her up and carry her, covered in pee and vomit and diarrhea, all the way to the city. I feel the urge to swear again.

Of course I'll have to carry Tira. What did I think, coming here? That a sick toddler could walk for two hours?

I thought Agatha would take Tira, that's what. I only meant to come and pick the lock for her.

I can't stall, arguing with myself, any longer. Malem's nights are longer than Seraffa's, but not endless, even if this one seems to be. Either I have to go back in there and get Tira or go back without her. One or the other. Now.

If only I could go back without her!

I think of Jumal, his face anguished as he looked at his aunt and cousin last night, and of Tira lying sick and alone in that disgusting hut, and I really, really want to hurt whoever made those laws. But first I have to get Tira out of there. I pull my sleeves down over the palms of my hands and hold them there. I hope Hamza was right about CoVir not being dangerous any more, I think as I run into the fever house like some idiot storybook heroine storming the enemy's citadel. I kneel and scoop Tira up and rise again in one motion, turn and race outside, kicking the door shut behind me.

I get all the way to the stone footpath before I have to expel my breath and inhale again. Then I remember to go back and lock the door so whoever comes with food tomorrow won't know anything's wrong. He'll think she's sleeping or dead when she doesn't answer.

Back on the path, I walk quickly. Luckily, Tira's small for her age, and gravity's on my side here. On Seraffa I'd never be able to do it. I begin to jog, holding Tira low against my abdomen, as far from my face as possible.

She whimpers at being jostled and squirms in protest, a little round fire against my stomach. I look down. Her eyes are shut, with crusty stuff around them. Her body shudders, her mouth opening in little jerks. She gives a stuttering cough, and a dribble of vomit slides down her cheek. She's choking! I kneel on the path and lie Tira face down over the water. Nothing more comes out that I can see. She's probably dehydrated but I don't have any drinkable water.

I pull off her wet, stinking gown. I'm tempted to toss it into the swamp but can't risk anyone finding it, so I tie it gingerly to my belt. Taking my own robe off, I wrap it around Tira and pick her up again. Her eyelashes flutter against her cheeks, long and dark like Jumal's. I wipe her little face gently with the sleeve of my robe. Her eyes open. She looks up at me.

"Mama," she cries, before her eyes shut again. I stare down at her.

"Mama…" It's barely a whisper this time.

"I'm here," I tell her. "I've got you." And I run. I use the low g, driving my feet into the ground and throwing myself forward, toward Agatha, toward help. Tira lies silent and limp in my arms.

"Don't die," I whisper. The words are torn from my mouth by the wind, tossed into silence. Not this one. Not this one, too.

My forearms begin to ache and then to tremble. I have to hold Tira higher, against my chest. She startles when I move her, too weak to cry.

"Hang on," I whisper fiercely, gasping for breath myself as I race on. "Help's coming." I reach the main road and push myself forward, faster. I have to get her to Agatha. Agatha will save her.

My legs have lost feeling, leaden weights jogging down the road. "Please," I pray to the silent night. I can't bear to look at the slack little face burning against my shoulder. "Please, don't let her die."

When I see the first buildings I weep.

"Almost there," I croak, as much to myself as to Tira.

I stagger into the first alley between two buildings and sink to my knees, laying Tira on the ground. Just for a minute, just till I catch my breath. She lies so still I panic and lean over her, searching for a breath. Ah, it's there, and it stinks! I laugh shakily under my breath, gathering Tira back into my arms.

"We're almost there," I whisper. My legs wobble when I try to stand, and I almost don't make it up. I peer up and down the street before leaving the alley.

The city is dark and silent. I stumble down the streets, hugging the sides of the buildings as much for support as for their shadows, listening for the sound of voices or footsteps. I hear the footsteps of the night watch just in time and flattened myself against a building, watching him cross the street a half-block down from me. It wakes me from my stupor of exhaustion. Quiet, I think blearily, trying to control my gasping breath.

I need to rest, but I'm afraid if I stop I won't be able to get up again. I push myself on. Tira hasn't made a sound since we left the swamp. She needs water. Keep walking, I tell myself, stumbling forward. Keep walking. Keep walking... By the time I reach Prophet's Lane I half-believe I'm destined to walk with Tira in my arms forever.

There's no one around. I stagger down the lane and tap once, lightly, on the door. It opens at once. Agatha pulls me inside and takes Tira from my arms. My legs buckle, as though Tira's weight has been holding me up. I sink to the floor and close my eyes. There's something I have to tell Agatha...

Water. Tira needs water. I'll tell her in just a minute...

"You have to get up now." Agatha is shaking me. "Shower and change your clothes. And Kia," she waits until I open my eyes and look at her, "I'm proud of you."

"Is she—"

"She's sleeping soundly. I got some water into her and she's held it down."

Agatha's waiting for me when I finish my shower. She holds out her hand. "Look at this." In her palm is a diamond. It draws the brightness from the single lamp in the hallway into itself and gives it back again like a tiny sun in the black of space.

How did she find it? Did she search my room?

"It was sewn into her robe," Agatha says. "I had to remove it to wash the garment."

What is she talking about? She washed the robe I left here? I stare dully at her, my thoughts sluggish.

"It's Tira's diamond. Her 'heart stone', they call it."

Looking more closely, I see that it's smaller than mine, though it shines with equal brilliance. "It's beautiful," I mumble.

"Does your father's look like this?"

Stupid with exhaustion, I almost shake my head.

"Kia, don't you know you can trust me?" She waits for me to reply. When I don't, she sighs. "I thought you were guarding a secret the day your father died, but I wasn't sure. And you were so young I thought it couldn't be important. I was wrong, wasn't I?"

"I have to get back to the inn." I take a step toward the door.

Agatha puts her hand on my shoulder, stopping me. "When I caught you staring at Lady Khalida's jewels, you were focused on them with such intensity, as though you were searching for something inside the flash of the gems, something personal. I knew then I'd made a mistake, that I should have intervened when you were young. But the Newtarian Embassy wasn't the time or place to deal with it. I intended to get back to you, but the Adept found you first."

"Because of the vision." It isn't me they care about. It's something they think I'm going to do for them.

"I don't know anything about prophecies and visions."

"You don't believe in the vision?" I'm not sure whether to feel relieved or disappointed.

"There's a saying: The Adept have visions, the Select have intuition, and outside the Order, it's all guesswork."

"Sounds like the same thing to me."

Agatha smiles.

I pull open the door and then stop, and look back at Agatha. "Don't let her die."

Agatha nods. "I won't."

"And… be careful. Don't kiss her."

# Chapter
# Twenty-One

I wake up with a scratchy throat, and feel my forehead. The room is freezing, so anything still alive feels warm, but is it warmer than usual? I get up and while I'm getting dressed, I sneeze twice and panic for half an hour, waiting for a third which never comes. My throat is better after breakfast, but what does that prove? The virus is probably already inside me, incubating. What if Agatha catches it? We could both die! What if we start another epidemic?

I force myself to calm down. There's nothing I can do now, anyway. What will happen, will happen. That sounds enough like the O.U.B. to make me want to gag, and that makes me feel like myself again. I get dressed and go for breakfast.

I can't go near Prophet's Lane for six days. I can't even ask about Agatha; I'm supposed to be angry at her. I hang around the dining room listening to every conversation at the inn, but no one mentions her. The innkeeper's wife is always full of gossip, surely she'd say something about Agatha visiting so-and-so, or being seen at the market.

What if they're both lying dead in the house on Prophet's Lane? By the third day, that thought drives me half-way across the city before I get myself under control and turn back to the inn. I have to continue playing the rebellious teenager.

On the fourth night I dream I'm Tira, innocently spreading the killing fever to those I love. In the dream, Tira/I am playing beside a white bed. I stand up and see Agatha lying cold and still—so still I become frightened. I grab Agatha's arm and shake it, calling her name. The door behind me opens and Owegbé walks in. She looks at me and holds out her arms.

I get up to run to her, but before I can, she crumples into a heap on the floor. She lies there as still as Agatha in the bed.

"Mama!" Tira/I cry in a baby voice, "Mama!" Neither of them moves. It's too late.

I wake up crying, and lie there the rest of the night, waiting for dawn. I inhale the cold sunlight when it finally arrives, like medicine.

Then I wait through the morning, and afternoon, and then the evening, until night falls again. All day I hear a small child's voice, my voice, crying for someone, but I have come too late.

On the sixth night I sneak out my window again and walk to the fever hut. Tomorrow is the seventh day. In the morning they will open the door to see if Tira has survived. She has to be there when they come. If they're still alive, Agatha will take her back tonight.

It's a rare moonlit night. I can see clearly down the path to the hut. Only there's nothing to see. I imagine a thousand scenes of Agatha and Tira gripped in the throes of fever or seized by a city guard, while I watch for them to arrive. I'm on the verge of heading for Prophet's Lane when I see a little body scampering toward me through the darkness.

Agatha's voice calls softly, "Tira be careful, don't fall off the path."

I stand up, grinning broadly, not knowing whether to laugh or cry. They're here! They're here and they're both healthy! I hold out my arms: "Tira!"

At the sight of me, or perhaps catching sight of the fever house, Tira skids to a halt. She takes two steps backward.

I let my arms drop. Of course she doesn't remember me, she was unconscious most of the time I carried her. Agatha emerges from the shadowing trees. Catching sight of me, she looks surprised, then annoyed.

"There's no need for you to take more risks," she scolds.

"Okay," I say. "You unlock the door."

She might have kept trying all night if I let her. She surrenders the lock pick ungraciously when I finally hold out my hand.

"Languages and thievery. Two things you can't learn." I grin.

"I can learn languages. Thievery you have to be prone to."

"Born to," I correct, yanking the door to the hut open.

"Not born to, Kia. Your father was an honorable man."

"How would you know?"

"I met him once. He was just what his name implies—merciful and kind."

"You met him once?" I end my sentence with a snort.

"I am a Select. I met him once."

I shrug and look around for Tira. Agatha, suddenly reminded, calls softly, "Tira."

She's standing on the path at the edge of the clump of land the fever house is built on, staring at the dark hut with wide, frightened eyes.

"Tira, come here." Agatha holds out her arms.

"No." Tira takes a step backward. Agatha starts toward her, and Tira backs up further.

"Stop!" Agatha cries, but she's too late; Tira slips at the edge of the island and topples backward into the water. We both race toward her. I skid to a stop where the land drops into swamp but Agatha plunges straight into the cold, muddy water crying Tira's name.

The swamp isn't deep near the island. Agatha can still stand, and after a few seconds of anxiously flailing through the water she finds Tira and hauls her to the surface. Tira splutters and coughs a few moments then gives a piercing shriek and begins to cry loudly despite our attempts to hush her. At last Agatha gives up and carries her toward the fever house. When Tira sees it she screams even louder and begins struggling and kicking to free herself. Agatha pauses uncertainly at the door. I just stand there. This is her plan. She wasn't happy to see me, so let her handle it.

"No! No! No!" Tira shrieks, sobbing. She clings desperately to Agatha. "No! No!"

"I can't leave her."

"You have to," I tell Agatha, but I'm sympathetic. I don't blame Tira for not wanting to go in there again, or Agatha for not wanting to make her. And Agatha doesn't know how bad it is yet. "It's only for the night. They'll come get her in the morning. We planned this," I remind her.

"The plan didn't include leaving a terrified child locked up alone in the dark."

"Yes it did." We just didn't know how hard that would be. "She'll be alright. There's nothing in there that can hurt her."

"She's soaking wet. I have to get her dry."

"You have to leave her here. You'll get CoVir if you stay in there all night. Tira's already had it, she's immune—" I stop myself, and turn away from Agatha, hunching my shoulders.

"I won't die, Kia," Agatha says. "I'm strong and healthy. The CoVir strain is no longer deadly as it once was. I've already been exposed and I'm fine."

"There are other diseases in the swamp. You didn't want Naevah coming here. You thought *she'd* die."

"Yes, I thought Naevah might get ill. Did you see her? How run down she was, with two two-year-olds and a household to care for without her husband? And on top of that, Tira so sick Naevah hadn't slept all night. Tira's fever broke three days ago and she's done little else but sleep since then. I'm well-rested, Kia."

Tira whimpers, the sound thankfully muffled against Agatha's shoulder now. She clings with a strangle-hold around Agatha's neck, her little legs circling Agatha's waist tightly. It would take both of us to pull her free, and we'd probably have to knock her out or something to keep her inside the fever house while we made our exit and locked the door.

"There's a chimney—that means there'll be a fireplace. I'll make a fire inside to dry our clothes and warm us," Agatha murmurs, stroking Tira's back soothingly.

"You didn't go in with Tira when they locked her in. How will you explain that?"

"I'll break the window."

"That's probably illegal."

"You know the mood of the city as well as I. When they see Tira's alive, they'll forgive me. They're not cruel people, only frightened. Crippled by fear, like children," she adds thoughtfully. She looks down at Tira, still stroking her back. Tira lies her head against Agatha's shoulder, quieter now. Her arms still cling around Agatha's neck.

"They'll put you in quarantine."

"I'm not sick. They'll quarantine me in my house. And I've already spent seven days with Tira, that's half my quarantine over already." She reaches to touch my cheek with her hand. I push it away. "Lock the door behind us," she says, carrying Tira into the fever house.

On the long walk home, I hear laughter. I turn all around, peering into the darkness. The night is empty and silent. I continue walking, faster now. The soft, mocking laughter comes again. Even when I start running, it stays with me. There's something familiar about the sound, but I can't place it...and then I do.

I thought I could save Tira. I hadn't considered that there would be a price.

I run through the night with my mother's laughter following me. I thought I could save her. I thought I knew the price. The wind stings my eyes and freezes on my cheeks the moisture it pulls from them. When the city appears ahead, I slow to a walk. You can't outrun death.

I never intended to trade Agatha for Tira.

# Chapter Twenty-Two

Where is Agatha?

She should have been here hours ago, carrying out the charade we planned, with apologies and promises and pleas for me to return to Prophet's Lane which I, after pouting a little, would agree to do. I can't go back until she comes; it would blow my whole we-had-an-argument-and-I-left story.

Of course, that was only the plan. A plan is the one series of events you can count on *not* happening. We should have made a dozen different plans; that way I'd know even more about what isn't going to happen.

At breakfast the innkeeper's wife told me the child who was ill survived CoVir and returned to the city healthy. She *smiled* at me, which is as jubilant as it gets with her. All morning I've heard people on the streets calling joyous greetings to one another as though they, as well as Tira, have recovered.

But nothing from Agatha. Nothing *about* Agatha. What's *wrong* with the rumor mill here? The innkeeper's wife is really slipping. I sit in the dining room of the inn, forcing myself to smile back at her, and order a noon dinner I don't know how I'll be able to choke down.

Most likely Agatha's quarantined at Prophet's Lane. Still, she could have sent a message to me. Something like, *"I'm very sorry about our quarrel and want to make up but I'm in quarantine now. P.S. don't worry, I'M NOT SICK."*

Is that too much to ask?

Or she's in jail. They don't convey messages from there.

The innkeeper's wife sets a bowl of fish chowder in front of me. It's steaming and smells delicious. I feel my appetite returning. As I pick up my spoon, a little girl skips into the dining room, calling over her shoulder, "Daddy, Daddy. Hungry!" The innkeeper's wife beams down at her as though she's a child vidstar.

I glance up—and gawk over my spoon at Tira.

"You'd never believe she was at death's door a week ago, would you?" the innkeeper's wife gushes. "And now she's a guest in my inn, with her father."

"I heard he was in the country," I croak, staring at Tira. What will I say if she remembers me?

"He was relieved of that duty as soon as his daughter fell ill. The High Priest himself radioed the message. He got back yesterday."

Tira skids to a halt, frowning at me. "No! Bad!" she says, backing up into a pair of legs that have just entered the room. She twines her fingers into her father's robe and pulls it around her, covering her face.

I look up to see Jumal's uncle at last, the man who rescued me from the Queen's wrath.

…And find myself staring at the priest who had, as a matter of course, cut off a man's head and a boy's fingers in the public square.

He's saying something, apologizing for something. "…doesn't usually act this way. I'm afraid she's never seen anyone of your complexion." He sounds embarrassed as he attempts to extricate Tira from the folds of his robe.

I open my mouth, but nothing comes out. I'm frozen in my seat, holding my spoon in a death grip halfway between the bowl and my mouth. I lower it to the table and uncurl my fingers.

The innkeeper's wife gives me an odd look before she leaves to get two more platters of food.

"Is this the girl who was sick?" I manage to say.

"Yes." He kneels down. "Tira, do you want to choose our table?" Then, when his offer has no effect, "I'll lift you up if you let go of my robe."

Tira's arms emerge from the folds of cloth and wrap around his neck. Her back is to me.

The angry line of that little back hurts. I know she doesn't remember the night journey back in my arms—no one but Agatha will ever know about that—but it's too bad she remembers me trying to make her go back into the fever hut.

He strokes her dark curls and murmurs, "What is it sweetheart?" I watch those hands, seeing them around the handle of an axe. Will he believe Tira if she says she saw me at the fever hut?

"I probably look like something from out of her fever dreams," I say, forcing a laugh. It catches in my throat. Can he hear how nervous I am? He visited me in jail. He must remember me, the one who escaped his punishment.

But he's also Jumal's uncle. He got me out of jail and was punished himself for it.

"Um, thank you for... The Select said you helped her, when..."

He looks at me over Tira's head. "I have been repaid tenfold," he says.

The innkeeper's wife returns with two more plates of food. Seeing us talking, she places their dinners at my table. Tira's father sits down politely across from me. After a few minutes of coaxing, Tira kneels in the chair beside him and picks at the food on her plate, glancing distrustfully at me now and then.

I force down a spoonful of chowder.

"My name is Prad Gaelig," he says. "And I didn't really do much for you. Our Queen… is a good ruler, but sometimes any ruler acts… in haste. That's why we have a triumvirate—the King, the Queen and the High Priest—to balance each other, to govern objectively."

Right, I think. And two of that balancing act are in bed together.

"You don't agree?"

"What if they all have the same bias?"

"Then perhaps it's a well-founded bias and should be considered seriously."

I think of Iterria, hot and dry and dying. When I look up, he's still looking at me, waiting for my answer. His eyes are friendly, Jumal's eyes.

"And if it isn't?" I ask. "If it's just prejudice or a misunderstanding?"

"What world doesn't have this problem?"

He's right. Almost all the Central Worlds are democracies, and several of them have been at war, planetside, for decades. Any government can control its people simply by keeping them in a state of heightened fear or outrage. I was shocked to learn in history class how simple and effective the formula is, and how often it results in a president's re-election. But even so…

"I was thrown in jail for no reason." That wouldn't have happened on democratic Seraffa.

"And when the Queen couldn't justify her action you were freed."

"It took a while." I sip at another spoonful of chowder. It's lost its taste.

"I'm sorry about that. It shouldn't have taken so long. Your Select didn't know how to appeal."

Hamza would have known. Is that why he's missing?

"I guess you're right," I say. Looking up I see the face of an executioner, and beside him, the daughter who was left to die. The child *I* saved.

Tira frowns at me, still suspicious.

"You must have been happy when they brought her to you," I say.

"I went to the fever house myself on the sixth morning."

The *sixth* morning? He knows Agatha wasn't there, then. I stare down at my bowl, aware of him watching me intently. "I thought it was supposed to be the seventh morning."

"I went then, as well."

He begins to eat, chewing slowly and nodding to Tira to encourage her to do the same. "The guards came too, on the seventh day, of course."

I gulp a spoonful of chowder down, choking on a lump of fish.

He leans across the table. "Why are you here at the inn, Kia?"

Just tell me what's happened to her, I think fiercely. Did you cart her off to jail? Are you here for me?

"Tira wasn't at the fever house—" Prad Gaelig watches me as he speaks.

"Daddy, I'm done."

"Just a minute, Tira."

"Daddy, sweets!"

"Tira—"

The door to the dining room opens and the innkeeper's wife bustles in. Seeing we've stopped eating, she clears the table.

"You will have coffee?" she asks Prad Gaelig.

"No, no," he protests.

"I've already made it. This is a special day, Prad Gaelig. And the little one wants a sweet. She should have one, after her ordeal. And you?" She looks at me. I shake my head.

When the woman leaves with our dishes, Prad Gaelig sits drumming his fingers on the table. Before he can speak the innkeeper's wife returns with coffee and a sweet for Tira. I'm ready to drum on the table myself by now.

"On the seventh morning?" I prompt him, when she finally leaves.

"On the seventh morning, your Select was there with Tira. She said she climbed in the window and nursed Tira through her illness." He cocks one eyebrow at me as if to say, but you already know all this.

"Is she alright?" I ignore the priest's qualifier, 'she said'.

"She was this morning. But she refused to leave the fever house. She said she would spend her quarantine there."

I stare at him, speechless. It isn't possible. Someone has forced her to do that. I stand up, slamming my hand onto the table and say, in a voice as quiet as the Adept's, "Who wants her dead?"

Tira pulls back, startled by the sound of my hand slapping the table. Her head knocks against the back of her chair and she wails. Her father gathers her onto his lap, trying to soothe her.

The innkeeper and his wife bustle in, eager to be of assistance.

"Nothing is wrong," Prad Gaelig says, "except that my daughter has had an exciting morning and it is past her nap-time." He stands up, holding Tira.

I step away from my chair and wait, not quite barring his way.

"I have an errand for you, if you would," he says evenly. "I cannot leave Tira while my family is still in quarantine."

I nod tersely. The innkeeper's wife frowns at my lack of civility.

"Come to my room in an hour, then."

I stand in the dining room after Prad Gaelig has left. It's inconceivable that Agatha *chose* to stay at the fever house. She said herself last night that healthy people aren't quarantined at the fever hut, they're quarantined in their home.

The Innkeeper's wife comes in to wipe down the table. "Your Select is quite the hero."

"Hero?"

"She spent the week at the fever hut, nursing Prad Gaelig's daughter back to health. Didn't he tell you? Or perhaps you already knew?" She aims a speculative look my way.

"No! I mean, I didn't know, but he did just tell me. I didn't know he told you."

"Of course he told me. He's staying here as our guest. Why shouldn't I be the one to take it to market? And indeed I did! Your Select is an example for us all."

"So Tira's recovery isn't a miracle after all," I can't help saying.

The Innkeeper's wife straightens. She turns to me with her hands on her hips. "Of course it's a miracle! No one survives the fever house. Your Select has been blessed by God for her courage and goodness. You should be honored to be with her." She narrows her eyes at me.

"Um, yes, I am. Did Prad Gaelig tell you anything else?"

"What else is there to say? The deed speaks for itself. As your Select told the guards, God protected her and Tira. A good woman, humbling herself and giving the glory to God."

"Right," I say. "But where is she now?"

To my surprise, the innkeeper's wife looks perplexed. "Why, at home, I imagine, where a woman ought to be. Oh," her face clears, "you want to apologize for your quarrel. So you should, without delay."

Apologizing to Agatha is the last thing on my mind. But the innkeeper's wife is nodding her approval.

"Yes, I will," I mutter. "I just thought she might be, you know, quarantined somewhere?"

"Quarantined? I suppose it's possible. Men are such fools. A woman protected by God doesn't need to be quarantined. Still, you can talk to her, just as long as you don't go inside."

She wouldn't expect me to go to the fever hut, so she must mean Prophet's Lane. Why would Prad Gaelig tell me Agatha's in the fever hut, and not tell her? Is it because Agatha's a hero, and locking up a hero wouldn't be popular? Or because he wasn't able to finish his story, and she isn't there now?

"I think I'll do that. I'll go talk to her. At her house." I add the location just to be sure.

The woman nods. "You're a good girl. A bit headstrong, but then a woman has to be."

Agatha isn't in the house on Prophet's Lane. I check every room to make sure she left no sign to suggest Tira was ever here. Before leaving, I bury the tool kit and put on the robe with my father's diamond sewn into it. If Agatha's in trouble, the house might be searched again.

Everyone I meet on the way back to the inn is full of praise for Agatha, but no one can tell me where she is. She's a saint, they all agree. Great. Cultural history 101: saints end up martyred.

"Prad Gaelig is waiting for you," the innkeeper's wife tells me when I get back to the inn. "I'll show you to his room."

Prad Gaelig invites me in and pauses, looking at the innkeeper's wife. After a moment the woman blushingly declares she has to get back to work. Prad Gaelig nods politely.

"A good woman," he says when she's gone, "but blessed with too much curiosity and too little discretion." He closes the door.

"Where is the Select?"

"I told you. She chose to stay at the fever hut for her quarantine."

"Why would she do such a—thing?" I prevent myself just in time from calling the hero of the day 'stupid'.

"She asked that a message be taken to the Queen and the High Priest: if she dies in the fever hut we are to send you back on the next ship to carry her ashes to the Order; but if she survives her fourteen-day quarantine, no one else will ever be sent to the fever hut."

I sit down. She wasn't forced to stay there. No, what Prad Gaelig said sounds just like her. I wish I hadn't withheld the word 'stupid'. "What did they say?"

"Nothing, yet. A guard was sent to the palace to deliver the message and receive her Majesty's orders. I myself took her message to the High Priest."

"Will they agree?"

Prad Gaelig's expression is not hopeful. "I haven't heard whether there's been an answer. I've delivered her message. The rest is speculation, and I've been warned not to speculate again on things that don't concern me."

"Why is she doing this?" I'd like to pound my hand into something again, but Tira's asleep on the other side of the room.

"You'll have to ask her. I've done what I can. It's only natural that a grateful father would make no secret of who had saved his child. If I know the innkeeper's wife as well as I think I do, half the city already knows what the Select did, and the rest will by tomorrow."

For a moment I don't follow him. Then I think of Hamza's unexplained disappearance and gasp. "You're afraid this will be hushed up, that she'll be left there to die in secret."

Prad Gaelig returns my gaze without comment.

"Has the King come back yet?"

"No."

"What if I talked to the High Priest?"

"He is very busy," Prad Gaelig says carefully. "He may not be able to see you for a couple of weeks."

"Would they let her be quarantined in Prophet's Lane? If she changed her mind?"

"Does she do that?"

I sigh. "Do you really have an errand for me?"

"I'd like you to let my wife know Tira is well. If I take Tira anywhere near our apartment she'll cry to see her mother. Show my wife this, so she'll know it's true."

He turns. Lying on the table behind him is a Malemese diamond. He lifts it tenderly, the concrete proof of his daughter's recovery, and brings it over to me. "It's Tira's heart stone."

I can see it more clearly today. It's slightly smaller than mine, but just as stunning. It appears softer, warmer this afternoon than it looked when Agatha showed it to me in the night, catching the brittle lamplight.

"Why do you call it that?"

"A heart stone? It's part of our faith. Our heart teaches us compassion, hope, endurance. It's the path to wisdom and self-knowledge. Therefore it's the path to God."

"That's the path to God?" I stare at the glittering gem. Sodum would love this.

"Not this." He closes his hand around the diamond, making its light blink out. "This is only a symbol. Like the cross and star the Select wear round their necks."

"What has the heart got to do with diamonds?"

"Vivid symbols make difficult concepts memorable. It's not always easy to remember the heart is valuable, especially when life has bruised it. So we use diamonds. Despite how backward we may seem to the Alliance, it has occurred to us that these gems are valuable."

He opens his hand to reveal the diamond again. "This one was my mother's. I hope Tira will acquire her wisdom one day."

"Does Tira share it with her sister, Liat?"

"Liat has her own heart stone. They're passed down through families. When someone dies, the next child born receives his or her heart stone. If there are none available within a family, the High Priest issues a new one to the family. That is a joyous occasion; it shows our population is increasing again. Liat was born second, she received a new diamond."

"Why give a child so young something so valuable?" And why is it just sitting on your table? I want to ask. My father wouldn't have had to know anything more about stealing than Agatha does, to walk off with one of these gems. Perhaps I'm wrong: he wasn't a thief, he just found it lying somewhere, left in the dirt by a child after her play.

"It's only valuable because it's Tira's," Prad Gaelig says. "Otherwise, what is it? A pretty stone. We have lots of stones on Malem. Dirt is more valuable than stones here."

"It may not be valuable here, but it would be on other worlds. If someone sold theirs, they could make a fortune."

He stares at me with a look that makes me wish I could take back my words. "If that happened," he says, pronouncing every word distinctly, "the off-worlder who bought it would be be-headed and the Malemese who sold it would be stoned to death. That's the punishment for desecrating a heart stone."

I stare back at him, wishing even more that I'd kept my mouth shut. And I'd been worried about losing two of my fingers!

"However, it's never happened," Prad Gaelig continues. "Not in my lifetime, and not that I've ever heard of. And what good would it do anyone? They'd give themselves away if they spent the money their sin brought them."

I want to drop it, but that word, 'sin', gets to me.

"Your Triumvirate could sell the diamonds. Malem could be a rich world. You could all live better."

"We like the way we live. How could we live better?"

I open my mouth to name a couple dozen ways that come to mind, but then I hesitate. I've been trained to view different cultures objectively. Despite their lack of luxuries and leisure, the Malemese, as far as I've seen, are content. Underneath the complaints and worries I've heard them share with Agatha, is a deep sense of community. They'd be shocked if she suggested any real change. They like her because she doesn't. Still, there's always the issue of farmable land.

"You could buy food. You wouldn't have to scrimp on coffee and jam and sweets and worry about having so little farmland."

"Yes. We do miss not having more of those tempting, unhealthy foods. But nobody on Malem is hungry. And we like being self-sufficient. When you become dependent on others, you have different things to worry about." He raises an eyebrow at me. "Nothing truly important can be bought. It has to be earned. That is what we believe."

"If you believe there isn't any value in possessions, why chop off a thief's hand? I saw you cut off a boy's fingers for taking something that belonged to someone else."

Prad Gaelig's face changes. I was prepared for anger after calling him on his hypocrisy, but instead it's grief that twists his features. "You don't understand. His crime was that he wanted what he hadn't earned, what he had no right to. Not because it was someone else's; because he wanted to get it effortlessly, undeservedly. I talked with him about it, how everything he got that way would be meaningless, until eventually nothing would have any value for him. I wouldn't punish him until he understood this about himself. Until he asked me to."

"He asked you to cut off his fingers?"

"He wanted to show publicly that he's changed. That he's no longer a thief. I was proud of him; he's begun to know himself, to decide who he wants to be."

I remember the boy's sharp bleats of terror and pain. My thoughts must show on my face because Prad Gaelig says, "There is no easy way to extricate yourself after you've done something wrong."

I wonder for a second if he can have guessed why I'm here. But that's impossible. Still, he's made me uncomfortable. "What about the man? Did he ask to have his head chopped off?" I ask sarcastically.

"Adults are punished when they are guilty. We have criminals and dissidents like any other world. We are a small community on a hard world, Kia, and by circumstance we're forced to live very closely together. Our resources are few and we must rely on one another. We can't afford to allow the self-indulgent to tear us apart. Nevertheless, I take no pleasure in what I had to do."

"What if he was sorry, too, and promised to change?"

"Some words and actions can't be taken back."

I think of Owegbé. It isn't her death that hurts.

"You think we are cruel and unforgiving," Prad Gaelig says, interpreting my silence as dissent. "But our laws are clear, unambiguous and they apply equally to everyone. That is justice. And we have no unfair division of wealth on Malem. Everyone must earn what they get, and everyone gets what they must have."

"How did Tira earn that?" I nod at the gem in Prad Gaelig's hand. Politics is interesting but what I really want is more information on the diamonds.

"I told you, this has no value except what Tira herself puts into it. That's how she will earn it."

On the bed Tira gives a deep sigh. "Mama," she murmurs from that dark, capricious place between waking and sleeping.

Prad Gaelig picks up a little pouch from the writing table and slips the diamond into it. He hands the pouch to me. "Thank you, in advance, for the comfort this will bring my wife."

Across the room, Tira stirs fitfully. Her father bends to wake her from her troubled dream.

I have no choice but to take the message for Naevah and leave.

# Chapter Twenty-Three

I get about three blocks from the inn before I see two men approaching me. My first thought is, how could I have been so stupid? I watched him cut off a man's head and still I let him convince me to walk out of his room carrying a Malemese diamond? Prad Gaelig is very convincing. Even when I see the insignia of the High Priest on the men's robes, even when they ask me to come with them, I have trouble believing he deliberately set me up.

"I'm delivering a message for Prad Gaelig," I say, and show them the pouch. They'd find it soon enough anyway, and I don't want them searching me for it; they might find my father's diamond sewn into the hem of my robe.

They look at each other, frowning and pursing their lips as though they have no idea what I'm talking about.

"I'll be happy to come with you as soon as I've honored my promise to the priest," I add, pushing my advantage. "You can come with me and see it done." Hah! If they refuse, they're refusing the request of a priest, and they can hardly claim I resisted arrest now. While they hesitate, I wave my arm in the direction of Prad Gaelig's apartment building and say, "We're almost there. He said it was urgent. If I can't deliver it, I'll have to return it and tell him so before I can go with you."

"Quickly, then," one of the men says. I set off at once. The sooner Prad Gaelig's diamond is out of my foreigner hands, the better.

Naevah cannot open the door so I announce my name as soon as I hear her knock back on her side of the door. "Prad Gaelig sent me."

"Is it true?" she says before I can tell her about Tira. I hear the catch in her voice.

"I saw her myself at the inn with your husband. He gave me this for you as proof." I slide the pouch under the apartment door, relieved to be rid of it. Naevah's cry of joy when she sees it is audible even to the guards, as are her sobbing words of gratitude. "I have to go now," I tell her, looking at the two men. I'm gratified to see their embarrassment.

"Where are we going?" I ask as they march me between them through the city, taking mostly back streets.

"The High Priest wants to talk to you."

They escort me to a building that looks like any other housing complex in the city. It has nothing of the opulence of the royal palace, even though the High Priest is apparently of equal stature in the ruling triumvirate. However, it is separated from the other buildings by cobbled streets on all four sides, giving it a measure of privacy rare here.

Privacy. Once I'm inside that building, anything could happen to me and no one would ever know. No one will even ask about me if Agatha dies in the fever house. As we approach the building I falter, looking around desperately. Two women are walking toward us. If I can catch their attention, they might remember—

We make eye contact and with a shock I recognize them. Mehda's mouth forms the word 'Kia' before Kaline nudges her quiet.

The guard grabs my arm and hurries me through the door.

"Is this whole building just for the High Priest?" I ask as they lead me toward the stairwell. I wish I'd done more research on the triumvirate, but I didn't think I'd need it in the short time I expected to be here.

"Priests and their families live here. The High Priest occupies the top floor."

Good. I'm not alone here. There's some comfort in that, even if he has hand-picked his neighbors. I'm used to climbing stairs by now, and the lower gravity helps, but by the time we reach the eighth flight I'm wondering why the High Priest didn't take over the first floor.

We step out of the stairwell into a large open foyer and take the door on the left. It opens onto a long, dimly-lit hallway. Several of the doors along the hall are open, showing meeting rooms furnished with a table and chairs. My guards escort me into one of the smaller ones.

The walls are gray metal, unadorned. Under the low, gray ceiling the room appears closed in, a room of secrets. There's a table in the middle, with a cushioned chair at one end—the only sign of luxury—and another plain metal chair.

The guards leave me standing inside the door, which they shut on leaving. I slump against it in relief. They didn't search me. The High Priest certainly won't. Nevertheless, it's only a matter of time before they find my father's diamond. Whatever the High Priest wants to know, I have to satisfy him quickly and get out of here.

It's a long wait. By the time the High Priest comes in I'm too indignant to be frightened. I look at him from my seat, not bothering to stand up.

"I have kept you waiting," he says in formal Malemese. "It could not be avoided." He sits on the cushioned chair.

"It is my pleasure to wait on the High Priest of Malem," I say, equally formal. "It could not be avoided."

# Chapter Twenty-Three

The skin around his eyes crinkles. "Is it also your pleasure to wait on the Select?"

"I was hired to teach the Select to speak Malemese during the voyage here. I expected to return with the spaceship." He knows as well as I why I didn't.

"Were you curious to see the planet your father visited?" His voice is smooth, his expression relaxed and pleasant, but his eyes are as cold and hard as the gray metal walls. He sits watching me like a reptile preparing to strike, while his voice implies shared confidences.

"My father visited many planets. It would take me a lifetime to see them all."

"Did your father teach you the language of every world he visited?"

"I know many languages. Would you like to continue in Edoan, Coralese, Salarian? Perhaps Central Ang?" This last is an insult. I regret it; I'm not here to antagonize the third most powerful person on this planet. Either he doesn't get the snub, or he pretends not to, though.

"I hope your father is well," he says.

"He died of CoVir. Which he caught here."

"I thought he had recovered."

"My father suffered recurring fevers after he left here. Eventually they killed him."

"So you did not want to come here," he says slowly. "Then you were sent. I wonder why the Order wants you here?" He appears to be talking to himself and I almost fall for it, because I've wondered the same thing myself. Which is, I realize, exactly what he wants me to be thinking.

"I told you. I was paid to teach the Select Malemese."

"Either you know or you don't." He ignores my interruption. "But you are a clever girl, so I shall assume for now that you do.

You see, I am being honest with you. It is a shame you are not being honest with me."

Does he think I'm part of some O.U.B. conspiracy against Malem? Or against him, personally? I meet his stare as calmly as possible.

"Why did the Order send you here?" he demands, his voice less friendly now.

"If the Order wants anything, it is only for the good of Malem." But I realize I'm no longer certain of that. Am I being used without knowing it? Agatha is a Select. Her first loyalty is to the Order, as Hamza reminded her when I was being dragged off to jail. And Agatha stopped protesting then…

The High Priest sits very still, his cold gray eyes watching me. Crazy and dangerous. That's what Hamza called him: dangerous. And where is Hamza now?

"Do you know why the Select insists on staying at the fever house?"

"No. I don't know." Some of my real feelings come out with that, sharper than I meant. This wasn't what we planned. Because Agatha only thought of it while waiting with Tira? Or because there had always been more to the plan than I knew?

"She's impulsive."

He smiles. "I wouldn't use the word 'impulsive' to describe a Select. Perhaps I haven't met enough of them?"

He already knows they aren't, so I don't answer. Didn't I wonder the same thing the first time I met Agatha? I thought it was all an act.

"You were in jail here. I had you freed when I learned of it. Did you know that?"

I nod.

"Then you know that I'm not unjust."

You had me brought here against my will today, I think.

"It wasn't your Select who insisted you be set free. Why was she content to let you stay in jail? Why didn't she want you to leave Malem? Have you asked yourself these questions?"

I am beginning to. I'm following where he's leading me, as hypnotized by his words as a rabbit caught in the spell of a snake. Until I remember Agatha running through the door of the Queen's meeting room to kneel at my side. It wasn't the High Priest standing outside that chamber after bringing her to help me. It was Prad Gaelig. Prad Gaelig and Agatha.

He frowns, as though he guesses my thoughts by my silence. "Your loyalty is admirable but misplaced. I would not want to find myself in your position." His voice is as cold as his eyes now. "I'd want to know what the Select intended for me. And what she intends with this little charade in the fever hut."

He's lying to me. It was Agatha and Prad Gaelig who argued for my freedom. But not until the ship had left. Is he right about that? Is the Order using me? Agatha knows about the diamond. Do they want her to give me up in return for water for Iterria? It makes more sense than the Adept expecting me to teach Agatha enough Malemese to represent the Order here.

"I will give you some time to consider." He stands up to leave.

"Has the Select been charged with a crime?"

"Not yet."

"On my world that makes her innocent."

"We are not on your world."

Is that a threat? I stand up, too, and meet his gaze evenly.

"Do you really believe she's innocent?" he demands.

"She saved a child's life," I remind him. "Whatever you accuse her of, do you really think your people will believe she's guilty?"

"Yes, that was clever of her, wasn't it?" he says smoothly. "I expect she was immunized before she left Seraffa."

# Chapter Twenty-Four

One of the guards returns and escorts me to a room further down the hallway. It doesn't look like the stone jail cell, but there's a cot and a small alcove to the side with a sink and a toilet, and when the guard shuts the door I hear an unmistakable click. At least the window has glass in it. I pace the room, feeling helpless. The High Priest is crazy, and no one knows I'm here except Kaline and Mehda, and they were too afraid of his guards to even acknowledge me. I stop pacing and hug myself, shivering. Am I going to disappear, like Hamza?

No, I am not. I take a deep breath. No one's coming to help me, so I'll have to get out of here myself. If I can escape and hide somewhere until the King returns, I can ask for his protection. Hamza trusted the King.

I think of the actionvids Etin took me to. If this was an actionvid, there'd be a way to escape. I walk to the window and look out onto an eight-story, straight drop to the street. Maybe not this way.

Overpower the guard next time he opens the door? Surprise will be on my side because I've been so meek until now... I think of the muscular guards who escorted me here and give up that plan. If I ever get home, I promise myself I'll take a self-defense course.

I go to the window again and look down. Way down. Vidheroes are insane.

From the window, the clouds look close enough to touch and thick enough to walk on, a strange, soft-textured landscape of rolling hills and valleys. I sigh at the thought of such an easy solution. All I'd have to do is break the window and hide in the clouds. Of course, they'd see the broken window and know where I was. They'd see...

What if I break the window and hide behind the door? It would look like I'd climbed out. When the guard goes to the window to look—

A sharp click at the door startles me. Even more startling is the person who walks in.

"Prad Gaelig!" I want to run to him until I notice how stiffly he's standing. "You didn't come to get me out."

"I can't. But nothing bad will happen to you here."

Right, I think. "How did you know I was here?"

He smiles. "Jumal told me. Mehda and Kaline told him they saw you being taken inside—against your will, they thought?" I nod. "Jumal was ready to break quarantine until I promised to come and see how you're doing."

I want to smile at the thought of Jumal threatening to break out and come get me, as if he could do anything against the High Priest.

"He's crazy, you know. Your High Priest. He imagines conspiracies everywhere."

"Maybe he's not imagining them."

I stare at Prad Gaelig. He looks sincere. "You think so too? You think the Select and I are involved in some kind of conspiracy against Malem?"

"It's happened before."

"A Select?" I don't bother hiding the scorn from my voice. "I don't believe you."

Prad Gaelig shrugs. "I can tell you what I know. Belief is up to you."

I should tell him to go. I don't need to hear more insinuations about Agatha's motives. But I do need to hear the truth about my father's visit. I look at Prad Gaelig. He's waiting calmly for my decision. I trust him. For no good reason I can give, but I do. It's probably stupid of me. "Alright. Tell me what happened during the plague. And about my father, when he was here."

Prad Gaelig nods. He sits on the end of the bed, since there's no chair. I sit cross-legged on the other end facing him.

"I was seventeen when the plague struck. I wasn't here at first. I'd taken my oaths as a priest that spring and was sent out to administer to the farmers for three years. I didn't know anything until messengers started to bring news from the city. That was before we built radio towers. We wanted to live simply, but the plague convinced us of the need for emergency contact." He speaks in a matter-of-fact voice, staring straight ahead.

"People were dying, the messengers said. Young people, strong people, not just the elderly and weak. No one knew why. We were a healthy people with no serious ailments aside from old age and injury, and suddenly we were dying." A look of pain crosses his face.

"I didn't believe it at first. I thought the messengers were exaggerating. But the fear in their eyes kept me awake at night. I began to think of my family, my parents, my little sister."

He pauses. His hands have begun to tremble. He clasps them together.

"People began to arrive from the city, fleeing the epidemic. When I saw the refugees I began to believe. I questioned everyone, hoping for a letter from the High Priest calling me back—I was desperate to see my family—but instead I received orders to remain in the country." He takes a deep breath, looking down at his hands as though he can see the letter there. "That's when I knew it was bad, worse than the reports, worse than I could imagine. Because they needed me to stay there. They needed some of us to survive."

"The King and Queen fell ill, and two of the princes. The other two princes were rushed out to the country, the eldest and the youngest, a baby not yet two. Our current king was sixteen when his father died. He married, as is our custom, before assuming the crown. His first task was to bury his family.

"No more messengers came, and no more refugees. People were being shot if they tried to leave the city. On the farms, we waited in silence for any news. We couldn't bear to talk about those we'd left behind; we couldn't think about anything else. We hated ourselves, hiding in safety while an unimaginable horror crept over everyone we loved."

Prad Gaelig stares at the window as though it's a vidscreen on which the bitter events of his youth are unfolding. My eyes are drawn to the window as if I, too, am looking into that past.

"After five months I could stand it no longer. I decided to go home.

"Things were even worse than I imagined. One person in every hundred was already dead, one third of the population was deathly sick.

"The High Priest was angry to see me, but he put me to work." His voice takes on a harder note. "I served as his secretary at the trial of the Select and the captain of the *Lightfoot*." He turns to look at me. "The *Lightfoot* was an Iterrian spaceship. It arrived on Malem three weeks before the plague, in the hire of the O.U.B., bringing a Select."

"You think he had something to do with the plague just because he was here?"

"She. And I know she did."

"Tell me the rest," I say with a slight shrug. He continues as though he doesn't notice it.

"The Select was a native Iterrian. She came to ask their Majesties to supply Iterria with water. They were willing to pay. But we didn't want foreigners living here, taking up even a small portion of our limited land to build their elevator to the stars, and who knows how many staying on to operate it. We'd told them that before. We came here to be left alone.

"At that time there wasn't any house on Prophet's Lane—no Prophet's Lane, in fact. The Select and the captain were staying as guests at the High Priest's complex.

"When the first few deaths occurred the captain wanted to leave. A priest was walking by their rooms and heard them quarreling. The Select refused to go. They had two weeks left before their time was up at the spaceport and she still hoped to convince us. The captain told her an epidemic was about to break out."

"How did he know?"

"How, indeed?"

"But you weren't there."

"No, I was on the farms then. But it was well documented at the trial."

"What did the captain have to say?"

"He denied it, until the Select confirmed what he'd said. Then he called it a hunch. Said he'd been on a lot of planets and 'knew the signs'." Prad Gaelig says this with such sarcasm in his voice that I can imagine the reaction it met with at the trial.

"What happened?"

"They were both jailed. By then nearly a third of the city was sick. People were desperate, traumatized by grief and fear. The High Priest used the spaceship's com-comp to broadcast our plight. He sent the lab analysis and magnified images of the virus we were finding in our autopsies.

# Chapter Twenty-Four

"The O.U.B. sent out a call for aid—but no one could identify the virus.

"Then Iterria responded. One week after they received our transmission, they'd done a review of medical data through human history and located a virus prevalent centuries ago on Earth that seemed to match ours: Acute Respiratory Syndrome, a member of the corona virus family. They were working on a vaccine. Were we still considering their request for water?"

"They didn't say that!"

"I saw the recorded transmissions at the trial." He meets my disbelieving stare calmly. "This is a story to you," he says, looking aside. "To us it was a holocaust."

"I'm sorry. It must have been horrible."

"It still is."

He studies the window silently. The sky is dark, threatening another storm. When he begins talking again, his voice is bitter. "Surprisingly enough, the Iterrians did develop a cure, in only one week. And they offered a trade: the medicine for a water agreement."

"But you didn't give them water," I say, horrified. Were they that stubborn? Could all those people have been saved? Could my father have been?

"We would have," Prad Gaelig says. "But their transmission was intercepted. The Alliance worlds were outraged. There were satellite meetings, orders, threats, counter-threats... Meanwhile our people were dying." He pauses, lost in his memories. When it seems he isn't going to continue, I shift on the bed. I'm caught up in it now, I want to hear the rest.

"Finally, Iterria agreed to give us the serum. The city went into a frenzy of celebration when it arrived. Patients in our hospitals began to recover, volunteers were trained to administer it to those who were ill at home. It was working. The dying was finally over."

"Your family?"

"My father and my sister both survived. My mother would have wanted it that way."

"I'm sorry." I let the silence lengthen before I say, "but it wasn't over, was it? People were still dying when my father arrived."

Prad Gaelig looks at me. "It isn't just a story to you, either, is it?" he says.

"No," I whisper.

"The captain of the second Iterrian ship wanted the Select and the first captain to return to Iterria to be questioned there. We probably would have done it. As far as the people were concerned, Iterrians were now our saviors.

"But the young Queen insisted the trial be held here. She didn't trust the Iterrians. She ordered the original ship to be searched. When they did, they found a secret compartment built behind a side panel under the captain's chair. Four small, empty glass vials were inside it. These were examined in a hospital lab. They contained traces of CoVir. And I was there at that time," he adds pointedly.

"The captain was clever enough not to leave fingerprints and he denied any knowledge of the vials—even under questioning."

"They tortured him," I whisper in horror.

Prad Gaelig observes me calmly. "So you believe that part even though I wasn't an eye witness."

"But not... not the Select?"

"No. The trial lasted two standard months. Everything I've told you came out. CoVir came to Malem aboard that ship and someone took it planetside to infect the first few victims. Both the captain and the Select denied any knowledge of it.

"The young Queen was for beheading them both, rather than risk letting the guilty one go free. She lost her entire family to the plague. The King and the High Priest wanted some degree of certainty before they offended either Iterria or the O.U.B., since both had also come to our aid. On the other hand, whoever was guilty had surely had assistance. The O.U.B. wanted Malem to join the Alliance; Iterria wanted a water trade agreement. One of them was willing to murder us for it. We wanted to know which one."

I glance at the window. It's getting dark. The overhead light panels have come on without either of us noticing. It feels strange to look around the room, to draw myself back from the past his words have invoked. His hands are clenched in his lap so tightly the knuckles are white. Tell me about my father, I think, but at the same time, I'm afraid to hear it.

"Then three new deaths occurred. And then five more. By this time everyone had been vaccinated. The trial was immediately adjourned while the King and the High Priest hurried to their council chambers for a full briefing.

"I went to see my family. I hadn't seen my father and sister during the trial. My father was ill when I arrived home. 'How can he be ill?' I yelled at them. 'Didn't he get the vaccination?' My sister began to cry. 'Weren't you vaccinated?' I grabbed my father's shoulders as he lay in his bed and shook him. He was limp between my hands and I came to my senses, eased him back onto his bed and begged his forgiveness. He died two days later. By then we knew that CoVir had mutated. The mutated strain swept through the city out of control."

Prad Gaelig stands up. He wipes his face as though merely tired but I've already seen the dampness on his cheeks. I blink several times to prevent my own eyes from spilling over.

"Jinna was sixteen." He turns to me. "How old are you, Kia?"

"Sixteen." I struggle to get the word out through a constricted throat.

"Are you ready to die?" he asks softly.

I shake my head, frightened, and lean against the wall away from him.

"Neither was Jinna. That was the last thing she said to me. 'I'm too young to die, Gaelig.'"

He turns and walks to the window. Looking out he says softly, more to himself than to me: "but apparently she wasn't."

He's silent a long time.

"Did you ever find out which of them did it?" I ask at last.

"The captain. The trial resumed three weeks later. He was sick—he'd become infected with the mutated virus and knew he was going to die. He made a full confession before us all, even naming his co-conspirators on Iterria. Several of them were quite high in their government, I understand. Before he died, he asked the Select to forgive him." Prad Gaelig turns to face me.

"Did she?"

"She rose and walked slowly across the room to stand in front of him. She wasn't well, but it wasn't CoVir. She tried to kill herself while she was in jail. She almost succeeded, with the help of a guard. Select can be very persuasive—he only came to his senses when she lost consciousness."

I stare at Prad Gaelig, my mouth open. A Select attempt suicide? I can't believe it. I want to tell him he's lying, that I'm not that gullible, but he continues, ignoring my reaction.

"'Do you know how many people you have murdered?' the Select asked the captain. 'Babies, young people at the beginning of their lives, parents with children to care for, the elderly who deserve a peaceful end…' She leaned forward suddenly and slapped him with such force it knocked him to the floor.

"He glared up at her, spat at her, called her a traitor to her world, reminded her that people would be dying there, too, of thirst, soon enough.

"'Not because of me,' she said in a terrible voice that frightened me more than any human voice has ever done. I hear it still, sometimes, in my dreams."

I shiver and draw back. I know the force of a Select's voice.

Prad Gaelig stares out the window. He whispers the words again, to himself, "Not because of me."

The door opens, startling us both. A guard comes in carrying a plate of food.

"Is it so late?" Prad Gaelig says. "I have to get back to Tira."

"What happened to the captain? Did he die of CoVir?"

"The High Priest invited him to a ceremony in the public square." Prad Gaelig stands up. "His body was cremated and sent back to Iterria. We didn't want his ashes on our soil. There are those who believe we were too merciful, we should have let him die slowly of CoVir."

"And the mutated virus?"

"It continued killing. No one was immune, not even those who'd survived the original strain. The little princess, our young King's daughter, fell ill. The Queen was distraught. She stopped caring what happened to the city, she sat by her daughter's crib day and night. The King considered sending her to the country but the Queen was beyond reason, she wouldn't let the child out of her sight. And he couldn't send a sick child to the farms, not even his own daughter.

"Then another ship arrived, bringing us a newly-developed antibiotic, specially designed to fight the mutated strain of CoVir. It weakened the virus, and boosted our natural immune system, giving those who had it a chance to fight it. People began surviving. It's what we still use today."

"And the princess?"

"The princess died three days before it arrived. She was…" he swallows, "she was two years old."

He's thinking of Tira. So am I, remembering her head on my shoulder, her body burning against me, my desperate need to save her.

"Was it—" My throat tightens. I have to swallow and start again. "Was it my father's ship?"

He looks at me blankly.

"Was it my father, on the *Homestar*, who… who came too late to save the Princess?"

Prad Gaelig looks away. When he looks back, his eyes are focused on me, not on the past, but they are still sad. "Yes," he says. Something inside me goes still and sick.

"Kia, your father brought us much-needed medical supplies and trained doctors. Many people survived because of him. including the Select he came to take home. She had been working in our hospital, nursing the worst cases, since her acquittal, and she caught CoVir. We had to force her to take the broad-spectrum antibiotics, which was all we had then. I believe she wanted to die, but she was a strong woman. Your father insisted on waiting for her to recover. He helped where he could. Every willing hand was needed. Then he, too, fell ill. He was a good man."

I nod, but it doesn't change the way I feel. I understand now the darkness inside him. My mother was right when she said he didn't want to live. I hated her for saying it, I didn't want to hear it—but even then I knew she was right. There's a lot I resented her for, that I understand now.

The guard is waiting at the door to let Prad Gaelig out, but I have one last question.

"If the Select was exonerated, why do the Queen and the High Priest distrust Ag— the current Select?"

"Don't you find it hard to believe that the Iterrians could fool the Order so easily?" he asks me. "How did the Order come to choose that particular captain and that ship to send their envoy here? Perhaps that Select was innocent, but was she being used by the Iterrians or by her own Order? The O.U.B. is known for its subtlety. It's a very small step from subtlety to manipulation. And I don't doubt that, given their unique abilities, the opportunity and temptation to take that step must be great."

# Chapter Twenty-Five

I eat slowly. The words Prad Gaelig used—opportunity and temptation—affect me in a way he couldn't have expected. I've made opportunity and temptation a way of life. And what for? Despite buying my way into university early with that first stolen ring, I won't graduate any sooner than if I'd waited and earned a scholarship. After the plain robes and lack of possessions on Malem, the things I bought with that second theft now seem silly and boring. As for Lady Khalida's bracelet, even if I hadn't been caught it wouldn't have saved my mother.

But I believed my reasons at the time. It's easy to convince yourself something you want to do is alright. And it would be even easier if you knew you couldn't be caught. Who would suspect a Select? Malem is the only world that even put one on trial. Prad Gaelig's right: that long ago Select might have been fooled by higher members of her Order, but not very likely by a ship's captain.

And if that's true, Agatha, too, could have been duped by the Adept on Seraffa and by Hamza into bringing and keeping me here. They might even have convinced her that turning me in is the right thing to do. Agatha believes in doing the right thing.

That's the High Priest's theory, but I still think the High Priest is a snake. He's locked me up here against my will, without any charges, which is against even their laws. He obviously doesn't want me to speak to Agatha to hear her response to his accusations. And his eyes—there's something wrong with him, something I instinctively distrust.

That doesn't mean he's wrong.

There's only one way to be sure. I set my empty plate on the floor and pull the blanket off the cot, winding it around my right hand and arm. Taking a deep breath, I raise my arm and slam it into the window.

The window doesn't break. Pound on it as I will, it remains intact. I try to kick it but it's too high. I look around the room: there's nothing I can use to hit or throw at the window. I go back to the window and pound against it with both hands in sheer frustration.

After several minutes I force myself to stop. The guard could come in to collect my dinner plate any time now. My dinner plate... I pick it up. No, the clay dish will shatter before it cracks glass this thick. I haven't been given a knife or fork but the spoon is metal. I scratch it along the glass. No good, it's too smooth and rounded. I need something sharp, like a fork or—

Or a diamond! How could I forget? I hike up my robe—and stop. What if someone comes in while I'm holding it? If the High Priest finds me with a Malemese diamond... I shudder. *The worst kind of sacrilege,* Hamza said. But the longer I stay here the greater the chance I'll be searched and it'll be found anyway.

I have to risk it. Quickly before anyone comes. I'm in such a rush to tear the pouch out of my hem, get the diamond out of the pouch, cut the glass and hide it again that when I tip the pouch into my hand I drop the diamond. It rolls across the floor. I scramble after it in a panic. By the time I manage to grab it, I'm terrified I've made too much noise chasing it. I'm tempted to stick it back into my hem again at once.

I take a deep breath to steady myself and scrape the diamond across the window. It leaves a long ragged scratch. I go over the jagged line again and again, digging deeper and deeper into the glass. Then I start another line across it, the two of them making an X. I work frantically, listening over the beating of my heart for the sound of the door opening behind me. Beads of sweat dampen my forehead. My hands are so sweaty the diamond slips in my grasp several times. The tiny scratching noise it makes against the window is almost deafening.

How long has it been since my dinner was brought? Hours, surely. Someone will come through that door any minute for the empty plate. Have I cut deeply enough to break the window if I hit it hard now? Should I try before putting the diamond away, to be sure? But the minute I break the glass someone might hear and come rushing in and see the diamond. If I put the diamond away and the window doesn't break I'll have to waste time getting it out again. I speed up, scratching up and down with an almost hysterical intensity.

The scratches themselves would give away the diamond now. A drop of sweat catches on my eyelash; I blink and the salt stings my eye. Enough, calm down. The window has to break now. It's only glass, however thick. I drop the diamond into its pouch and the pouch into my pocket. I re-wrap the blanket around my hand, turn sideways, and gripping my blanketed wrist with my other hand I swing both arms as hard as I can against the window, hitting the center of the X. The window breaks with an enormous crash, shattering out from the center all the way to the casement, glass flying everywhere. Small shards catch in my hair and robe and in the blanket but miraculously miss my face and eyes. I run behind the door.

Any second a guard will come rushing in. It's almost impossible to stand still, with every nerve on edge. Why doesn't he come? Come, I think desperately, open the door!

# Chapter Twenty-Five

No one comes. The door stays shut. Maybe there's no one in this hallway this late in the evening? Cautiously, I shake glass slivers from my hair, my robe, the towel. Still nobody comes. What if I've been locked in for the night, they don't care about dirty dishes? I look at the dinner plate on the floor beside my bed. It isn't much of a weapon but better than none at all. I put my ear to the door: no footsteps. I race across the room, grab the plate and scurry back to my position behind the door. Then I wait some more, feeling foolish.

I'm acutely conscious of the weight of the diamond in my pocket. If I'm caught I'll be searched; they'll want to know how I broke that window. I look around the room, but they'll also search it. I pull up my robe and tuck the pouch back into the hem, knotting the thread I broke to get it out. There's a small area of the hem that isn't sewn where the pouch used to be, but I can't do anything about that.

It feels like hours have passed. Could a person fall asleep standing up? Would that person fall over? Would she wake up while falling in time to put her hands out and not break her nose? I don't like my nose, it's too small, but it would look even worse broken.

Stop being stupid, I tell myself severely. I'm tired, my thoughts are wandering. I have to keep alert.

At last the door opens. Behind it, I hardly dare to breathe. It opens wider. The guard sees the window and rushes across the room toward it.

I tiptoe very quietly around the door.

He hears me anyway, and turns with a bellow, but I'm through the door and pulling it closed before he can cross the room. The door shuts, cutting his voice off abruptly and completely. Has he had a heart attack or choked? I wonder, before I realize the room must be soundproofed. No wonder no one heard me break the window. I turn the lock and smile when it clicks home. Let him yell all he wants.

I'm standing at the end of a long, dark hallway. At the other end a muted glow of light indicates the foyer at the top of the stairwell. A single guard stood there when I was brought up and there's probably one there now, unless I'm very lucky and he's the one locked in my room. In any event, there were two more at the bottom of the stairs guarding the door outside.

I pull the blanket from around my arm and fold it over my shoulders and around my back under my robe, making myself look heavier, more muscular. Then I walk briskly down the hall toward the stairwell. I'm almost the same height as the guard; with any luck the man at the end of the hall won't even look up as I pass him. He's expecting the other guard to return with the dirty plate. Good thing I grabbed it. I pull my hood over my head and forward so it covers my face when I turn my head sideways, and hold the plate low, with both my hands under it where they won't show.

If you carry yourself with assurance people seldom question you, I tell myself firmly, quoting Sodum's wisdom. They'll see what they expect to see.

"'Night, Yosil," the guard calls to me. I walked purposefully across the foyer without answering. There's a box elevator, its door invitingly open, beside the door to the stairs, but I don't know how to run it and any hesitation will give me away. Besides, I was brought up by the stairs. The elevator might only be for priests. I push the stairway door open. My scalp prickles under the hood, conscious of the guard's eyes on my back until the door shuts behind me.

Eight stories is a long way down. What if I run across someone on the stairs? It's late at night, the priests and their families probably use the elevators, and it turns out I'm lucky. But as I start down the last flight of stairs, I still haven't come up with any ideas for getting past the two guards.

I open the door just wide enough to peek through. Only one guard is visible. Is the other one there, out of sight, or is he occupied somewhere else in the building? I look at the guard again. It's the one who was at the central square for the executions, the big one with the broken nose and the heavy, scowling eyebrows. I shut the door. I might not have much time before the second guard comes back. I'll have to try to bluff my way past this one. I pull the blanket out from under my robe. The lighting's better in this foyer, too good for me to pass as a guard. I'll pretend to be a visitor, leaving late. I push the door open and walk confidently toward the door.

"Hey! What are you doing there?" broken-nose calls before I've crossed even a third of the distance.

"They told me to leave this way," I call back, keeping my face averted and my pace quick but not visibly hurried.

"They did?"

"Take these stairs and go out the front entrance, they said." I keep walking, resisting the urge to speed up. I'm half-way to the door now.

"Wait! Who said it?"

"They did. Upstairs." Almost there.

"Stop! Who are you?"

"I'm in a hurry." And I break into a run for the door, with broken-nose racing to catch me. I'm closer to the door, though. If I can just get outside, where I can scream, where someone might see me! He'll sound the alarm, but he might not leave the door unguarded to chase me down the street. I reach for the door handle—

And run smack into the second guard, diving for me from the side. My hood falls back, revealing my face. He grabs my arm. I

217

twist sideways, but he's too strong. Without thinking I jam my knee upward.

The guard's eyes widen. He gives a little "oomph!" and his grasp loosens. For a second I stare at him, wanting to apologize. Then I twist free and grab the door—

Too late. Broken-nose has reached me now. He grabs my arm from behind and before I can dodge again he pins me against the door.

The second guard straightens slowly and takes a step toward me, his face twisted in fury.

"Sorry," I mutter. It doesn't change his expression in the least.

"No!" Broken-nose says. "The High Priest will want to see her. You might get your revenge later, but not tonight. Let's go."

They drag me up the stairs between them. The guard at the top stares as we come through the door.

"What do you think, letting this one escape?" yells the guard I kneed. "Are you sleeping up here?"

"She didn't come by me!"

"Of course she did. There's only one way into the stairway."

"The only one who passed here was Yosil, carrying the prisoner's supper plate."

"Idiots, both of you! Go open the door to her room and let Yosil out. You're lucky we caught her."

# Chapter Twenty-Six

Broken-nose comes for me the next morning. He holds my arm tightly enough to leave a bruise as he walks me down the hall to the meeting room. This time the High Priest doesn't keep me waiting. He sends the guard outside and stands there, examining me. Not a muscle in his face or body moves. I stare back, trying to stand equally still.

"Where were you planning to go?" he asks at last. His voice is cool, as though he doesn't care what my answer is. I raise my chin, staring him eye to eye.

"I thought I'd go to the Queen and ask her why you could imprison me without cause when you wouldn't let her."

He looks surprised, then laughs. "You are an amusing person, Kia Ugiagbe," he says. His smile dies abruptly. "Did you know that the Queen is also looking for you?" He sees my expression and nods. "I thought not. But you don't seem very surprised, either. What do you imagine she wants with you?"

"I can't imagine what you want with me."

"Perhaps I am trying to save myself some trouble. If Queen Sariah doesn't know where you are, I won't have to concern myself with getting you out of jail again. However, I'm finding you just as much trouble here."

"Why don't you let me worry about keeping out of jail, then?" I suggest.

"It would weigh on my conscience."

"Yes, I imagine you do have a problem with that."

"How did you break the window?"

"I kicked it." He might believe this if he knows I'm used to stronger gravity. Not if I look eager to explain that to him, though. "It's only glass." I shrug.

He watches me without so much as blinking. "No matter," he says at last. "I wouldn't do it again, though, if I were you. Glass is precious here. Replacing it will be coming out of the guards' pay." He pauses. "They're not very fond of you at the moment."

I shrug again. If they were permitted to harm me, they would have last night. But I get the message—my arm is still sore from broken-nose's hold on it.

The High Priest's hands on the table twitch slightly. He has large hands, with long fingers. His pose is casual but there's tension in those hands, in the veins standing out against the skin. When I look up his eyes are icy although he still speaks casually. "It's foolish of you to make enemies here. Who will protect you when your Select is dead?"

"She isn't dead," I say as calmly as I can.

"Come now. You don't really think she'll survive two weeks in the fever hut, do you?"

I look back at him without answering.

"Perhaps you don't care if the Select dies? Perhaps you've thought about what I said yesterday, and realize she was using you? Or you already knew it. Is that why you left and went to the inn?" He leans toward me, his hands balanced lightly on the table as though he's itching to use them to force the answers out of me.

"She isn't using me. She isn't planning anything."

"Are you naïve? Or do you think I'm stupid?" His voice is harsh. I have to force myself not to back away from him. Never let a bully see you're afraid—Owegbé's advice, ironically.

"Her goal is to bring Malem into the Alliance, we both know that. Of course she has a plan for accomplishing it. I want to know how this little drama at the fever hut plays into it." He leans across the table, glaring at me. "Just like that other one, scheming, calculating…" He stops and pulls himself back, steadies himself with a deep breath. "I'd like to know why the Select and the Queen are both so interested in keeping you on Malem." He looks at me as though I'm an irritating puzzle.

I remain silent. Even saying I don't know why would sound like agreeing that there's a reason. Something he said earlier bothers me, but I can't concentrate on anything but the thought: he wants Agatha dead. It's in his eyes, his hands, his voice when he says *the Select.*

"I see you need more time," he says, with barely-concealed anger. "Think carefully before you cause me any more trouble."

He turns to the door. Before he can reach it, it opens. I hear the surprised intake of his breath and look up. Jumal is standing in the doorway.

"What are you doing here?" the High Priest demands.

"I believe I've already done it," Jumal says, looking past him at me.

I hold my breath. My stomach feels giddy at the sight of him, but I'm terrified of what the High Priest might do. Did Jumal break quarantine? I try to count the days in my head, but so much has happened…

"I'm glad to see you survived your quarantine. Your uncle has sent you—?"

"I'm not here on my *uncle's* behalf."

They stare at each other, the tension between them so thick it makes my stomach clench. Don't punish him, I want to cry, but strangely it's the High Priest whose face is going pale.

"I'd like to talk to Kia alone," Jumal says.

The High Priest locks eyes with him a moment longer, then growls, "See if you can talk some sense into her, then." He steps past Jumal through the door and nods to the guard to shut it.

"Jumal," I want to run and throw my arms around him, but the Malemese don't touch. "Now you're imprisoned, too!"

He crosses the room. "Have they hurt you?" His voice is tight, angry.

I shake my head, too choked to speak.

He reaches for my shoulders and pulls me to him. It overwhelms me then, how frightened and alone I've been. I lean against him, shaking, my tears dampening his chest.

"Hey, it's okay," he says. His hands grip my shoulders. I nod and struggle for control. He holds me a minute longer and then steps back, releasing me. "Sit down," he says. "Tell me."

"Are the Queen's guards looking for me?"

He nods.

"Ag—the Select—is she—is she still alive?"

He rolls his eyes. "No doubt about that. Her insistence on staying in the fever hut has stirred up the whole city. Troops of people march out every day to see if she's still alive. Everyone's calling her 'the angel who saved the miracle child'." His voice softens, mentioning Tira.

I laugh. It comes out a bit shaky. "I'm surprised she hasn't come out to set the record straight that it's God's work, not hers."

"Oh, she's made that clear. The guards at the fever hut are sick of hearing it."

"Guards? They're forcing her to stay in there?"

"Just the opposite. They're waiting for her to take so much as one step outside so they can grab her and haul her away to be quarantined in her house."

I shake my head. "Why don't they just go in and get her?" I wish they would. Every minute she's in there, exposed to... ugh!

"Not even the Triumvirate would order someone healthy to enter the fever hut and touch a person who might have CoVir. When the incubation period's over they might do it, though."

What would he say if he knew I did just that? But I didn't get CoVir. Maybe Agatha won't, either, despite what the High Priest said. I imagine her inside that stinking, disgusting hut, and shudder.

"She sings," Jumal says.

"She sings?" I look at him blankly.

"A little off-key," he says. "The people sing with her. Hymns and lullabies. She must have learned them while visiting. We often sing while we work."

She's singing. I'm here, terrified she's dying, and she's there singing. I don't want Co-Vir to kill her, I want to do it myself!

"She does it to let them know she's alive," he says. "To reassure them."

Yeah, that's Agatha. I laugh. It comes out a little shaky. "The High Priest thinks she's hatching some devious plan in there, to force Malem into the Alliance."

"But you don't think so?"

I look straight into his eyes. "I don't think this Select could do anything that would hurt anyone, not even under orders. And she's smart. She doesn't always come across that way, but she can't be fooled."

"I rather thought she came across that way."

"Well, you know," I grin self-consciously, "her... accent might fool some people."

Jumal grins before he resumes his serious expression. "So you don't believe there's any basis for the High Priest's concerns? She'd never do anything even potentially harmful to Malem, under any circumstances?"

I blink. *If the potential benefit is greater than the potential risk of harm, and that risk is very slight...* Agatha's own words. But why is he asking? *Potentially harmful?* He sounds like the High Priest, grilling me. I lean back in my chair. "You were sent here."

He didn't come for me at all. I don't want to believe it.

"No," he says at once. "It's not like that. But I have to ask."

"Because you're training to be a priest. You're working for him." I can't believe I let him hold me, I cried against him.

"You've got me completely wrong." He takes a breath. "What do you want me to do, Kia, to show you?"

"Get me out of here." I don't look at him. I might as well be saying, *nothing,* and he has to know it. It's not like the High Priest is going to listen to a seventeen-year-old.

"Where will you go if I do? You're safe here."

"I need to see A—the Select. I need to talk to her. To ask her what she thinks she's doing!" I'm on the verge of crying again, but not in front of him. "The High Priest doesn't believe she'll survive the fever hut."

"He said that? Those are the words he used?" Jumal leans toward me, his face tense.

I nod miserably.

"Then she will die." He looks down, his expression glum.

"No one can predict that!"

"The High Priest has a remarkably accurate track record for doing just that."

"What are you telling me?" Select Hamza warned us against the High Priest. Agatha said he was afraid. A Select, afraid? I hadn't believed it. "Why? Why does he want her dead?"

# Chapter Twenty-Six

"He doesn't want her dead. He just doesn't want her to succeed."

"At what?"

"At whatever she's doing. At bringing Malem into the Universal Alliance."

"Why doesn't he want Malem to join the Alliance?"

"It would be the first step to losing our way of life. Just what our ancestors came here to avoid."

"I have to talk to her!" I have to warn her the High Priest is plotting her death.

He frowns. "It isn't a good idea. There are guards in the streets, people at the fever hut…"

"Is that what she said about helping Tira? '*It isn't a good idea*?'"

He sighs. "Okay."

"Okay? You can get me out?"

He gets up and knocks once on the door. It opens immediately. "Ask the High Priest to join us," I hear him say quietly.

"I'll have to send a guard with you, of course," the High Priest says when Jumal tells him he wants to take me to talk with the Select. I can't believe he's even considering it. I can't even believe he came in when Jumal asked for him.

"The Queen's guard will recognize yours," Jumal says. "She'll know Kia's been with you while she was looking for her."

The High Priest's eyelids lower slightly. A muscle in his cheek twitches. I keep my face neutral.

"Go at night. You're not afraid of the dark, are you?" He glances at me, his lips twisting upward slightly, into something like a sneer except he doesn't let it get that far.

I deliberately hesitate. Let him think I'm the timid fool he imagines, just because most off-worlders are used to cities lit up at night and find the darkness here creepy. "I'll wait till tonight," I say. "But if the Select sees me with your guard she won't tell me anything. You want me to find out if she has a plan, don't you?"

The High Priest gives me a measuring look. "So now you're listening to me?' He glances at Jumal approvingly. "I'll tell my guard to stay back. And… your uncle can go with her instead of you. He knows the way, and the Select knows him. She'll talk in front of him."

Jumal looks at me.

My lips part to say I want Jumal with me, but what if that makes the High Priest change his mind? I *have* to warn Agatha. I nod without looking at Jumal.

# Chapter Twenty-Seven

I pace my room. By my reckoning, Agatha has less than a week left of her quarantine. If the High Priest plans to make her death look CoVir-induced, he'll act soon. Unless he knows he doesn't have to, unless Agatha's already burning with fever, already dying. I try not to think of that, try to focus on Jumal's reassurance, but he's not there. A person can be healthy one day and the next...

What if Agatha's already dead and the High Priest's plan is to have me be the one to find her? That would explain why he agreed to let me go.

By the time Prad Gaelig arrives I'm so anxious I snap at him. He glances at my untouched dinner. "I have to wait on the High Priest's command," he reminds me calmly.

"Did *she* wait on orders from the O.U.B. to save Tira's life? Did she?" I whisper, the words hissing from my mouth like insects, powerless to do any real harm and furious in the attempt.

"You are upset," he says, his voice even. I remember that this is a man who administers punishment, however reluctant he claims to feel about it. I bite my tongue, because I still want to fume at him, until he steps closer and adds in an undertone, "I will do what I can."

Broken-nose joins us at the door. The three of us walk through the dark city without speaking, and into the even darker countryside. Whenever I glance back, Broken-nose is watching me, his solid eyebrows furrowing over narrow, suspicious eyes. Prad Gaelig ignores him but my back prickles under his watchful stare.

It has been raining. The sound of our feet squelching through the mud on the swamp islands fills the night. Each time we pull free of the sucking mud to take another step, the stench of rot rises from the ground like tiny gasps. Prad Gaelig and the guard carry palm lights, which cast an indistinct light on the path in front of our feet and throw everything else into even darker shadow. The black forms of trees loom eerily around us, elongated, twisted ghosts in the night, separated by shining pools of deeper darkness just beyond their roots. Where is the crowd of people Jumal told me came every day? The High Priest can do what he likes here at night.

My legs tremble as we approach the fever hut. It's dark and silent, just as I remember it. The guard stops on the last clump of land before the swamp island on which the hut stands. Prad Gaelig and I go on alone.

"Agatha," I call when I reach the hut. Prad Gaelig looks at me, and I remember he's never heard Agatha's name.

There's no answer from the hut.

"Select," I call again, louder.

Tira hadn't answered, either. I picture Agatha lying inside on the floor in a puddle of her own vomit and excrement, burning with fever, like Tira. The guard won't come and unlock the door if there's no answer. He'll drag us away and leave Agatha to die. I take a deep, ragged breath and opened my mouth to shout—

"Is that you, Kia?"

"WHAT ARE YOU DOING HERE?"

Silence greets my outburst. Then, through the door, Agatha says, "I was about to ask you that."

She's smiling! I can hear it in her voice. The sudden transformation from the image of Agatha dying to the sound of her joking makes me want to scream.

"You're crazy! You know that?" My voice is shrill in the darkness. I don't care if the guard can hear it all the way on the next island.

"It has been suggested. Not quite so blatantly."

"What are you hoping to prove by dying here?" I demand, lowering my voice but still angry.

"Actually, I hope to prove something by not dying here. But whatever happens—Kia, listen—I want you to remember what we were talking about the last time you saw me at Prophet's Lane. You must return—"

"Yes, I remember," I interrupt quickly. "I was just telling Prad Gaelig that tonight. When someone does you a good turn, you should return it. Good for good."

There's a pause, then Agatha says, "Hello Prad Gaelig. Is your family safely out of quarantine?"

"Yes, thanks to you they are all well. And if I can I will return a good turn for a good turn, Select."

"You already have: you brought Kia to me. I'm sure that wasn't easy. Otherwise, you wouldn't have come at night."

It was Jumal, I think, and I wonder again how he did it. I remember the High Priest's face blanching, and something else, what was it…

"It wasn't my doing," Prad Gaelig says. "The High Priest asked me to accompany Kia. He thought she might not know the way."

What does Prad Gaelig think, I wonder? I'd like to see his expression, but it's too dark.

"How considerate of him," Agatha says. "Kia isn't always good with directions."

"There are times when good instincts will take you closer to the goal than good directions."

"My philosophy also."

"Was it instinct or direction that brought you here, Select?"

"God, of course."

"Yours or mine?"

"Ours."

Prad Gaelig is silent a moment. "Not many see it that way," he says.

"Perhaps the problem is too great a reliance on directions, Prad Gaelig."

"Do you think you and I could resolve it—by instinct?"

"I think we must try."

"What are you talking about!" I hit the wooden door with my fist, impatient with their riddles. The threat here is real, not mystical. "How is staying in there going to make the Malemese join the Alliance?"

"I don't know," Agatha's voice through the door sounds surprised. "What made you think it would?"

"Well isn't that your intention?"

Agatha doesn't answer. Finally, when I'm ready to bang the door again, she says, in Edoan "Kia, what's the most effective way to control people?"

"Through fear." I remember my cultural lessons.

"Exactly. And what are the Malemese most afraid of?"

That's a no-brainer. "CoVir." I glance at Prad Gaelig. The High Priest no doubt sent him to monitor our conversation, but he doesn't seem upset with us speaking Edoan. It's hard to know who's side he's on.

"With good reason, in the past," Agatha agrees. "And this place, this fever hut, is at the core of that fear, the physical symbol of it. It stands here like a hideous monument to those who

CoVir has killed. I realized that when Tira walked out of here—skipped out, actually—into her father's arms. The faces of the guards—like they'd been released, a nightmare lifted—all those clichés that sound silly and trite until you actually see them in someone's face.

"Then I heard someone say, 'I'll spend my quarantine in here' and it was me talking—another cliché, but that's what it was like, like waking up in the middle of sleep-talking. I was horrified, until I saw that shadow of fear drawing over their faces again as they looked at me. Then I knew I was right. Because when I walk out of here, I'll take the fear out of this place with me. It'll just be an old, useless building in a swamp, and I hope they'll tear it down and be free."

She stops abruptly. A small, embarrassed cough sounds through the door. "It's something that has to be done, not talked about. I think I'm right. I hope so. Sometimes you have to go on that."

An image comes to my mind of her singing lullabies through this door to the people who have come here despite their terror of this place, and them joining in. Singing together against the fear. My throat closes.

She misinterprets my silence. "The worst that can happen is that they won't believe it."

"No." I grit my teeth and force myself to speak calmly, "The worst that can happen is that you'll be dead. The High Priest is going to make sure of it."

"Kia, the High Priest is a man of God—"

I risk it. I have no choice, she's so stubborn, so idiotically naive! I switch back to Malemese, and in a low voice only Prad Gaelig and Agatha can hear, I say, "The High Priest told me you will die here."

"Kia, you are too suspicious," she answers in Malemese. "The High Priest would not—"

"Yes," Prad Gaelig interrupts, his voice as low as mine. "He might. I'm sure he hopes God will take care of it for him, and wishes it weren't necessary, and will regret it as he regrets every execution. But when this door opens three days from now I think you will be dead and CoVir will be blamed."

There's a long silence within the hut. I lean forward until my cheek is almost resting against the door. "You have to come out now," I whisper hoarsely around the tightness in my throat.

It occurs to me suddenly that perhaps this is the plan, that Prad Gaelig is here to get me to coax Agatha outside the hut, where they can kill her. I turn to look at him—

"It is against the law to break quarantine," Prad Gaelig says. "You cannot leave now."

I let my breath out, ashamed.

"Calm yourself," Agatha says gently. Her voice is almost in my ear as though she, too, is leaning into the door. "If I am to die, I will; and if not, I won't. It is in God's hands."

She's determined to die. I want to scream at her, 'Die then, in this filthy hut on this cold, ugly world! I hope you get your wish!' I open my mouth to hurl the words at her...

And find I can't speak. A sense of loss lies suffocatingly over me and my attempts to push it aside are useless. In a small, tight voice I say, "It matters to me."

There's another pause, but when she speaks Agatha's voice is under control. "Prad Gaelig, if anything happens to me, you will see that Kia is sent home on the next ship?"

"I will."

"Trust him, Kia."

Prad Gaelig touches my shoulder. "There's another way out of here," he says quietly.

I shake his hand off my shoulder. "I'm not leaving. I'm going into the fever house with her. The High Priest can't kill us both."

"You will do no such thing," Agatha says, at the same time as Prad Gaelig says, "Nothing would be more convenient than to have you both die of CoVir in the fever house." His voice is low, reminding me of the guard waiting on the next island.

"You can't stay with me, Kia," Agatha says.

I lean against the door again. It's cold and damp, slimy with mildew, and smells of the swamp and the night, dank and fresh at the same time. "Agatha, you're not safe," I whisper in Edoan. "There's a guard at the edge of the path. He's strong. Remember the guard on the dais at the beheading? That one."

"You're sure?" she answers in Edoan.

"His nose is broken. His eyebrows meet. He's the tallest man on Malem."

"And he's the High Priest's guard?"

"Yes."

"He's the one who searched your room, just before you were let out of jail."

"Not the Queen's guards?"

"It was that one, and another with him. They had different insignias. I thought it denoted rank, but perhaps it was different services."

"He'll kill you if I leave."

"He won't. Believe me."

"I want to stay."

"You have a different task." Her voice drops, so low I strain to hear it, even though no one but us can understand Edoan. "Kia, you must give back the diamond. Find out who it belonged to and make them take it back."

"It was my father's. He gave it to me."

"It wasn't his to give. However he came by it, it has to go back to its original owner."

When I don't answer Agatha's whisper grows even more urgent. "Did it bring your father any happiness, Kia? Has it made you happy?"

*Take it… I'm free at last…* My father's words come back to me. The diamond was a burden to him and it's a danger to me. "It's all I have left…" I can barely get the words out. …*of him.*

"It belongs here, on Malem. Put things right, Kia."

My eyes sting. I'm aware of the diamond lying in the hem of my robe, a small, hard lump, as bitter as the lump in my throat that keeps me silent.

"Prad Gaelig will tell you how to escape the guard. You have to leave now."

I glance nervously at Prad Gaelig. "How do we know we can trust him?" I whisper. "He's a priest. The High Priest is his superior."

"Do what Prad Gaelig says, Kia," she says, switching back to Malemese.

If only I could see Agatha's face. Is there a hidden message behind her words? Does she mean 'go along with him', rather than trust him? I wish Agatha could see Prad Gaelig, the inquisitive angle of his head, the unwavering firmness in the line of his back. He might be our friend, but I can still see his hands gripping the handle of the axe. Even a Select can't read a person through a closed door, so how can she be sure?

Prad Gaelig steps forward. "It's time," he says. "You have to get as far as possible from here while it's still dark."

I touch the door of the fever hut. Agatha will never let me inside. "You'll stay here?" I ask Prad Gaelig.

"I'll stay here until morning, when others will come."

"And every night?"

He hesitates.

"Every night till she comes out alive. As she did for Tira."

"Every night," he agrees.

"Alright." I lean against the door. "I'll do what you want, Agatha, if I can. But I don't know where to start."

"You know, Kia. In your heart, you know."

I'm about to protest, to insist she just tell me how to go about finding the person, but Prad Gaelig clears his throat impatiently beside me.

"Stay close to the walls of the hut and work your way around to the back." he whispers. "I'll stay here where the guard can see me. You'll have to walk through the swamp. It's dangerous. The path's under water and the swamp is deep on either side."

"How will I see it?"

"You won't. You have to know where it is."

"It's a secret path? For the priests?"

He looks uncomfortable. "Yes."

I don't ask him why the priests need a way to come here secretly, but I wonder how many people they've helped die of CoVir. And then, why he wants me to take the path.

"It runs from island to island, as the other one does, but it zigzags," he says, not appearing to notice my hesitation. "When you're directly behind the hut, put your foot in the water and feel for the path. When you find it, head toward the nearest island to the left. On the other side of that, head for the nearest right island. Then the nearest to the left again. Two more to the right. The next one is left again. Then three to the right, one left, four to the right, and left, each time adding another to the right before one to the left until you've circled around to the edge of the swamp and reached dry land."

"One left, one right, one left, two right, one left, three right. Got it."

"Good. Don't be fooled by the size of the islands. Any clump of land in the right direction, just keep to the pattern. The path will take you to dry land well to the east of the road we came here by. Follow the summer star, the brightest one in the sky— there it is, see it?" He points without raising his arm. I look up and nod. "Good—walk east under it, through the fields. That will lead you back to the city. Give me your boots." He pulls from beneath his robe a pair of knee-high slippers and offers them to me. I stare at them.

"Your boots," he repeats. "I can give you ten minutes, maybe fifteen. Then I'll throw a stone into the water, over there," he nods in the opposite direction of the secret path, "and I'll leave your boots at the edge of the water."

"You thought this out before we came," I say, making no move to take the slippers he's holding out to me.

"Jumal did," he says. The corner of his lip twitches into a half-smile. Jumal's half-smile.

*Don't be afraid, I won't let anything happen to you*, I hear Jumal say, and despite everything, for no intelligent reason at all, I feel myself smiling back. I take the slippers. They're firmer than they look, and smooth—waterproof?

"Go to my apartment. Jumal is waiting for you, he'll take you somewhere to hide."

"Where?"

"I don't know. I don't want to."

"I can't put him in danger for me."

"He won't be in any danger. Repeat my instructions."

There's no time to argue, so I repeat his instructions, but I promise myself not to let Jumal risk himself any more for me. Hiding a fugitive from two of the Triumvirate has to be treason.

"When you get to my apartment, tell Naevah to gather as many people as she can and bring them here." Prad Gaelig's voice is barely audible. "Tell her they must hold a vigil here day and night, until the Select's quarantine is over."

"Does Naevah know…"

"She won't ask why." He looks at the door of the fever hut through which his tiny daughter came running into his arms.

I nod. "Goodbye," I say, softly tapping the door. It's so inadequate. I want to tell her—I want to beg her to come with me…

"Kia—"

I lean in, right against the door. "I'm here," I whisper.

"Remember this: you are worth more than you know. Believe it."

I swallow. You too, I want to say, but I can't get it out.

# Chapter
# Twenty-Eight

Behind the cabin, beyond even the dim glow of the palm light, the night is pitch black. I align myself with the middle of the hut and walk straight forward, feeling the way with my feet on the slight downward slope to the water.

A dark shape appears suddenly in front of me. I throw my hands up. The sleeves of my robe pull on branches: a tree. Prad Gaelig didn't mention a tree in my path. Did I walk at an angle? How would I know? Behind me the hut has vanished into the night. I'll have to find the hidden path by touch when I reach the water.

I push the branches aside and make my way around the tree then stop, holding the end of a twig. I run my hand along it until it joins a thicker branch, and measure off about the length of my leg. I bend the branch quickly back and forth until it cracks, and pull it free. I can almost hear those fifteen minutes he said he'd give me ticking away, but now I can move faster, sweeping the ground ahead of me. It's not as good as a real cane with autosensors, but better than nothing.

When I reach the edge of the island I sit down. The cold dampness of the groundcover seeps through my robe and jumpsuit. How deep under water is the path? Leaning forward, I poke the twig into the swamp, swishing it left and right. It meets no resistance so I scuttle sideways and dip it in again. After two more tries I feel something solid blocking the twig's path. I lower my feet carefully into the swampwater.

The path is more than a foot under water; my slippers sink into the freezing water with only an inch to spare. They are waterproof, but the cold goes right through them. Holding my robe up, I move my right foot sideways till I reach the other edge: about two feet wide. Carefully I rise, extending one arm for balance. My left foot slides an inch sideways as I stand up. The rocks are flat but slippery with slime. I can't make out any clumps of land in the darkness. The pattern will help me locate the path from each island, but not stay on it.

I fight back a sense of blindness that nearly overwhelms me. I try to step forward. My feet are frozen to the path. It's just a walk-strip, I tell myself, and it's not even moving. Still, I can't make myself move forward. What if it stops abruptly and I plunge into the water far from land? What if it leads me deep into the swamp and ends, marooning me where no one will ever find me?

I back up carefully and sit down on the island, catching my breath in a single sob of relief when I feel firm ground underneath me. I can't do this.

Broken-nose will take me back to the High Priest, and he'll keep Prad Gaelig with him. No one will send Naevah and her friends out to guard the fever house, until it's too late. Behind me I hear the murmur of Prad Gaelig's voice talking to Agatha, camouflaging my escape. Ahead there's only darkness, and the deep silence of still water, and the putrid smell of decomposing vegetation.

And the remote possibility that Agatha might survive this, if I can send help. I stand up and inch my right foot forward along the path, and then move my left foot forward gingerly, feeling my way with my feet as well as the stick.

I have to hurry, put distance between myself and the guard. If Prad Gaelig knows of this path the High Priest's guards will, too. But every inch forward is weighted with the heaviness of fear, every step deeper into the treacherous swamp is harder to take. I force myself forward, silently repeating Prad Gaelig's instructions until I'm clambering up onto the first clump of land, crossing it with legs grown steadier on dry land, then once again bending over the water, searching it with my stick for the secret path. How long will the guard be fooled by my boots and a stone? Will he come down this path, just to make sure? Or leave me out here to die?

I follow the path over five clumps of land for more than an hour when I notice the sky is clearing. Moon and stars blink sleepily through breaks in the cloud cover, helping light my way. I try to speed up, conscious of the passing time, and hurry over another clump of land. I step onto a rock on the other side which my twig locates.

My foot slips sideways and I plunge into the cold water, dropping my stick. Where's the path? My hand grabs for the rock—a single rock, slippery with moss. I lunge for the land. The bank is muddy and falls away steeply. Clumps tear off in my hands as I try to stop my fall. I sink underwater, holding my breath, fighting to keep from panicking.

My feet touch bottom. Something bumps against my legs. I reach down to push it aside and feel an arm, a human hand. I kick wildly, lunging sideways and propelling myself up from the bottom despite the weight of my sodden robe. As my head breaks above water I fling my arms over the stone path and heave myself up onto it, scrambling backwards onto the land and uttering little bleats of terror, *uh, uh, uh.* I run to the center of the island, dripping and shivering, and stare at the water. A dark lump floats up beside the pathway.

# Chapter Twenty-Eight

The thing in the swamp doesn't move. I realize I'm in more danger of freezing than from it. I struggle to pull the soaked robe over my head. My hands shake as I pull off my slippers and tip out the water.

I shudder with cold, my teeth chattering uncontrollably as I wring out my robe. It must be someone who had CoVir. But no, they cremate those who die that way. I don't want to go near it, let alone walk past it, but I have to take the path. I have to get to Prad Gaelig's apartment or I'll freeze to death. Before I can change my mind I walk down to the water and crouch at the edge of the path staring at the still, black shape. Its clothing billows around it, unlike soaked wool. I lean forward…

And jump back in horror as I recognize the blue and white habit floating on the water.

Hamza! Oh, God, it's Hamza!

Dead, beside the priests' secret pathway.

I turn, peering into the darkness behind me. The guard might be coming for me. The High Priest's guard, loyal only to the High Priest. He'll have to kill me now, I know about Hamza. I yank on my slippers and pick up my sopping robe. Maybe I can push Hamza further out, so no one will know I've seen him.

Immediately, I am ashamed. I remember him holding my arm in the square, supporting me when I would have fallen, guiding me home after the beheading. He was unpleasant, but he was always concerned about our safety. I can't just leave his body lying in the water. I crouch at the edge of the land. There's my stick, bumping against the rock I slipped on. I grab it, and manage to snag a corner of Hamza's robe, and gently pull him toward me. Holding my breath, I grab one of his legs and pull him up onto the land.

Now what? I can't bury him, and he's too heavy for me to carry, I'd never make it. I drag him behind a tree and pile leaves on top of him, hoping he'll still be here when I get back with someone I can trust. I bow my head and try to think of something to say.

"You were honest and loyal to your Order. You did your best to protect us. I should have thanked you," I say, through chattering teeth.

There's no time for more. I hurry across the clump of land and step onto the pathway, heading toward the island to the left. Then four to the right. Or is it five? I can't think...

Four! Yes, four. Concentrate on the pattern. Only on the pattern.

∽

Naevah and Jumal answer the door together on my third knock. They stare at me a moment, shivering and wet and stinking of the swamp, then Jumal pulls me quickly inside.

As soon as I've delivered Prad Gaelig's terse message, barely comprehensible through my chattering teeth, Naevah hands me a clean robe and underclothes and sends me to shower. Nothing has ever felt as good as that hot water washing the mud from my hair, easing the shivers from my body.

Jumal is waiting when I emerge wearing Naevah's robe, carrying my own robe and jumpsuit under my arm. He makes a face. I rinsed out as much of the swamp mud as I could, but they're still pretty rank. I shrug. I have to take them with me. It isn't safe for Naevah to be found with my jumpsuit, and I can't leave my robe behind. My father's diamond lies in its hem like a secret vice. How will I ever find its owner and return it, without admitting my father's crime?

I'm gulping down a plate of food Naevah prepared for me when a loud knock shakes the door. We all freeze.

"Take her to my room," Jumal whispers.

I pick up my bundled clothes and the plate of food and follow Naevah down the hall.

A bed, a table, a chair. Not even a closet to hide in if they search, and I don't doubt they will search the apartment. I hear Jumal speaking in the front room and tiptoe to the door to listen.

"It smells like swamp in here."

"My aunt has been spending her days outside the fever hut," I hear Jumal say, "giving moral support to the woman who saved my cousin's life. You have an objection to that?"

"No, no," the voice says quickly, at the same time as a second voice says something I can't make out.

"Yes, I know her. Why?" Jumal's voice is cool, almost disinterested.

"She's missing," a man's voice says. Incredibly, he sounds hesitant, almost stuttering.

"Yes, I heard. The Queen's guards have been searching for her for several days. You think I wouldn't know that?"

"No... I mean yes, of course..."

"What's interesting is that you are the High Priest's men. So now he is searching for her, too, when he wasn't before. What should I think of that?"

The guard mutters something too low for me to catch, but I'm not really listening, I'm too horrified at Jumal's tone. He's taking his act too far. How can he think he'll get away with it?

"You want to search my home?" Something in the way he emphasizes 'my' conflicts with the tone of amusement in his voice. It gives me goosebumps, like the sound of a fork scratching a metal plate. It is followed by silence. I can almost feel the guards' discomfort, perplexing as it is.

"Alright," Jumal says, "But tell the High Priest that I may choose to remember this."

Alright? Alright they can search the apartment?

There's a shuffling of feet from the uncomfortable guards, then the unmistakable sound of their footsteps following Jumal across the living room. I close the bedroom door quickly and whirl around. A bed, a table a chair. A window, but the apartment's too high up for that to be any use. I stand, frozen for a second, hearing the footsteps coming closer…

"The last room is mine," Jumal's voice says. I hear the door open. Heavy footsteps enter the room. I hold my breath.

"May I?" the guard asks. A corner of the bedcover trembles. I close my eyes.

The blanket is pulled aside, revealing Jumal's pajamas bunched up in the middle of the bed. I know because I put them there.

"Satisfied?" Jumal asks. I wish I could hear a quiver of relief in his voice, but he's as cool as ever. It ticks me because I myself am sweating and limp with relief as I listen to the guards' receding footsteps. When I hear the front door shut with unnecessary loudness, I heave the mattress up and climb out from my hiding space between it and the bedboard. Jumal comes into the room, grinning.

"Your mattress is going to smell of swamp," I say, pulling my robe and jumpsuit out with me. I fail to wipe the smile off his face, so I cave and grin back at him, acknowledging the little thrill of success at having outsmarted them together.

"You took a huge risk," I say, laughing, "with that arrogant, outraged act. And they fell for it!"

"No risk at all," Naevah says grimly, coming into the room. "You were the only one at risk, Kia. Tell her, Jumal."

Jumal looks abashed. "I knew she'd pull it off," he says. "She's quick on the uptake."

"Tell me what?"

# Chapter Twenty-Eight

"It really isn't important."

"Tell me what?"

"Okay, okay." He frowns at Naevah. "I'm just a commoner—"

Naevah gives a soft snort.

"—but my brother is the King."

# Chapter Twenty-Nine

It hits me in the gut. All this time I thought I knew him, or at least, was getting to know him. It was all a lie?

"You're the heir to the throne?" I stammer, and for a moment I hope he's going to laugh and call me "duckling" or something equally stupid for falling for it.

Instead, he shrugs. "I'm hoping my brother and his wife will take care of that."

I stare at him, unwilling to believe it. But a lot of things make sense now, like the way he spoke to the High Priest and the guards, and the fact that they all listened to him.

I was going to confide in him, tell him about my father's diamond, and finding Hamza's body. And now I find out he's practically one of the Triumvirate? The Queen is his sister-in-law; they're family. How can I trust him now?

"That's why I didn't tell you," he says, and I think he's reading my thoughts until he adds, "Don't look at me like that. You're the only one who looked at me and saw *me*, not my brother's crown. And now you don't."

How did I look at him? I glance up into his eyes above that crooked grin, and I flush and look away. I looked at him like my heart was in my throat, choking me, whenever he looked at me. Like we might get to be, I don't know, something more than friends. Like

I hoped we would. I'm such an idiot. Did everyone see it? How could they help seeing it? And all along they knew he was the king's brother, the heir to the throne, and no way was he ever going to look back at a dumb off-worlder making eyes at him. And now he's sorry because I won't make a fool of myself any more? He was laughing at me from the start, with his "quack" and his "duckling".

"You're wrong," I tell him. "I didn't see you at all, or I'd have known you were a jerk."

His mouth falls open, like he can't imagine why I'm *royally* ticked.

Naevah laughs. "Be careful what you wish for," she tells Jumal.

He turns and stalks to his room. I stand there, not sure what to do. I've lost the one person I thought might help me return the diamond, without telling anybody.

*I can never let myself think I'm above the law,* he said. If he wouldn't set aside the law for Tira, he won't even hesitate for me. I get it now. A king who thinks he's above the law is a bad king, and Jumal might someday be king. I respect that. But I can't show him a stolen Malemese diamond and ask him to keep it secret.

"You better get some sleep," Naevah says. "You'll have to leave before dawn. You can sleep with me."

I nod. I'm beyond exhausted, but the minute I lie down and close my eyes I see Jumal laughing at me. And when I push that image away, I see something so much worse I forget my humiliation. Hamza's swollen corpse swims before me, blue and white robes billowing in the fetid water. Is that what they intend for Agatha? For me?

Jumal probably still intends to take me into hiding. It's not against the law because I haven't been accused of anything. But I don't think there's anywhere on Malem where I would be safe.

I stare at the High Priest standing over Agatha. As his fingers tighten around her throat he turns to me. "I am trying to save myself some trouble," he says in a voice devoid of emotion, as if killing Agatha is an aside, something to do with his hands while talking to me. "I don't want her to tell the Queen where you are."

"Quack," says a voice behind me. I don't turn around. Even though I hear it clearly, I know there's no one there.

Suddenly Agatha raises her head to stare at me. In a choking voice she gasps, "You know who it is. You know it in your heart."

Her head falls back. She lies still in the High Priest's grasp, the stiffness of death creeping over her. No! No, no, no! I back away, weeping.

The High Priest is coming for me, now. He grabs my shoulder and shakes me, crying—

"Wake up!"

I shudder and open my eyes. Naevah is leaning over me, jiggling my shoulder. "Wake up. You're having a nightmare," she says.

"Thanks. Thanks for waking me," I mumble, still groggy with sleep and shaken with the terror of the dream.

I lie in bed with my eyes open, listening as Naevah's breathing lengthens into the deep, slow rhythm of sleep. Waiting until I can get up and dress, and tiptoe out without anyone noticing. I can't go into hiding with Jumal. Agatha's right: I have to give the diamond back. Neither of us will be safe until I do.

I pull on my jumpsuit, which has dried and lost most of the swamp-smell. My heavy woolen robe is still damp, so I take the one Naevah loaned me, after pulling the pouch out of the hem and sealing it into my jumpsuit pocket. I take some rice bread and goat cheese on my way through the kitchen, hoping I'll be able to repay Naevah later, and leave.

Outside, I find my way by touch as much as sight, running my fingers along the hard, rough clay bricks of the buildings as

I creep through their dark shadows. I've gone only a few blocks when my path crosses a set of guards. I hear their footsteps in time to draw back into an alley before they turn down the street I was walking on.

The second set catches me completely by surprise. I'm certain I've been seen, they're no more than a hundred yards away. I crouch in the recess of a door holding my breath. They pass without stopping, so close I could have reached out and touched the nearest one.

Why are there so many guards patrolling the city? Are they all looking for me?

Well, let them look. I'm heading for the last place on Malem they'll expect me to go. I continue even more carefully.

The third patrol on my route is easy to avoid. They're busy talking to a Malemese citizen. I hear the woman's voice arguing loudly before there's any danger of being seen. I listen long enough to learn that a curfew has been placed upon the city for three days: no one may leave their homes between midnight and dawn. The woman being harried home by guards protests repeatedly that she's only been visiting her daughter-in-law, whose baby is colicky.

I lean against the building, shivering in the night wind, after they've moved on. Prad Gaelig's plan to send people to the fever hut day and night has failed. No one will be keeping a watchful eye outside the hut while Agatha sleeps. I want to turn and race to the fever hut. But what can I do? No one will be there to hear if I raise an alarm and I can't stop trained guards. Everything depends now on my returning the diamond, and even that might not be enough.

I begin to run, measuring the distance in heartbeats, the sound of life, and willing that life into Agatha. All I can think is that I hate my father's diamond, with its trail of losses. If I can't find its owner I'll just drop it somewhere. Someone will find it.

Only it might be the wrong someone, and all their laws might fall down on an innocent head. I curse under my breath as I run.

I stop a block from the palace to catch my breath, approaching more carefully. The usual two guards are lounging at the wall, chatting together under the lamp above the gate, only occasionally glancing out into the street. Just as I hoped, no one expects me to come here. Keeping to the shadows, I make my way around the grounds, following the wall.

The sky is getting lighter by the time I reach the back of the palace, where the woods abuts the stone wall. I search until I find a low branch hanging over the wall, and leap to grab it. Using it as a rope I haul myself up and crouch on the stones, surveying the grounds. There are no guards in sight. They're probably all out enforcing the curfew and searching the city for me. I laugh under my breath as I lower myself into the palace grounds. But dawn has already broken. Servants and cooks will be stirring and soon the palace will be full of people. I run lightly into the palace woods, where I will be safer than anywhere else on Malem while I try to figure out what it is I supposedly "know in my heart".

The trees are short, only twelve to fifteen feet high, more like bushes except for their thick, squat trunks and wide branches. When I touch a tree trunk it feels uneven, covered with lumps and bumps which accentuate its mottled gray and dark purple coloration, but the bark is surprisingly smooth despite the knobs. They grow together in circles of five or six trees, their branches intertwined, with smaller shrubs all around. I crawl into the center of one of these clusters and make myself as comfortable as possible.

Dawn has dispelled the curfew, at least. Naevah will go to the fever hut, with as many people as she can convince to join her. Agatha will be safe during the day. And I am so tired…

It's late afternoon when I awake. A light drizzle is falling, but the leaves of the trees deflect most of it. I take out the cheese I got from Naevah's kitchen and bite into it. It crumbles in my mouth, its tangy flavor making me even hungrier. I tear off a hunk of the rice bread, looking around as I chew it. My head brushes against a low tree branch. It shivers, its broad silver leaves tipping a rivulet of cold raindrops down my neck. I pull the hood of my robe over my head. The drizzle is tapering off but even so, I'll soon be soaked.

I hope that's the worst thing that happens to me, I think, as I stare dismally through the leaves at the falling rain. I go over everything Agatha said about returning the diamond. There isn't a single clue there, except for that infuriatingly smug, *you know it in your heart*. Why didn't she just tell me if she knows? Or does their stupid vision show me miraculously solving the riddle? Won't they be ticked when I don't!

I cross my legs, ignore the water the movement shakes from the leaves, and close my eyes in a meditation pose. I imagine myself sinking down into my heart and looking around…

I jerk myself awake at the sound of footsteps and voices.

"…I'm just saying I'm glad he's back. All these extra patrols through the city, the night curfew…you'd think we had a monster among us, not a saint, saving a child's life and talking her place in the fever hut…" his voice trails off. They're moving past me; his companion's voice is low, I can't make out the words. But this one's voice is still loud with indignation: "Don't tell me you weren't glad, too, to see the King come back this morning. He'll sort this business out!"

I'm still sitting stock-still when they've moved on. The King is in the palace? Forget all that heart and visions crap. I've got a plan!

Dusk on Malem is only a hyphen between daylight and nightfall. The moon rises grimly behind a gauze of clouds before the sun has even made its exit. Iterria follows the moon, glaring down intermittently through the clouds. I crawl out of the bushes, ignoring the dripping leaves. For a moment I stand there, staring at the palace. This is even more dangerous than going into the fever hut after Tira. I remember trembling the first time I met Sodum in his shop, and I want to laugh.

If this doesn't work it's almost certain I'll be beheaded. I look back at the woods. I'm safe in there. I could just stay there…

Then I remember Agatha tapping her finger on the other side of the fever hut door, whispering good-bye to me… and I start walking toward the palace.

For once I appreciate the veil of clouds over Malem's sky as I sprint across the grounds to the back of the palace. I examine the building, looking for a ground floor window into a darkened room. When I find one, I hesitate before it. I can't see any way to open it from the outside. This will be the second window I've broken on Malem where glass is in short supply and precious. The first time was kept quiet because the High Priest didn't want it known I was there, but this will be different. Even if 'break and exit' isn't a crime, 'break and enter' surely is; especially the 'break' part.

I lean against the window, peering inside. The door to the room is shut. If only I had my tools with me! I'll have to rely on the Malemese' disregard for interior locks and hope I'm lucky. I wrap my left hand in a fold of my robe, my mouth pursed in a thin line of disgust. Only suckers trust in luck. And vidstars, but my opinion of them has plummeted now that I've experienced adventure first-hand. Agatha might really die. I might, too.

I take a deep breath, break the window and hoist myself inside.

It takes forever to find the back stairs. I creep around the main floor of the palace in the dark, opening doors on sitting rooms, reception chambers, even a huge banquet hall. The rooms are all large, but true to the style here, half-empty. My footsteps tiptoeing in the hall, the squeak of a hinge that needs oil, even my breathing as I peer into the cavernous rooms, all echo back at me alarmingly. At one point I duck behind heavy drapery just in time to escape the notice of a servant making his last round, turning out the lights. I peer after him in the darkness until the light he's holding begins to rise. I've found the back stairs.

I wait for him to get wherever he's going before I climb the stairway. It leads to another hallway. I look around for guards but there are none in sight. My private audience with the Queen was on this level, though, so I assume the royal suites will be on this floor. I tiptoe down the hall to the first door. There's no lock. A ruthless off-worlder could really clean up here. If my father *was* a thief, he could have come home with pockets full of gems and made us rich. It's a shame, really. After tonight the guards will probably never be so lax again.

My hands sweat so much I have to wipe them on my robe each time before I grasp a door handle, and my heart stops every time I open the door. I'm not so sure of this plan anymore. Even when I find the King, he'll probably call his guards to shoot me before I have a chance to talk to him. But I keep opening doors. The first three are unoccupied bedrooms, the next a sitting room. I carefully open the fourth door.

And stand still with disbelief. It's furnished as a nursery, complete with a crib, a little cot, a child-sized table and chairs. There are two wooden puzzles half-solved on the table beside a little cup and plate. A rag doll smiles from the crib and painted balls and little wooden animals all lie about the room as though waiting for a child to come and play. I sneeze, clasping my hand over my nose at the last moment and turn it into a muffled snort. Everything is heavy with dust, the only visible sign of the fifteen years that have passed since any child has played here.

I am looking at sorrow so tangible it has taken on a life of its own. CoVir, as thick as the dust in this room, weighs down every impulse toward joy in this palace. I back out of the room, silently shutting the door.

I stand there, staring at the closed door. I'm aware of the sound of my breathing, a deep, constant sound, tied to the living present. Otherwise, all is silent and still. Only the breathing...

...Two sets of breathing, slowly becoming asynchronous. My neck prickles with the sense of another presence behind me.

# Chapter Thirty

I stand still, holding my breath. The breathing behind me continues. My throat closes, frozen like the rest of my body. Only the other set of breathing can be heard now, louder and harsher and closer than before. A guard would not stand silently behind me. A guard would grab me and raise the alarm. Someone or something else is in the hall with me. I can feel its intensity boring in on me. I dare not turn around.

"How dare you?" The voice is low, a hoarse whisper of barely-suppressed rage. I force myself to turn.

My breath comes back to me in a gasp. The Queen stands behind me, near enough to touch in the dark hallway. Her face is as gray as the dust and twisted into a death-like grimace. She wears a white robe which accentuates her unnatural paleness, and her uncombed hair floats in a tangled black web about her head and shoulders. Her hands are curled into claws beneath the ruffled sleeves of the gown.

For a moment I can't decide whether she's real or a nightmarish apparition. She raises her hand. I stare at it, frozen with terror. The clawed hand trembles before me.

"Answer me," her terrible voice rasps again.

I open my mouth. Nothing comes out.

"How dare you enter that room!" The Queen's entire body is shaking now. Her arm jerks as mounting rage overcomes her rigid self-control. I stand there shaking, my knees so weak I'm afraid I'll fall down before she has a chance to hit me. What was

I thinking, coming here? What in the universe was I thinking? I'm going to die for this.

"Sariah?" The King's sleepy voice precedes him through the open bedroom door. He comes into the hall and sees us. "Guards!" His voice echoes in the empty hallway.

I fall on my knees. "I need to speak to you, Your Highness!"

"You may talk at your trial." The Queen snaps.

"Now. In private." It comes out a croak, my throat so dry I can barely push the sounds out. "Please, listen to me. The Select's life is at your mercy!"

"She made the choice to risk CoVir. Every life is at its mercy." The Queen glares at me, "And at the mercy of the law, which you have broken!" Her voice rises, frantic with rage. It's that room, the princess's room. She'll never forgive me for seeing it.

I hear boots pounding up the stairs.

"What's going on here?" the King asks with deliberate calm. "Do you know this person?"

"She's a servant to the Select." The Queen makes a dismissive gesture with her hand.

Behind me, I hear the guards running down the hall toward us. "Please, Your Highness! Please! The Select has done nothing but good for your people!" I'm sobbing, I can't help it. Agatha's life as well as mine is at stake, and I've blown it, completely blown it!

A guard's hand drops on my shoulder, pushing me down as his other hand twists my right arm behind me. Pain shoots up my arm.

"Search her for weapons," the King says.

I am yanked to my feet. Behind me I hear the click of a lead-arm. I stand still, trying hard not to shake while one of the guards pats me down.

"No weapons, Your Highness."

"Very well." He looks at me. I make myself look as pathetic as possible, which isn't hard at the moment. "Bring her into the… the breakfast room."

I glance at the Queen. Her face is turning purple. Her mouth forms a thin line of rage as she turns to follow her husband into a room down the hallway. The guard pushes me forward, his hand still gripping my shoulder.

They stop me just inside the room. At the far end a large bay window is curtained against the night, with a broad, padded chair and foot stool on either side of it. The only other furniture is a small, square table, large enough for four to dine at, though two of the chairs have been pushed against the side wall. Three light globes, recessed into the walls, activate as we enter, casting a dim light over the room.

"Close the doors and step back," the King says. The guard with his fist bruising my shoulder hesitates, as though he wants to object.

The king raises one eyebrow.

The hand drops from my shoulder. I hear them shuffle back to wait by the door.

I bow—or should I curtsey? It's a little late for either—as the Queen settles on one of the chairs against the wall, the King standing near her. He looks expectantly at me, and I can't say anything. Because now I'm certain whose diamond my father took, but I still have no idea how to return it. It has to be done carefully, in private, so no crime can be recorded. And this is definitely not the audience for it.

"You may start by telling us how you got in here this evening."

He can't really imagine their palace is well-guarded? "I… I broke a window—but I'll pay for it," I add quickly, aware of the guards listening behind me, "—at the back of the palace. I'm sorry. I had to see you."

"We have doors for that."

"—alone."

"So now, because you are getting your wish, you will think your criminal act paid off." The Queen shoots an angry look at the King, which he ignores.

"I believe the Select's life is in danger." I look at the King as I say it.

"So do we all," the Queen says.

"Not from CoVir. From the High Priest."

A look of astonishment crosses the Queen's face, quickly followed by outrage. Before she can speak the King says sternly, "You make a serious allegation against the head of our faith."

"I have reason to think it, Your Majesty." I hesitate. Is it safe to speak in front of the guards? The King nods sharply for me to go on, so I explain that I was abducted and held against my will by the High Priest since the night after Agatha announced her intent to stay at the fever house. This draws a second look of outrage from the Queen. "He told me the Select is going to die in the fever hut," I finish.

"What were his exact words?" the King asks.

"'You don't really think she'll survive two weeks in the fever hut, do you?'" I recite the words reluctantly. They sound more like speculation than a threat; it was Jumal's reaction that made them alarming.

"That's it?" The King asks. "On that comment alone you accuse him of contemplating murder?"

I open my mouth to tell him about Select Hamza, but before speaking I glance sideways. The Queen's face is rigid. She's staring at me with a mixture of rage and fear.

What if she was in on it? She would deny it, and the body would be gone when the King's guards arrived. And those who murdered him would know I had seen his body.

I look back at the King helplessly. "Has he ever been wrong?" I ask. But Jumal's damning comment doesn't sound very convincing coming from me.

"All the more reason to respect his wisdom," the Queen says coldly.

I hate to do this. I've been the center of a family feud before and I hate to do this to him, but it's nighttime and there's a curfew, and Agatha's alone. "Jumal agrees with me. What if we're right, Jumal and I? What if she's murdered and you were warned and you didn't try to stop it?" If the King hates the O.U.B. as much as the Queen does I'm dead. We're both dead, Agatha and I.

Am I being paranoid? I sound paranoid. Everyone down here can't be a murderer. I look at them closely: the King looks thoughtful. The Queen looks furious, but not... not secretive; not alarmed so much as insulted. I take a deep breath, and I make my choice: "Like the other Select."

"You are saying the Select who is missing has been murdered?" the King says. He looks ready to order the guards to haul me away.

"I have proof, Your Majesties." I close my eyes. If the Queen was involved, I'm lost. I open my eyes and look directly at the King. "I found his body. I can show you—your guards—where it is, but they have to come with me to the fever hut to guard the Select."

I hold my breath while the King examines me. What is he thinking? Did he know my father? Did he hate him, blame him for his daughter's death as the Queen does? Anything, anything at all could tip the balance...

He nods, and I breathe again. "I will send two of my men with you. If you can show them a body, I will make sure the Select is protected." He holds his arm out to the Queen.

"I will wait here while you arrange it," she says. "I have something to say to this girl."

The King looks about to protest. The Queen raises her chin. "The house guards are at the door," she says. She leans back in her chair, watching me through narrowed eyes as the King leaves the room. As soon as he's gone, she orders the guards to wait outside and close the door. They do so reluctantly.

This is my chance to talk to her alone—and I'm not sure I want to. I've got what I need. The guards will come with me to protect Agatha as soon as they see Hamza's body. I don't have to give up my father's diamond.

The pouch burns in my jumpsuit pocket.

*Put things right,* Agatha said. Still I hesitate. If I tell, offer the diamond to her, will that save Agatha's life, or condemn us both? Everything depends on the Queen and I don't trust the Queen. It occurs to me that it's fortunate I was in jail when Hamza went missing; no one can pin this on me.

Her face looks weary and older in the dull light. She leans against the back of the chair as though needing its support. I follow her gaze to the line of curtains, staunchly holding back the night. The sweep of an arm could undo their vigilance and darkness would flood in over the dim wall lights. I lift my arm a little toward the nearest globe, accidentally casting a shadow over the Queen's face. She startles. I drop my arm. The same fear that I surprised there once before stares out of her wide dark eyes.

My father's voice whispers: *Take it, Sariah, it's yours.*

I take a deep breath. "Your Majesty, there's something I have to tell you."

"It is too late." Her voice is low and tight. "That's what I stayed to tell you: it is too late. Keep your secret, if you wish to live."

I am tempted. More than I've ever been before. And I am very good at succumbing to temptation, believe me. But I hear Agatha's nagging voice say, *Put things right,* and my own voice, promising, *I'll do it.* Those may be the last words we ever say to each other. Before I can change my mind, I reach into my pocket and pull out the pouch. My fingers curl around it in a protective fist. Protective and possessive. I force them open to reveal the little leather pouch that I have shown no one in all the years I've had it.

"I was at my father's bedside when he died, Your Majesty. He gave me this, in secret trust."

The Queen stares coldly down at my palm. "Your father stole one of our diamonds?"

"I don't believe so, Your Majesty. His last wish was to give it back to you." I avoid her eyes. I'm telling her I lied when she questioned me four weeks ago. But if she accuses me of it, she's admitting it's hers.

She has to admit it. She has to take the heart stone back. How has she concealed its loss for so long?

"He told you it was mine?" She laughs. "I have my heart stone." She flashes her diamond ring at me. "The heart stones of the Royals pass from King to King and Queen to Queen this way, always on display for the people we serve."

Am I wrong? Was my father speaking of someone else? I hear heavy footsteps coming down the hallway toward us. My open hand trembles. The Queen sits smiling carelessly at me.

"I advise you to put it away."

The footsteps stop outside the door. We hear the King's voice as the guards open it.

"Hide it, quickly," the Queen hisses.

I close my hand, concealing the pouch in my fist as the King enters with two of his men. I don't turn around. I stare at the Queen, waiting...

"Stop," she says. "We haven't finished talking."

The King gives her a puzzled look. "Wait outside," he tells his men.

The Queen watches the King as his men depart. Her face is indecisive. I see it harden: an off-worlder sneaking around our rooms at night. What is her word worth? The Queen's decision is as clear as though she said the words out loud. I have to make her change her mind—but how?

"Tell him your story." The Queen leans back casually, a mocking smile on her face. I can still see fear at the corners of her eyes, beneath the scorn. The King won't see that. He'll want to believe his wife.

As much of the truth as possible, I remind myself.

I hold out my hand, exposing the leather pouch to the King. The Queen looks eager to take it now, she's only waiting for me to tell my story so she can deny it. Her eyes are already taking on a false look of outrage.

"The Select told me to give this to you when I spoke with her at the fever house."

The Queen draws a sharp intake of breath. The King's attention is fixed on my palm. He hesitates a moment, as though he, too, is afraid of what I might say.

Then he reaches for the pouch. My fingers curl reflexively as he does; I have to force myself to let him take it. He sees the gesture and looks at me. Behind him, I see the Queen clasp her hands together in her lap, her knuckles white with the force of her grasp. I open my hand for the King.

The King unties the thongs of the pouch and tips the diamond into his hand. He stares down at it for a long moment, before he looks at the Queen. She looks back at him, barely breathing. Her eyes are wide in her pale, still face.

"How did the Select come by this?" he asks, still looking at his wife.

"She found it in the fever house." I glance at the Queen. "The Select will confirm this, if necessary." God, I hope not, I think, looking steadily into the Queen's eyes. I hate using back-up. It's never reliable.

"It must have been left there by a distraught parent whose child died," I add.

The King looks at me. I give him my most innocent look, the one I practiced for hours in the mirror before my interview with the Adept.

He looks back at the Queen, then down at the diamond. "By the time she realized it was missing," he says slowly, his voice so low he might be talking to himself, "she had forgotten where she'd misplaced it."

"Yes," the Queen says, leaning toward him.

Gently, as though she is still that grieving woman, he places the diamond in her hands and folds them together around it. She bends her head. He draws his thumbs across the corners of her eyes, wiping away the dampness that gathers there.

I turn away to give them privacy, and let my breath out slowly. I'm right. I should have thought of it earlier, but I was so sure it was the Queen's diamond.

"It is a miracle," I hear the King whisper.

"Well." The Queen says, sounding a bit uncomfortable.

I feel myself warm a little to her.

# Chapter
# Thirty-One

"Two of my men are waiting to go with you," The King says, breaking away from his wife and coming up to me. "They have been told what you claim you will show them."

"And they'll come with me to guard the fever hut? And the Select who found the heart stone?" I'm pushing it, I know.

He raises an eyebrow. I feel reprimanded but I don't back down. "You are a persistent person. Yes, they will go with you to guard her until she comes out. I can spare them one night."

I'm halfway through "Thank you, Your Highness," when his words hit me. One night? I calculate quickly. He's right, this is her last night there, and suddenly I'm desperate to leave. He sees it in my face.

"Show them your proof, first," he warns me. He opens the door and signals to his men: "Go with her."

We are stopped several times on our way through the city. The patrols let me pass, reluctantly, only when they recognize the King's men. I watch the King's guards go from surprise at their persistence, to irritation, to thoughtfulness after the third encounter. The fourth patrol doesn't stop us, which frightens me more than being stopped did.

"Hurry!" I urge the guards, breaking into a jog. They increase their speed without any questions. When we reach the road out of the city, I start running.

I lead them to the secret path—the priests' shortcut to the fever hut—and then I wonder if that's a mistake. The High Priest must know by now that I took this pathway to escape his guard. We are utterly alone, without even the possibility of witnesses to curb the High Priest's actions. What if he's already sent his men to meet us on the route? Would he dare dispose of a King's guard? But it's more likely he's sent someone to take care of Agatha before we arrive, so I strike out onto the first underwater pathway, calling them to follow.

It's pitch dark outside the little beams of the guards' hand lights. I have to focus on finding the hidden path. When I realize the next island is the one where I buried Hamza in leaves, I fight down the urge to vomit as a vivid memory of his billowing robes and bloated body comes back to me. I have to force myself to lead the King's men over behind the tree. The smell assures me the body is still where I left it.

Their hand lights play over the body as I describe finding it in the swamp and dragging it over here. I choke on the words, fighting a rising panic. "We have to get to the Select!" I finish.

They don't answer. They don't believe me, any more than the King—

I hear a voice, loud enough for me to catch some of his words, and I realize one of the guards is calling for back-up. On his comradio.

"Does the High Priest have a comradio link with his guards?" I shout at the other guard.

The expression on his face gives me my answer. I take off running. He calls to his comrade to deal with the body, then I hear his footsteps pounding right behind me.

We have to slow down at the edge of the island; the trail is too treacherous for racing full out. I want to scream with impatience as I jog the interminable zigzags from island to island. Beyond

The Occasional Diamond Thief

us, the swamp is ominously silent. Is Agatha sleeping, unaware of the danger she's in?

Is she still alive?

The guard grabs my arm, pulling me to a stop. He snaps off his light and whispers, "Quiet." I nod. The fever hut lies just ahead.

We approach the final island cautiously. The sky is already lightening to gray, enough for us to see the stone hut. There's no guard in sight.

Am I wrong? Was it all in my head, this suspicion? A figment of my imagination because I didn't like the High Priest? I'm going to be horribly embarrassed, I think, as I hurry across the island toward the fever hut—

And see the door hanging open! I race forward. When I reach it I hear the muffled sound of bodies struggling together, the heavy gasping of a single breath. The King's man grabs my shoulder, pushing me behind him as he runs into the dark stone hut. I rush in right behind him, my eyes following the arc of his light as he swings it around the dark interior: stone walls slick with mould and mildew; the slate floor, slippery with slime; a single, narrow cot, covered in a crusted mire that looks as vile as it smells; a broken chair, discarded in the corner; and there!—the High Priest's guard, bending over Agatha!

Agatha thrashes on the floor, her hands clutching at the guard's beefy fists, which grip her neck. I catch a quick sight of her bulging eyes staring desperately up at us before the King's guard rushes forward with a shout, blocking my view. The High Priest's man lets go of Agatha, reaching for his lead-arm, but the King's guard already has his in hand.

"Stand aside!" he shouts.

"She was having a convulsion!" the guard cries. "She called for help. I was loosening her robe so she could breathe."

266

# Chapter Thirty-One

Agatha lies on the floor beside the broken chair, sucking in gasps of air with a desperate noise. The harsh rattle of her breathing fills the stone hut. The sound of that rattle terrifies me. "Don't die!" I scream, running to her.

The moment's distraction is all the murderer needs. He rushes the King's guard, knocking his lead-arm aside, and envelopes the smaller man in a crushing bear hug. I see him bring his forehead smashing down against the guard's face. The crunch of bone and the guard's cry of pain bring me leaping to my feet. I look around desperately, searching for the fallen lead-arm, for anything!—as he slumps to the floor. When the High Priest's man bends down to finish him off, I bring the chair down on his head. He staggers back, dropping his weapon. It skitters across the floor, lost in the darkness. With a swipe of his arm he throws me against the wall and turns back to the King's man.

"Stop!"

A hand light sweeps over us. I look up groggily, beyond the two men struggling together, toward the door.

"I said, STOP!" The blast of a fired lead-arm shatters the air above us.

The two guards fall apart.

"Kia! Are you hurt?"

"Uhh," I croak, my voice still hoarse from having the wind knocked out of me. I recognize the voice—how is it possible?—but it is. I want to laugh with relief but it comes out part hiccup, part cough. "Y..yes," I gasp, squinting into Jumal's hand light.

"The Select...?"

"I...I am well." Her voice sounds even worse than mine but I'm so relieved to hear it I do laugh this time, although it sounds more like a series of hiccups.

"You," Jumal's light catches the High Priest's man, "don't move. And you," the light moves over to the King's guard. "Why are you here?"

The man tries to speak but with what looks like a broken nose pouring blood, his words are indecipherable. I tell Jumal the King sent him with me to protect the Select, and that another guard radioed for reinforcements. Jumal gives him the lead-arm to hold on the High Priest's guard and comes over to me.

The gray rectangle of the open door has lightened into a bleak Malemese dawn, enough to let me see his face. He looks concerned, and yes, he can't help it—he wrinkles his nose. I struggle to my feet with his help, and lean against him. I don't care if the Malemese don't touch, he's saved my life and I'm hopelessly happy to see him, so I throw my arms around him. Who would have thought I'd be rescued by a handsome prince? And prince that he is, he hugs me back, even though he must be suffocating with the effort not to breathe. I hurt all over from the force of my fall, but I prolong that hug until his eyes are tearing up, partly because it feels so good to have his arms around me, and partly because it serves him right for making me hide under his mattress while he calmly led the guards into his bedroom. When I release him he coughs a couple times, trying not to. I smile and go to Agatha.

"Ugh! It stinks in here," I say, helping her up.

She sighs and nods. "There's no getting used to it. They might as well tear it down."

"Come outside and get some fresh air." I slip my arm under her shoulder and behind her back, supporting her. Jumal is already pushing Broken-nose toward the door, ignoring his loud protests. The King's guard—Broken-nose two, I guess—waits for us to preceed him, one hand holding his bleeding nose and the other holding the lead-arm.

Agatha stops walking. "I am in quarantine."

I laugh and take another step, but she doesn't move. She's serious.

"It's morning." I point to the increasing light in the doorway.

"I have to wait for the priest to officially let me out."

I should have let him strangle her, I think. I open my mouth to tell her I'm not staying in here—

"I am the King's representative. I declare your quarantine over," Jumal says from the doorway, in a way nicer tone of voice than I would have used.

"Jumal," Agatha says, in a chiding tone—

"He is," Broken-nose-two says. "He has the authority. Keep moving. Please."

Agatha looks at him, at the blood dripping steadily below the hand over his nose, and lets me help her to the door.

I hear the voices just before we step outside. Even so, I'm not prepared for what I see. Dozens of people—I squint, my eyes accustomed to dark—maybe a hundred, crowding onto the island in a steady stream along the path. Naevah's in front, with Liat on her hip and Prad Gaelig beside her. They brought them, they brought everyone! The innkeeper's wife is on Naevah's other side, proudly holding Tira, who clings to her neck and does not look happy at all to be here. The innkeeper walks beside his wife looking no more pleased about it than Tira. I recognize some of the people I saw at the inn—did the innkeeper's wife bully her customers into coming and lock the door behind them to make sure they did? I wouldn't put it past her.

I see the women I visited with Agatha, and their husbands, and so many more they become a throng of silent brown faces, elders, young people, parents with children in arms, all coming to see Agatha triumph over her quarantine.

And then, while I'm gaping at all the people, another amazing thing happens: the sun comes out. I look up, expecting to see a momentary break in the clouds, but a high wind is blowing them away, leaving a clear sky.

The people catch sight of Agatha and a cheer goes up. "She's alive! She's alive and well!" those in front pass on to those behind, and the cheering grows. Agatha grasps my arm to steady herself. I pull her forward into the sunlight and hold her from falling as the crowd erupts in shouts of joy, increasing in volume as those too far to see her grasp the significance of the cheering and join in. Several babies including Tira start to wail, adding to the din.

The crowd ripples and I catch sight of the High Priest surrounded by four of his guards pushing their way to the front. The look on the High Priest's face as he stares from his bound guard to Jumal to Agatha turns every paranoid thought I had into intelligent reasoning. I tense for a moment until I see men with the King's insignia pushing their way through the crowd: the reinforcements have arrived. And—my eyes widen—the King is with them! He notices the High Priest and gives him a measuring look as they both approach the fever hut.

Agatha, shading her eyes from the sun and gazing on the cheering crowd with an expression of amazement, has not seen either of them. She holds up her hand. It takes a while for the noise to subside.

"Thank you," she says. Her voice, despite its hoarseness, carries over the crowd as only a Select's voice can. "The fever hut is no longer a death sentence. CoVir is beaten! No one must ever be sent here again."

A shocked silence follows her words. I see those near the High Priest glance at him nervously as he glares at Agatha. Before he can speak the innkeeper's wife, who isn't close enough to see her priest and can't resist the opportunity to star in an unfolding drama, raises Tira in the air like a torch and cries, "Praise God! And burn down the fever hut!"

Naevah reaches quickly for her sobbing child as wild cheering breaks out again, punctuated with cries of "Burn it down!", "The plague is over!", "Burn down the fever hut!"

"NO!" The High Priest's voice is almost unrecognizable in his rage. The King, however, has now reached him. He murmurs something into the High Priest's ear that turns his face gray as the King's men quietly surround them.

"Burn it down," I hear Prad Gaelig advise the King as the royal guards escort the High Priest and his men away.

"So be it," the King says, and the cry is taken up across the island.

The flames are still crackling loudly, the hut a fetid torch in the center of the island, when Jumal finds us. I look at Agatha, leaning on my shoulder. Her eyes are closed, her face white with exhaustion. "I have to get her home where she can rest," I tell him. "Can you help me with her?" He slips his arm under Agatha's other arm and together we half carry her down to the path through the swamp.

It's a long way. I tell Jumal and Agatha about finding Hamza's body, and that I was too afraid to talk about it—and that's all the explanation I give for not telling Naevah and him about it, and for leaving their apartment. I can't mention the diamond without betraying the Queen's secret, and without that it just sounds like I didn't trust him. Which is true, although I feel crummy about it now. Then I remember he lied to me about who he was, and I can't say that without giving away his secret to Agatha, so I just mutter, "I guess neither of us gets an A+ in honesty."

Agatha says "Hmmm," and I say, "You have your secrets too," and we all walk on for a while in silence.

"Thank you both for saving my life," Agatha says when that has gone on long enough, and we're back to our good points. I describe (sketchily) trying to convince the King to send two guards with me to find Hamza's body and protect the Select. Jumal says—a little unfairly, since we've moved on—that when he didn't hear from me (emphasis there) he got worried and decided to come to the fever hut to find out if I'd gone there.

And after that we're back to silence, but we've reached the city by now. From time to time I glance at Jumal but I don't know what to say next, and apparently he doesn't either. Jaro would start up an easy conversation without a second's thought but I can't think of a thing to say that doesn't sound idiotic. Like, it's the first sunny day since I got here, and despite everything, I just want to stretch my arms up to the sunshine, but am I going to talk about the *weather*?

Agatha doesn't seem to notice. It's taking all she has left just to keep walking, holding on to both of us. But I am more and more painfully aware, with every silent step, that Jumal and I have nothing to talk about.

Why should we? He's the heir to the throne and I'm a foreigner. He'll never leave Malem, and I can't possibly stay here.

So, honestly, what is there to say? That's what keeps me silent.

We reach Prophet's Lane, and then we're at the door. Agatha hands me the key and I let us in and we lower her onto a chair and she thanks him for everything, and he leaves.

The end.

But then I jump up and run outside after him.

"Why did you do it?" I blurt out "You risked your life for us."

"For you," he says.

"Why?"

# Chapter Thirty-One

"You really don't know, do you?"

"Don't know what?" I hate riddles.

He shrugs. "People will always take risks for you, Kia."

He leaves me standing there, staring after him as he walks down the street and turns the corner and is gone.

# Chapter Thirty-Two

I wake up the next morning to thunder. I groan and roll over, but the thunder continues. It sounds pretty distant, just a low, steady rumble that goes on and on—

I sit up and listen. …On and on…

I jump out of bed and run to the front room, where Agatha sits calmly at the table drinking a mug of tea.

"What's happening?"

"A ship is landing."

"A spaceship?" I say idiotically. "Landing here?"

She smiles. "Apparently."

I race to my bedroom to dress.

All I can think of as I try to hurry Agatha through Malem City to the spaceport is: what if it leaves before I get there? Which is ridiculous because it won't have even cooled from landing yet, but even so, couldn't Agatha walk a *little* faster?

A lot of people are headed to the spaceport. We find out why when we overhear two men discussing the possible reasons a ship from Iterria would dare land here, and a third speculate on whether there'll be trouble.

What kind of trouble? I wonder. Then it registers: a ship from Iterria. Is it landing without permission? I shake my head. I don't want to know. I don't care about their stupid dispute or whether or not Malem joins the Alliance. All I care about is that I'm on board when that ship leaves. I glance at Agatha. She looks worried. I speed up. We're almost there. I can see the edge of the field ahead, at the end of this street.

What if the King and Queen order the ship off-planet before I can fight my way on board? Because that's exactly what I intend to do. No matter what it takes I'm getting on that ship before it leaves. I'll climb over anyone who gets in my way!

I break into a run, sprinting to the end of the street—

It's there! Solid and real in the middle of the landing field. I can hardly believe my eyes. I want to run across the field toward it, but it's just landed; waves of hot air still emanate out around it, and the hatch is closed.

A small crowd has already gathered. Half-way down the field a ring of guards, their weapons held ready, surround the King and Queen as they face the ship. More guards patrol the perimeter, warning us back. Agatha catches up to me and we stand at the edge of the field, watching the ship as it cools down. I chew my lip with frustration, willing the hatch to open.

At last it does. A hush falls over the crowd, every face tense, straining to see. When the hatch is fully open a figure steps into its arch. I recognize the blue and white of the O.U.B., but can make out little else through the crowd of Malemese around me. I wriggle my way forward, pulling Agatha with me.

"You!" I hear the Queen cry. "How dare you come here again!"

"Where are my people?" the figure in the hatch asks without so much as a glance at the Queen.

I'm close enough to see her now, but I wouldn't need to; I'd know that voice anywhere. A loud voice would carry across this tensely silent field, but hers ricochets over the crowd with the controlled force of a whiplash. The stillness of the Adept's features is frightening, her voice a cool veneer over the frozen fire of her eyes. People around me step back, and I'm tempted to do the same except for Agatha's ramrod straight back beside me.

The Adept looks over the field full of people, ignoring the guards' lead-arms as though they are toys. Her question hangs over us. She does not repeat it.

Agatha starts forward. The guards allow her to pass. I take a deep breath and hurry after her. I'm not exactly crazy about this direction—the one thing I didn't expect to have to climb over to board this ship is an angry Adept.

She sees us coming. Her gaze lingers on Agatha, moves on to me—and I miss a step and nearly take Agatha down with me, because who would think a totally expressionless face could convey such relief?

"There is one missing," she says, her voice as commanding as ever, so I must have been mistaken. She looks back at the King and Queen and their guards.

She talks like she owns us. It's annoying, but right now, with an angry Adept facing down the Malemese, I'd rather be one of the owned than one of the accused. Especially when I remember being jailed, and being afraid my hand would be cut off, and having to get Tira out of the fever hut, and arriving just in time to prevent Agatha from being murdered. And finding Hamza's body…

"You've come too late for him, Adept," I call to her. If this is her idea of a rescue, she's bungled it. We'd be dead, too, if we'd had to wait for her.

The Adept turns to me, standing with Agatha beside the King. I narrow my eyes, not retracting my words or my tone. She should have been here. She should have come with us, not sent us all unsuspecting into danger.

"So. Another death on my soul." Her voice is so low the meaning of the words follows a beat after her voice. "Tell me, child."

The field is silent. Even the wind has died down, as though it, too, is waiting to hear what I will say. I wish I'd kept my mouth shut, now that the pull of her intense focus is trained on me. I take a breath and open my mouth—

"Enough," the King says. His voice is firm, steadying. The Adept glances at him and I am released. I still want to tell her everything, but now I want to for my own reasons, and in my own way. I look at the King, cool and in control, and I admire him tremendously.

"Yes," the Adept says. "You are right, Your Highness. This is not the time or the place."

The King turns to his people. "Go home," he says. He waits a few minutes as the crowd begins to disburse, then turns back to the Adept: "You may disembark."

The Adept inclines her head and steps out of the ship.

For a grueling two hours Agatha and I stand in a private room in the palace, going over everything that has happened since we arrived. Well, not everything—I omit the parts that involve the Queen jailing me, and returning the Princess's heart stone. The Queen is, after all, sitting between her husband and the Adept, listening to our testimony. Prad Gaelig is called in to verify his part in it all when we're done, even though the Adept has already confirmed I'm telling the truth—mostly. She leaves that word out, but I'm pretty sure she knows it's not the whole truth. She lets that go, for now.

At last we're dismissed. We'll have to appear at the High Priest's public trial and execution—I flinch at the word—and repeat our testimony. The thought makes me sick, but when I look round at the faces in the room, there isn't even the tiniest possibility I can get out of it. If I even suggested wanting to, they'd be shocked at my lack of ethics, wanting a man to be condemned without the opportunity to face his accusers.

As soon as we reach Prophet's Lane, I offer to make dinner and disappear into the kitchen, leaving Agatha with the Adept. I delay there as long as I can, but finally I have to either announce that dinner's ready or explain why I stood in the kitchen while it cooked to ashes.

I bring the platter of somewhat dried-out fish and vegetables and set it down on the table. "So I'll let you enjoy—" the Adept cuts me off with a nod toward the third chair. I sit down with them.

"Has the Queen's loss been redeemed?" she asks. And so begins my second grilling.

It's rather quieter than the one at the palace. The Adept asks a question, waits till I look at her, and reads the answer in my face. An efficient use of words—or lack of them.

"Good," she says, with an air of finality, when she's satisfied. "Then we have nothing more to worry about."

Nothing to worry about? I stab a piece of fish on my plate. What did she have to worry about? She wasn't even here—

I stop cold, the fish halfway to my mouth. A rush of understanding leaves me dizzy. "You were there…!"

"I was," the Adept agrees.

"Tell me what happened."

The Adept looks down. She takes another mouthful of food. I notice my own fork shaking in the air in front of me and lower it to my plate. "I have a right to know," I say. "Whatever happened here, it killed my father."

The Adept nods once, as much to herself as to me.

"We were walking across the landing field, your father and I, on our way to the *Homestar*. If it had happened earlier, there might have been time for Sariah to reconsider, or Itohan. But we were already leaving when she came to speak to him.

278

"She was so young, barely eighteen. She had a vulnerable beauty that could stop a man's heart. And your father… he was a man with a large heart.

"She reached out to him, and he stopped. Slowly she opened her fingers. Nestled in her palm was a single, perfect Malemese diamond.

"She demanded he take it. 'It was my daughter's,' she said. 'Every time you look at it, I want you to remember she's dead because of you.'"

"That's not fair!" I cry.

"It is not," the Adept agrees. She takes a forkful of vegetables and chews. "I told him to come away, but he insisted he wanted to help her.

"'Then leave her alone,' I said to him, and I told her she was young, she would have other children.

"'Never!' she cried. 'My daughter is dead. If I can't be her mother, I won't be anyone's mother!'

"'It seems that way now,' I said, trying to be reasonable.

"'What did you do to save my baby?' she screamed at me. 'It was you who brought this plague on us!'

"I flinched, and that was my undoing. Your father saw my guilt, even though I had been exonerated, and he was furious. He lost his faith in that moment, because of me. He accepted the heart stone even though I called him a fool and asked him how he dared to take it."

She stops talking, as if the story's over, as if she can leave it at that.

I push my plate aside and stare at her. She eats calmly and methodically.

"Why? Why did he take it?"

She shrugs, opens her mouth to say something trite like, how can we know another's motives? Like she isn't an Adept.

"I need to know why."

"Not because he coveted it, if that's what you're thinking. And not because of its value, he never would have taken money for it. I believe he took it for her, so *she* wouldn't have to look at it every day. And because he thought she might be right. His ship suffered mechanical problems on the trip; he had to stop for repairs. It delayed him a week, and in that week the princess died."

"That wasn't his fault!"

"No. But responsibility is a subtle thing. We rarely get it right. Some people deny responsibility for anything; others err on the side of accepting too much."

"Surely he knew it was against the law? That he could be killed just for having it?" Agatha says.

"He knew. And so did Sariah. I think that was her plan, to have him found with it, and I believe he knew that, too. But in the end she didn't go through with it. She let him leave."

I stare at her, unable to speak. He was prepared to die here, was willing to? He would never have returned to us, never have seen Owegbé again, or taught Etin and Oghogho the trader business, or had any time to know me at all.

Anger rushes through me so fast it takes my breath away. "He was prepared to sacrifice us," I say, the words choking me. "And you were prepared to let him."

"It was a moral decision, and his to make. I tried to talk him out of it, but we do not impose our morals on others; that is not our brand of religion."

"Oh? Then why am I here?" I glare at her.

"Because you chose to come."

"Some choice I had."

"And who is responsible for that?"

Sodum taught me, tempted me. Agatha helped me, even encouraged me to steal that last bracelet. I could blame them, I have blamed them for my being here. I want to say my choices weren't my own, but I can't. Sodum made it easy, but no one made me do it.

"I'm responsible," I say.

The Adept smiles. "You are your father's daughter."

I swallow, unable to speak. My father's daughter. No one has ever called me that, and meant it as praise. I draw in a shaky breath.

"She couldn't have another child," Agatha says slowly. "Not without everyone knowing she didn't have her daughter's heart stone to pass on."

"Yes."

"Couldn't you… Couldn't you have brought it back here later?"

"I tried. Your father wouldn't speak to me, or any Select, after Malem."

I nod. I guess that's where I got my distrust of the O.U.B., from him. I finish my meal in silence, sitting between a Select and an Adept. I glance at Agatha, who put herself at risk for others, again and again, and at the Adept. *But not because of me,* Prad Gaelig still remembers her saying.

"He was wrong," I say. They look at me. "My father. And the Queen. You didn't bring the plague here. It wasn't your fault, just because you were on the ship it came on."

Her eyes remain calm and expressionless, as always, but her mouth twitches into a smile. It's kind of creepy, that Adept smile, like she's doing what the situation calls for. But that's the point: they do what should be done. It's less a matter of ideals than a matter of training. The Adept couldn't have knowingly brought death here; she is totally lacking the emotional triggers that would let her justify murdering the innocent. I smile back at her, a real smile, eyes as well as mouth, and for a moment—just an instant—the corners of her eyes crinkle.

# Chapter Thirty-Three

"The High Priest kept me prisoner while the Select was in the fever house." That's where I start when I'm testifying at the High Priest's trial: after my trip to jail, and definitely after Tira's "miraculous survival" in the fever hut. I tell about finding Hamza in the swamp, and end with finding the High Priest's man strangling Agatha.

I force myself to look at the High Priest from time to time as I must, accusing him to his face. It makes my stomach ache—I don't know whether from anger at what he did and tried to do to us, or from pity, because he's about to be beheaded. Both, I guess.

I try not to look out over the square. The size of the crowd is unnerving; everyone in Malem City must be here. They stare at us without warmth. Five days ago Agatha was their hero, they burned down the fever hut for her. And now we're outsiders again, exposing their dirty laundry to them.

Broken-nose steps forward, his mouth set in a grim, resigned line. He sticks to his story—that he rushed in to rescue Agatha from convulsions—despite our witness against him. The Select was having convulsions in her sleep, he says. He heard her from outside the hut, and wanted to help. Of course it's ridiculous: no one's allowed to go inside the fever hut while someone infected with CoVir is inside. I guess he wasn't hired for his brains.

The King's guard, Broken-nose-two, climbs up on the raised platform in the center of the square to stand beside us. An ugly black-and-purple bruise extends from his swollen, bandaged nose across both his eyes to his upper lip. He confirms my story, describing the scene when we entered the fever hut and the fight that ensued. The damage to his face is proof of his story.

The King, seated with the Queen at one end of the platform, calls out for all to hear: "Guilty of attempted murder."

The evidence against the High Priest is less conclusive. I am asked to describe exactly where I found Hamza's body. Broken-nose-two and the other guard the King sent with me testify where and when they saw the body. A medic confirms Hamza died of a blow to the head. But nothing links the murder to the High Priest except the secret path, and every priest knows of that, as well as their guards. No one witnessed Hamza's abduction. The trial drags on.

"We cannot conclusively prove who killed the Select," the King proclaims at last, his face tight with exhaustion and frustration.

The Adept speaks for the first time: "Let me try."

I bite my lip to prevent myself from laughing at the understatement, and look away, wishing I could leave. The Adept's focus is intimidating even when you're just an observer.

The Adept looks at the High Priest, and then across at Broken-nose, with a cool, appraising eye. The High Priest turns to stare at his guard at the same time as the Adept turns her dreadful scrutiny upon him. The silence lengthens. The guard sinks to his knees. Sweat runs down his forehead. He looks like a blade of grass caught in the focus of a magnifying glass trained to the sun. Slowly he curls over upon himself, until his head touches the floor of the platform. Nobody moves to help him.

The square is very quiet. I begin to sweat in sympathy.

"I killed him."

The High Priest's man has not moved. His voice is muffled and without expression. It does not seem to have come from him.

"He's crazy!" The High Priest raises his arm, which shakes violently, and points toward the Adept. "She's making him say it!"

"I killed him at the order of the High Priest," Broken-nose chokes out.

The Adept turns to the High Priest. "Is this true?" she asks.

"Of course not!" the High Priest sputters, but then he makes the mistake of looking at her. Apparently he's never had the focused stare of an Adept trained on him before. He blanches.

She doesn't repeat her question, but her eyes never waver from his, and she doesn't let his eyes waver from hers. His face turns gray, but his lips are clenched tightly together.

I wish more than ever that I could leave. The Adept's calm has a tick-tock feel to it.

"Is this true?" she says again.

"YES!" he cries. The word explodes from him, an admission of guilt and a scream of triumph. "And they should thank me! I did it for Malem, to keep us pure, to keep us free of the contamination of other worlds! The next plague they infect us with won't attack our bodies; it'll sicken our souls! He was plotting! They both—" his head jerks as though he means to glare at Agatha but can't escape the Adept's mental hold—"both plotting against us! You'll see! You'll wish you'd listened to me, all of you!" He gives an inhuman shriek of laughter and falls silent as the Adept looks away.

"What have you done to him?" the King demands.

"Lanced the truth out of him. It is not fatal. He has had poison in him so long, he is sick without it."

The King gives her a long look. "And you didn't force a false confession?"

"No one can force another to lie. Lying requires imagination and imagination depends on freedom of thought. I cannot even force the truth out of someone who truly doesn't want to tell it. Fortunately, in our hearts we all want to spew out our own truth. I merely encourage that."

The King glances at the Queen, then back at the High Priest, who is smiling hideously and rocking back and forth on his feet.

"Guilty of murder, self-confessed," the King proclaims. "Execute them."

"You dare?" the High Priest cries.

"I dare not," the King replies. "Neither you nor I nor anyone on Malem is above the law."

I try to think of Hamza in the swamp, of Agatha being strangled in her sleep. I want these two men punished. Only, I don't want to have to watch. I'll never accuse anyone of anything again, I resolve to myself—and realize why the accusers have to be present.

A priest climbs up onto the platform to stand beside the High Priest and his man. Beside me, Agatha already has her eyes closed, her lips moving in prayer. The Adept is also murmuring a prayer, but her eyes are open. Probably she's in some religious trance that removes her from her surroundings. I feel justified in squinting until my eyes are almost closed. Nevertheless, I hear the thunk of the axe digging into wood, once, and again, and again. I will hear that sound the rest of my life.

As soon as the bodies have been carried away, the King and Queen stand up and announce the new High Priest. Prad Gaelig makes his way through the crowd to the platform, an expression of astonishment on his face. At every step people touch his arm, clap his back, congratulate him. When he mounts the platform, they break into cheers.

Nice touch, I think, glancing sideways at the King. Always leave 'em happy.

He turns and catches me looking at him, and arches a single eyebrow at me.

# Chapter Thirty-Four

"What are you doing with that?"

I look up quickly. The Adept stands at the doorway to the bedroom I'm sharing, once again, with Agatha. I should have shut the bedroom door. Wait, didn't I?

I can't get used to living with an Adept. I'm never sure whether 'Please make me a cup of tea' is a request or a subliminal command. I haven't felt inclined to refuse and find out. On the other hand, I haven't felt inclined to refuse.

"I'm packing." The box of tools Sodum gave me, which I was just about to put into my spacebag, burns in my hands.

The Adept keeps staring at me. I want to shove the box out of sight but I can't move. Doesn't the woman ever turn herself off?

Agatha walks in. She takes the box from my hands and tucks it into my spacebag. "God had a use for this," she says. "It saved a child's life. As Kia saved mine."

She smiles at me, a small, slightly pained expression.

The Adept's face softens. "You did well here, child," she says. "Very well."

I clasp my hands behind my back. "How are the negotiations going?" I ask her.

"Quite well." The Adept allows a note of satisfaction into her voice. "I believe we will be sinking the first shafts for the sky elevator within the year. The Select and I will be able to return to Seraffa in two years at the outside."

"But Malem hasn't joined the Alliance."

"No. This is not an unqualified success."

"They are helping their neighbors on Iterria," Agatha murmurs. "Many members of the Alliance do far less."

"True."

"The High Priest thought the Malemese would lose their religion if they joined the Alliance," I say.

"Nonsense," the Adept replies.

"Prad Gaelig says if you destroy a religion, you destroy its people."

"We are not trying to destroy the Malemese." Her expression is neutral, but I've begun to notice she talks just a tiny bit faster when she's ticked. You'd have to live with her to hear it.

"Prad Gaelig has a point," Agatha says, looking at me. "Losing their religion can destroy a people's sense of identity, the way they differentiate themselves."

"No one is trying to undermine the Malemese religion."

There it is, just a smidgeon faster than normal.

"But Prad Gaelig's job goes beyond that. His job is to increase their faith. As is ours," Agatha adds.

"This is the outcome you were after all along!" I grin at Agatha.

Agatha looks uncomfortable. She glances at the Adept.

"We strive to follow God's plan," the Adept says. "Presumably, this was the outcome He was after."

For no reason that I can actually see, I get the impression she isn't completely happy with Him about it.

"Will you have another task for me, then?" Agatha asks. "When we leave Malem in two years?" She keeps her face very still, as though the answer is of little concern to her.

"We will both pray about that," the Adept replies. Her voice has slowed back to normal.

Agatha looks downcast. A tiny worry-line creases her forehead.

I seal the top of my spacebag and begin its inflation. Standing up to leave, I look around awkwardly. I said goodbye to Jumal last night. I don't think he'll ever be King. I've seen the way the Queen smiles at the King now that she has the diamond she needs to pass on to her next child. Even so, I'm going home and Jumal is staying here and nothing can change that for either of us. And now the same is true, at least temporarily, for Agatha and me. I straighten resolutely.

In three steps Agatha is at my side, her arms around me.

"I'll see you again, on Serrafa," I mutter.

Agatha tightens her embrace. "Of course you will," she says, "God doesn't build bridges that won't hold." And then, as if she can see right inside me, she says, "Your brother will be there when you get home. The captain will contact him as soon as you reach space."

I hug her back, blinking fiercely.

The Adept appears not to have noticed. Which means she saw everything. I straighten and let go of Agatha.

"Another assignment," the Adept says, looking at Agatha thoughtfully. "That may depend upon whether you can secure a good translator."

Agatha smiles.

I grab my bag. "Excuse me," I say, heading for the door. "There's a ship waiting for me."

# Acknowledgements

I am grateful to all the people who have supported and assisted me in the writing and publishing of this book. My husband, Ian, for his belief in me and his careful line-editing, my daughters Amanda, Tamara and Caroline and son-in-law Steve, for their enthusiasm and suggestions, and my family, Richard, Linda and Peter, Pete and Jan, for their love and support. My life is blessed for having all of you in it.

Thanks are also due to my fabulous Launch Team, for their comments, their enthusiasm and their critiques throughout this process. I would be amiss not to mention you by name: Sue M., Lori C., Barbara and Isabelle S., Jenn A., Linda S., Marsy B., Karen D., Marsha B., Jennifer C., Robin M., Tom and Kenzija K., S. J. F., Karen G., Mande W., Stacey G., Joy W-M., Dominick M., Amber M., Rebecca B., Mary-Ellen M., Judee S., M. E. T., Namita M., Jo J., Melanie M., Barbara P., Terri R., Michael M., and Joseph M. Thank you all so much!

I also want to mention my publisher, Brian Hades, of EDGE Science Fiction and Fantasy Publishing, and publicist Janice—thank you both for being so professional and so great to work with! And I can't not mention Brian's lovely wife, who started the whole ball rolling. I am lucky to be able to work with people like you.

Last but not least, I am grateful to the excellent people at Expert Subjects: William Sudah, Marija and Cath, for your artistic and technical expertise. Thank you for making my book beautiful.

It takes a whole community to create a book. Thank you all for being my community!

# About the Author

J. A. McLachlan was born in Toronto, Canada. She is the author of a short story collection, CONNECTIONS, published by Pandora Press and two College textbooks on Professional Ethics, published by Pearson-Prentice Hall. But science fiction is her first love, a genre she has been reading all her life, and The Occasional Diamond Thief is her second published Science Fiction novel.

Here's what readers are saying about J. A. McLachlan's first science fiction novel, *Walls of Wind*:

*"There's a new master of truly alien SF, and her name is J. A. McLachlan. THE WALLS OF WIND is doubtless THE debut novel of the year." – Robert J. Sawyer, Hugo- and Aurora –winning science fiction author*

*"If you read no other "alien" authors this year, don't miss WALLS OF WIND." – Bookreporter*

*"O. S. Card got into the alien hive mind in the latter books of his "Ender" series. Octavia Butler did the same in her "Wild Seed". No other writer I know of comes close to J. A. McLachlan depicting the thoughts and emotions of two truly alien species and their society as well as the environment in which they live." – SFWriter*

*"This book is a fascinating look at what it takes to learn compassion and understanding of those different from ourselves. It is beautifully told from different points of view, and enforces the idea that everyone is of value. I highly recommend it. " – D. Warde*

Find *Walls of Wind* on Amazon at:
http://www.amazon.com/dp/B00IPOP5GC
Find J. A. McLachlan and her books on her website:
http://www.janeannmclachlan.com

If you enjoyed reading The Occasional Diamond Thief, please leave a review on Amazon.com. Your review is important to me, and I read them all. ~Frequently, actually.

Post your review of *The Occasional Diamond Thief* at: http://www.amazon.com/dp/B00NF9NYJM

Happy reading!

~ *J. A. McLachlan*

# To The Readers of This Book

I just want to say that the title of this book is a gross exaggeration. Technically, I am NOT a diamond thief, even if I did take a few things that weren't mine, and perhaps they did have diamonds on them. But I have stopped doing that, so I do not think it's fair that the title of this book is "The Diamond Thief."

I was going to suggest that all of you email the author and object to this unfair title, and force her to make a retraction, but I don't like relying on back-up. So I took matters into my own hands and wrote "Occasional" across the top. Just to set the record straight. Now you know.

If you agree with me, you can write a review of this book on Amazon, and in your review, you can say that you don't think I'm a thief. I would appreciate the support, and if Jaro sees all of you saying good things about me, he will have to give me at least a B+.

But if you see another book by this same author with the word "thief" in the title, you and I will know that she is not open to subtle hints. Jaro has already demoted her to D- for calling me a thief, and if she does it again, she will be an F-. You can still read the book, because if I am in it, it is sure to be an EXCELLENT story, but I wouldn't associate with her if I was you. She's had her warning.

~ Kia